Sabotage at Cedar Creek

The Little Red Truck Mysteries
Book Two

Sabotage at Cedar Creek

JANICE THOMPSON

BARBOUR
PUBLISHING

Published by Barbour Publishing, Inc., 1810 Barbour Drive, Uhrichsville, Ohio 44683, www.barbourbooks.com

Our mission is to inspire the world with the life-changing message of the Bible.

Member of the
Evangelical Christian
Publishers Association

Printed in the United States of America.

DEDICATION

To Billie and Shirley Moseley, the real owners of that gorgeous property east of Mabank. Thanks for so many wonderful memories on that amazing patch of land. You are loved and missed.

SCRIPTURE

God sets the lonely in families, he leads out the prisoners with singing; but the rebellious live in a sun-scorched land.
PSALM 68:6 NIV

CHAPTER ONE

"Tell me what you think. . .really."

I brushed a loose hair from my face and glanced up at my best friend, who gestured to the freshly painted exterior of her new vacation rental as she spoke.

"I think it looks great, Tasha," I responded as I gave the property a solid once-over.

Tasha's brow furrowed, as if she didn't quite believe me. "*Great*, as in 'I'm your best friend, and I have to say that'? Or *great*, as in, 'Wow, this place is really coming together. You're going to keep it booked all summer long and make a ton of money'?"

I did my best to respond quickly so she wouldn't read too much into whatever expression happened to flit across my face as I pondered my response. "*Great*, as in *great*. Amazing. This place is going to be full all summer long."

She released an exaggerated sigh. "You didn't mention the money. I really need the money. I've got a mortgage now, you know."

Oh, I knew. My best friend's newly acquired mortgage to fund this vacation rental was a key topic of concern these days, often worming its way into other conversations. Like, when she bartered with me over items she wanted to purchase from my family's antique store, Trinkets and Treasures. I heard a lot about her mortgage during those moments, which was why her new place was currently filled to overflowing with furnishings she'd gotten for a song from our shop. Not that I minded. She deserved the best with this new venture of hers.

I offered what I hoped would be a confident look. "It stands to reason that if you keep it booked, you'll make the money, so I will pray that is the case."

"*If?*" She shot a doubtful look my way.

Good grief. This girl. "Tasha, don't worry. Have faith."

"Oh, I have faith." She groaned, and worry lines creased her brow. "We just need to get past this final inspection on Monday morning, and we'll be good to go."

"What's the inspection for?" I asked.

"It's something that's recommended for vacation rentals before the property goes live. The inspector is going to walk me through a checklist of things to look for regularly to keep the house safe for incoming guests."

"Sounds good."

"Yeah, but I feel like there are still way too many things to get done between now and then."

I knew my BFF well. If I didn't turn this conversation in a positive direction ASAP, she would fall into the depths of despair. She tipped in that overdramatic direction regularly. And her new home did look great. Well, it would, anyway, after we finished painting the ceiling and trim work, and wrapping up our work on the bathrooms.

"You're hesitating." She gave me a panicked look.

"No hesitation. Just thinking about all of the things I need to do once I get home. But I wouldn't worry if I were you. This place looks great, inside and out."

"It does, doesn't it?" She released a lingering sigh, and for a moment my friend was back. No worries. Just a peaceful countenance on that freckled face.

I took a swig of water and gave the house a closer look, as if viewing it through the eyes of potential guests. Tasha couldn't have found a prettier piece of property in Henderson County if she'd tried. The old two-story house was nestled against a lush acre of land that gave off a "secluded and serene" vibe.

Flowering dogwood trees were tucked neatly beneath rows of oversized, stately pines. They provided a natural canopy to filter the late-afternoon sunlight. The leaves from a nearby oak tree cast dappled shadows across the front lawn, which still needed a bit of tending but not much, thanks to my brother's handiwork in the front garden. All in all, this place was really looking magnificent.

Through a gap in the foliage, I could almost see the neighbor's ranch-style home in the distance. It, too, added a bit of picturesque charm. Thank goodness, the elderly Mr. Reeves kept his place in pristine condition, which would probably make guests feel even better about their decision to vacation here. This area really felt like a slice of heaven, and beautifully situated near the water meant it was a coveted rental property in these parts. In other words, Tasha had nothing to worry about. Though, I suspected that wouldn't stop her.

We walked around the side yard of the house, taking it all in. The real showcase, of course, was in the backyard. At the far edge of the property, a newly renovated pier extended out over the tranquil waters of Cedar Creek Lake, the boards creaking quietly against the late-afternoon breeze overhead.

Granted, the deck at the far end still needed a little work, but I had no doubt we'd get that done before the first guests arrived. They would love this place, regardless. How could they not? It provided a nostalgic reminder of simpler times and practically shouted, "Hey, come spend a few lazy afternoons fishing or watching the sunset with your loved ones."

I could almost picture parents, children, and even grandparents with poles in hand, whiling away the hours.

In short, Tasha's new property was perfection, and I knew my bestie had to be deliriously happy that she had actually pulled it off. Now, to finish those last-minute touches so she could list it online and start recouping some of the money she'd spent by mortgaging and renovating the place.

Tasha chattered on and on, sharing her list of things still needing to be done, but I only heard about half of it. My back ached from the work we'd already done, and beads of sweat trickled down my back, causing further distraction. I took another sip from my water bottle. The heat was relentless, making the air thick and heavy, and I found myself wishing for a cooler spot to have this discussion.

"You still okay to spend the night tonight?" Her eyes sparkled as she asked the question. I could read the excitement there. She might as well be asking me to her fifth-grade slumber party.

I nodded. "Yeah, it's going to be fun. I'll run home and shower and change, and then I'll come back with dinner. Bessie Mae's frying up a mess of catfish and hushpuppies, and I'm sure there'll be a jug of sweet tea in the mix, so I'll bring all that when I come back."

Tasha settled onto the porch swing and laughed. "You never sounded more southern than you do right now, talking about your aunt's cooking. You just c'mon back with that mess'a catfish 'n sweet tea, ya hear?" More laughter followed.

"I'll take that as a compliment. . .*honey.*" I laid it on thick with the *honey*. Not that I minded her comment. I'd never shied away from my East Texas heritage, especially when it came to catfish and sweet tea.

"If you throw a cobbler into this story, I'm really going to swoon."

"Peach cobbler," I said. "Bessie Mae's on a roll with peaches this week. She's been canning, freezing, and pretty much peachin' up anything she can think of, including her homemade salsa. It's been pretty miraculous to watch, honestly. The woman has a gift." One I hoped to inherit.

"Yum." A thoughtful look came over Tasha's face. "Hey, peach salsa might go well with the catfish."

"I'll bring a jar. But before I can come back, I actually have to leave. You gonna be okay here by yourself? I know there's still a lot to do."

"I think I'm okay for now. We've got the Sunday school class coming in a couple of days to wrap up loose ends, so I'm not too worried about getting it all done by my lonesome. Besides, Dallas is coming by to check on the AC unit any minute now." Her cheeks flushed pink as she mentioned my younger brother's name. I'd been noticing that more and more lately. Or maybe she was just overheated. It was sweltering out here.

I swiped at my forehead with the back of my hand, hoping to brush the perspiration away. I needed a shower. ASAP. "Hopefully Dallas will get it fixed before we settle in for the night. Otherwise it's gonna be a hot one."

"We could always sleep out on the back balcony. That might be fun."

"In ninety-five-degree weather?" I countered. I hated to burst her bubble, but my days of sleeping outdoors ended with my two-year stint in the Girl Scouts. And the only badge I'd earned was for camp avoidance.

"I'm sure Dallas can figure it out. He's so good at all that stuff."

Should I tell her that my brother had never been terribly good at handyman stuff until she needed him to be? Nah, I'd let that lie there. Right now, I had bigger fish to fry.

CHAPTER TWO

Fish to fry. Ha. Aunt Bessie Mae would love that one.

I reached for my water bottle and took a swig then gave Tasha a quick nod. "I'm headed out. See you in a couple hours."

"With a mess'a catfish and a jug of sweet tea."

"Yep." I took several steps in the direction of my 1952 Chevy truck, lovingly named Tilly. Her bright red paint shimmered under the late-afternoon sunlight, and for a moment I found myself transported back in time to my childhood. Back in those days, Tilly had belonged to my grandfather. Oh, how I loved riding alongside Papaw on his many trips into town. These days, I rode solo in Tilly. I wouldn't trade her for the finest car in town. Not with so many memories attached to her.

I climbed behind the wheel, determined to remain focused on the task at hand. Get home. Shower. Grab dinner. Head back.

The heat inside the truck was brutal, so I hand-cranked the window down. Right away, the overpowering scent of blooming azaleas wafted through the air.

I turned on the truck and adjusted the AC vents. Not every '52 Chevy had AC, but I'd added it to the reno a few months back. No way I'd survive in Texas without it.

Seconds later, Tasha appeared at my open window, brow wrinkled in concern. "You seemed a little worried earlier. Are you concerned we won't be safe in the house by ourselves tonight?"

"Of course. We'll be fine." I pressed my water bottle against my neck in an attempt to cool myself down.

Still, the flicker of concern in her eyes made me second-guess my response. I knew she had concerns about the homeless man who had set up camp here a couple of weeks back, but the police had that situation under control. I hoped.

"I'll bring Riley with me." I set my water bottle into the cupholder to my right. "She'll protect us."

Tasha didn't look convinced. "I love Riley, but that dog is about as useless as a wooden frying pan."

"True, that." I laughed. "But I'll bring her anyway. A barking dog always scares away would-be intruders."

"So you *are* nervous." She released an exaggerated breath. "I knew it."

"Nope. Not at all." Though, I was a little nervous that she had her sweaty arm up against my clean truck.

Tasha's gaze shifted to the ground then back up at me. "I guess this would be as good a time as any to tell you that I had another certified letter from Belinda Keller this morning."

"Really?" My heart skipped a beat as she mentioned the name of the former owner's daughter. The woman had been a pain from the get-go, but I was sure she would eventually let go of the notion that the house should have come to her. Apparently, some folks didn't give up that easily.

"Yeah. She says she's going to take me to court." Another dramatic sigh followed. I'd come to expect this sort of over-the-top reaction from my BFF.

"She's just bluffing. You're the rightful owner now. She has no claims to this property, even if her parents did once own it. Or am I misunderstanding all of this?"

"No, you're understanding it correctly. The house was left to her stepbrother, Anthony. He was the only one named in the will. She was left out, which got her very upset."

"Ouch. Are you sure?"

"Yep. Anthony showed us the will at closing in case she tried to pull any shenanigans. He's named right there, in the very first paragraph. She's actually named too but only to state that no provision has been made for her."

"Oh my."

"I know. I guess this sort of thing happens a lot after family squabbles. But from what he said, she's been threatening legal action since she learned he was going to sell the place."

"But he sold it anyway. To you." The cool air from the vents finally worked its magic, and I relaxed a little.

"Yep." She nodded and leaned against my door. "He wanted to be rid of it. And the quicker, the better. That's why I got it for such a great price."

"I see." I paused to think through this situation. "But I can kind of see why Belinda would be upset. I mean, if my parents left the ranch to my brothers but omitted my name from the will, I'd be worked up too."

"Except she'd had a big falling-out with her family years prior." Tasha swatted away a mosquito. "Made their life miserable, from what I was told. Things got so tense when her father passed a few years back, her stepmother talked about putting a restraining order out against her."

"Whoa."

"And when her stepmom got sick last year, she tried to move in with her, like she owned the place. But she didn't, of course. And Anthony put a stop to that. He saw that she was just looking for a free place to stay. He says she's always been like that, the kind who takes advantage of others, which is why I'm nervous she'll try to do the same to me."

"She was mooching off of her dying stepmom?" I asked.

"Yep." Tasha released a sigh. "This place has quite the history, doesn't it?"

"Sounds like it."

"Anthony said he wanted to dump the house because there were so many hard memories here. I've never seen anyone so happy to be rid of a place."

"That's rough. Family drama can be so messy." Not that I'd experienced much myself. We Hadleys were a pretty amiable lot. Well, unless you counted the occasional squabbles between my two younger brothers. Gage and Dallas had a way of going at each other from time to time.

"She doesn't have a leg to stand on," Tasha said. "And she needs to get over it and leave me alone."

"Only, she's not leaving you alone, sounds like."

"Right. I'll tell you all about it when you get back." Tasha patted my door, as if to send me on my way.

"Okey dokey." I shifted the old truck into drive, just as my brother's Ford F250 pulled into the curved driveway alongside me. He flashed a smile, and I hollered a quick "Get that AC fixed before I get back, ya hear?" then headed down the driveway toward the street.

As I pulled away from the house, I gave the property a quick glance and tried to see it through the eyes of potential guests, not as the weathered hoard it had been a few weeks back, when we started the renovations. What a mess it was back then, still overloaded with the former owner's belongings.

The big two-story home now exuded charm and character, especially with the tranquil waters of Cedar Creek Lake shimmering off in the distance. Its exterior, freshly painted in pale buttery yellow with sage green shutters, gleamed in the late-afternoon sunlight, which created jagged ribbons of light. Windows, once boarded up or adorned with cracked panes, now glistened with fresh paint.

Weeks of work had gone into this project. The expansive front porch, adorned with intricately carved railings, offered the perfect point of entrance for guests. And that big porch swing promised cozy evenings spent sipping sweet tea and admiring the neighborhood.

All in all, I'd say this place was perfect, not just for would-be vacationers but for the community at large. It was a sure sight better than the rickety old house it had once been.

Yes, Tasha had nothing to worry about. Her home would be filled all summer long. Folks would come for the lake views and that amazing wraparound balcony, which offered sweeping views of the water on the west side, and the surrounding countryside from the other three angles.

The inside was quaint too—sort of a blend of nostalgia and charm. We'd swept every dusty corner clean and polished up the hardwood floors that had been worn smooth by previous generations.

As I reached the stop sign at the end of the road, I found my thoughts shifting back to Belinda Keller, the latest thorn in Tasha's flesh. She'd grown up on this lakefront property in Payne Springs. No doubt she had wonderful memories here. It must be weird, to be excluded from the family will. I wondered what she could have possibly done to cause that.

Determined to push her out of my mind, I took off down 198 toward the bridge and over Cedar Creek Lake, toward our family's property east of Mabank by just a few miles. I rolled the window back up, fully relishing in the cold air now pouring out of the vents.

My gaze shifted to the fields on either side of the highway. Summertime in this neck of the woods was always beautiful, but nature had really outdone herself this year. Flowers were in full bloom in every field, and fishing boats dotted the sparkling waters of the lake off in the distance. My relationship with Mason—the sweetest guy in Henderson County—was in full bloom too. I was so blessed to have him in my life. Our family's antique store—Trinkets and Treasures—was up and running, and all was right with the world.

The narrow road leading into Payne Springs meandered through this lovely, picturesque landscape, towering oak and pine trees framing it out on either side.

I loved how the sunlight left dappled patterns on the road. Every now and again I'd pass a ranch, where weathered wooden fences bordered the roadside. Horses and Angus bulls grazed in the late afternoon sunshine under the wide Texas sky.

I found myself overcome with such feelings of gratitude for where the Lord had planted me. There was no place else I'd rather be than here, in the Cedar Creek Lake area.

A couple of minutes after I passed over the bridge onto dry land, my phone rang. I put it on speaker the minute I saw Mason's name on the screen and responded with a playful, "Hey, you."

"Hey to you too." His thick Texas twang grabbed hold of my heart, just as it always did. "Still at Tasha's place?"

"Nope." I tapped the brakes as I approached the corner of 198 and 334. "Headed home to shower and grab some food to take back."

"For the slumber party?" He chuckled.

"Yeah. It'll be fun. Like a campout."

"Only, indoors. With AC."

"AC is questionable," I explained as I turned onto another country road with slightly narrower lanes. "It keeps cutting out. Dallas just stopped by to look at it."

"Your brother works on air conditioners now?" Mason asked.

"My brother works on whatever will win him brownie points with my best friend," I explained. "He was probably up all night looking at YouTube videos to impress her with his AC prowess."

"I see how it is. He'll do anything to impress the gal he's crazy about."

"Pretty much. But I think he's also there because he's nervous that homeless guy might show up again."

"Conner?" Mason paused. "There's no need to worry about him. I ran into him at the church, and we had a good talk."

"Seriously? What was he doing at the church?" I'd known Conner Griffin since we were kids. He'd always been trouble but no more so than lately. I couldn't quite picture him showing up at the local Baptist church, to be honest.

"I'll tell you all about it later. But I'm pretty sure he won't turn back up at her place. He was just staying there when it was empty because he had no other place to go. I guess there was a time when he used to work for the family, so it was a familiar spot."

"But now he has a place...at the parsonage?" That still struck me as odd.

"Yeah." Mason's words interrupted my thoughts. "But that's too long a story to tell right now."

"Tasha also seems really nervous about the daughter of the man who owned the house before she bought it. Apparently, there's been some trouble there. Threats, even."

"I thought the house belonged to the grandmother of one of Dallas' friends?"

"Yes, the widow Keller. Do you remember her?"

"Barely," he said.

"Her stepdaughter Belinda is saying she has rights to the property."

"I think in the state of Texas the house automatically goes to the kids unless there's a will stating otherwise," he interjected. "I learned all about this after my dad passed last year. That's how I ended up with his place."

"Ah, right," I said. "Well, in this case there was a will, and she wasn't in it."

"Ouch."

"I think she was estranged from the family. I don't think she's a happy camper about losing out on the house, though. From what I understand, it went to her stepbrother, Anthony."

"That had to hurt."

"I know."

"Well, there's not much she can do about that. Tasha closed on the house. It's hers."

"It is. And tonight—for this one night—it's mine too," I interjected, right as I pulled onto my street. Off in the distance I saw the family ranch, fields the prettiest shades of forest and kelly green underneath the afternoon sun.

As I pulled into the driveway, my cattle dog, Riley, came bounding toward my truck, as she always did when I arrived home. Her striking mix of brown and black fur shimmered in the late-afternoon sunlight as she chased my truck up the drive.

Seeing that sweet dog's tail wagging was all the incentive I needed to shift gears—literally and figuratively.

"I'm home, Mason. Gotta go."

"If you need anything tonight, please call me."

"I will," I promised. . .and then ended the call. Hopefully all would go well and I wouldn't need anything at all.

CHAPTER THREE

I arrived home to find Mom and my great-aunt Bessie Mae up to their eyeballs in canning jars that were full of beautiful east Texas peaches, each jar brimming with lovely golden slices. The kitchen brimmed with the luscious, sweet aroma of the ripened fruit. My stomach rumbled just thinking about it. Bessie Mae was like some sort of modern-day Pied Piper, wooing us with her sweet treats. And I, for one, always took the bait with no apologies.

Mom took one look at me in my ragged state and clucked her tongue. "RaeLyn Hadley, you look like something the cat dragged in."

"Thanks, Mom." I closed the back door behind me and took a few steps in her direction. "I'll take that as a compliment."

"Well, I didn't mean it that way." Her nose wrinkled as I drew near in my messy clothes. "Sorry you misunderstood. And what's that. . .aroma?"

"It's almost a hundred degrees out today. I've been working hard. In the heat."

"And it shows."

I fought the temptation to plop down into one of the chairs at the kitchen table. Mom would scold me for dirtying up the chairs with my messy self, so instead I headed to the shower, leaving the two of them to their work.

Twenty minutes later, dressed and sporting clean, wet hair, I made my way back into the kitchen. The jars of peaches had been pushed aside to make room for Bessie Mae's oversized fryer. Minutes later, the scent of sizzling catfish permeated the room. I walked over to the fryer to take a little peek inside.

The golden fillets sizzled and cracked in that bubbling oil. My favorite part was that crispy coating with its deep amber hue.

I sniffed, breathing in the tantalizing aroma. My stomach rumbled. I couldn't take it much longer.

Still, I must wait. I wouldn't be eating with the family, after all.

I had to remind my mother that I planned to take food back to Tasha's place, not have dinner with everyone else. This didn't sit well with her.

Her lips curled down in a pout. "Gage is on a date. Dallas is fixing Tasha's AC. Jake and Carrie have gone to a ball game with the baby." She lit into a conversation about how she didn't think the baby should be out in this heat.

"And Logan?" I mentioned my brother who lived in the trailer on the far side of the property.

"Probably proposing to that girl."

"Mom." I chided her for referring to my brother's girlfriend as 'that girl.' "Meghan is amazing. If she and Logan end up together, we'll throw the biggest engagement party ever!"

My mother's eye roll revealed her thoughts on the matter.

"And don't worry about me." I opened the fridge and pulled out a cold water bottle. "I'm only going to be at Tasha's place one night, so it's not like I'm running off and leaving home for good."

"Soon enough you will be." A melodramatic sigh followed. If I didn't know any better, I'd say that Mom and Tasha were kin. "Before we know it, Mason will be popping the question and you'll be planning for your big day."

"Whoa, whoa." I put my hands up. "We've only been dating three months. You've already got me marching down the aisle?"

"I wasn't born yesterday. I can see where things are headed."

"Mom." I planted my hands on my hips and stared her down. "Four months ago, you were after me to find someone to date. Now I have. I've got the most amazing guy ever. And you're still not happy?"

Worry lines creased her brow as she kicked back with, "Oh, I'm happy. I'm very happy."

"You might want to tell your face." These words came from my father, who had managed to slip into the room mid-conversation without being noticed.

"I'm thrilled for you and Mason," Mom said as she pulled drinking glasses from the cupboard. "But I also see the writing on the wall. My kids are growing up and leaving me."

"Hardly." My father snorted. "Do I need to remind you that all five of our kids still reside on the Hadley property? And none of them appear to be moving on."

He wasn't wrong. My brother Jake and his wife lived in the little house next to ours—the original Hadley home from the 1930s. And Logan probably wasn't moving on from his trailer anytime soon. My younger brothers most definitely weren't giving up their cushy situation here in the big house.

"I'm definitely not going anywhere in the immediate future," I countered, "so you can put that messy little thought right out of your mind."

Mom sniffled in exaggerated fashion. "I just know the day is coming, and I'm trying to psychologically prepare myself."

"Right now, could you psychologically prepare yourself for an evening alone with Bessie Mae and me?" my dad asked. "It'll be quiet but nice. Kind of a fun change." He reached for one of the glasses and filled it with ice then poured tea over it.

"We missed you at the shop today, RaeLyn," Mom said, completely ignoring my father's words. "We were busier than usual."

"Thanks for covering for me. Hopefully we'll be done with Tasha's place soon and life can get back to normal."

"Dot brought in a really pretty water pitcher set to place on consignment. Oh, and Nadine Henderson came by with some gorgeous candlesticks. Very pricey, I'd say. She says she's got a lot more stuff to get rid of."

"That poor Nadine is probably purging after her husband left her." These words came from Bessie Mae, who lifted the basket of fish out of the oil.

I cringed when she mentioned Nadine's name. The woman had really been through it over the past few months, ever since her husband's unfaith-fulness had become a matter of public record. Clayton Henderson might be the richest man in the county, but right now he was enemy number one to almost everyone in Mabank. We didn't look kindly on cheaters, no matter how much money they had.

Bessie Mae dumped several large golden pieces of catfish onto a plate with a paper towel on it. "I don't blame her a bit. I'd hate to think that new gal would get all of her pretty things."

Thank goodness the conversation shifted. Before long Bessie Mae offered me first dibs on the food and even helped me fill a thermal lunch bag with enough for a feast for Tasha and me. She even tossed in some peach salsa and a couple of thermoses filled with fresh sweet tea.

"Now, you girls have a wonderful time tonight," she said. "Make it a real slumber party like you used to do when you were kids."

"If Dallas doesn't get the AC fixed in the house we're sleeping outside on the balcony," I said. "So it'll be more like a campout."

"Sounds like fun! You should take the inflatable mattress, just in case."

"Great idea."

Mom dove into a story about how they often slept outside when she was young. She seemed to be enjoying this jaunt down memory lane as she tickled our ears with her over-the-top nostalgic tales.

I raced back to my bedroom and grabbed an overnight bag then stuffed it full of the things I would need for my stay. Minutes later, I headed out, pausing only long enough to grab an extra jar of peach salsa from the pantry. Then I headed out the back door and toward the driveway.

I made a quick stop in the carport shed to grab the inflatable mattress. Then I called Riley's name, and my beautiful girl appeared, tail wagging and ears perked with excitement. I placed the mattress and overnight bag in the back of the truck then opened the passenger door. Riley jumped right in, wriggling with joy.

I made my way back to Payne Springs as the sun began to set in the distance. Riley settled down onto the bench seat and rested her head in my lap as I drove. Before long, she had drifted off.

I was feeling a little sleepy too. A good night's sleep would do me good after all of the physical activity of the past few days.

I pulled onto 198 and made my way toward Tasha's place. By now, the sun was changing colors, painting the sky in a gorgeous mixture of colors that captivated me and almost made me drift off the road.

I turned onto her street and made my way to her place at the end. I passed the house just before hers—a spacious ranch-style home on an expansive, well-kept property.

Under the cover of dusk I caught a glimpse of a man walking along the edge of the property. I recognized the elderly man, Bob Reeves, a longtime owner of the pristine property next door to Tasha's. I offered a wave, but he didn't respond, though he did glance my way with what could only be described as a scowl. Odd.

Tasha had mentioned that he wasn't terribly friendly toward her. But why?

I pulled into her driveway and shifted into park.

A short while later, with Riley at my side and my arms loaded down with food and sweet tea, I walked up the front steps of the beautiful old home. I would have to come back for my bag and air mattress later.

I examined the house for the first time under the colors of the sunset and thought it was lovely at this time of day. Tasha's guests were going to love it here.

A couple of raps on the door brought no response from Tasha, so I stuck my head inside and hollered out, "Anyone home?"

Nothing.

I stepped inside and noticed right away that it was still stifling in here. Maybe Dallas wasn't as skilled at AC repair as we'd hoped. I took a few tentative steps into the room we'd dubbed the parlor and accidentally rammed my knee into the leg of the player piano in the dark.

My heart leapt to my throat as it began to play "Let Me Call You Sweetheart." Loudly. This startled Riley, who started yapping. At this point, I almost dropped the food. I managed to hold onto it, but the pain in my knee proved to be quite the distraction. I hobbled up and down with an "Ow, ow, ow!" trying to get my bearings.

Then, just like that, the piano stopped playing.

CHAPTER FOUR

"Tasha?" I called out, now feeling a little unsure of myself.

No response.

I set the food down on the coffee table and made the decision to text her. Seconds later, my phone dinged and I read the words, "Back balcony. Bring food."

Ah. That made sense, considering the heat inside the house.

I grabbed the food and tea once again. Then I made my way up the stairs and into the master bedroom, where French doors led to the balcony. This was quite the feat with my arms so full, but I arrived without mishap.

I found her sitting in one of the oversized wooden gliders facing the water.

"Hey, you!" she said. "I'm hungry."

"Me too. It's kind of dark out here." I set the food down on the small table between the two gliders.

"I know. I've been enjoying the sunset. It's unbelievable, like God took a paintbrush and pulled together the most glorious shades of orange and pink." She released a lingering sigh. "Magical."

"Sure is." I settled into the other chair and shifted my gaze to the skies. "I got a pretty good look at it on the way over. I love that you're west of our place. Makes for a pretty drive."

"Mm-hmm."

"Sorry it took so long."

"It's okay. I enjoyed the stillness. I rarely get quiet moments to myself. Between my parents and the crowd at the family restaurant..." She sighed.

"Oh, I get it. My world is chaotic much of the time too." I turned my gaze out to the water, where the sunset lit the ripples with a golden glow.

"Half the time I'm wishing I could keep this house for myself, and the other half I'm hoping for guests to keep it filled. But for now, I'm just enjoying the solitude."

"I understand." I paused. "Should I ask about the AC?"

She groaned, my cue to leave the topic alone. "He tried. But no luck. I need to call someone who does that sort of work, I guess. But something crazy happened. We entertained ourselves with the player piano."

"I bumped into it as I came in and got quite a shock."

She laughed. "Well, you would've been even more shocked if you'd shown up an hour ago when your brother and I were singing a harmonious rendition of 'Let Me Call You Sweetheart'."

"Oh my."

"It was actually very..."

"Hokey?" I offered.

"I was going to say sweet." A moment of silence hung in the humid air between us. "He's been very kind these last few weeks, and I appreciate it. It was nice to have a moment that didn't involve work."

The pause that followed made me wonder if she might finally be ready to reciprocate his feelings.

Just as quickly, Tasha seemed to change gears. "Is that Bessie Mae's fried catfish I smell?"

"It is. Want to take it inside or eat out here?"

"Here is better. There's a little bit of a breeze coming off the lake. It's not too bad. Let me run inside and grab some plates. I'll get some glasses of ice for that tea while I'm down there."

"Thanks."

She returned moments later and flipped on the small porch light, which offered just enough of a glow to make the scene feel eerie. We moved to the patio table and dove into our meal.

"So tell me more about this certified letter you got," I said between mouthfuls.

"Just got it this morning, and I've been so busy, I haven't had time to process it. Belinda Keller is claiming her stepmother wasn't in her right mind when the will was written. She believes her brother coerced her into changing it. Belinda really believes this house was always meant to come to her."

"It's a little late for that, I'd say."

"I hope you're right. But I'm going to call my dad's attorney to make sure Belinda doesn't really have a case. I'd hate to advertise the place for rent only to end up losing it in the end."

"You won't lose it." I rested my hand on hers and hoped I was speaking the truth.

Tasha took a swig of tea and leaned back in the chair. "While you were gone, I looked up Belinda on social media."

"Oh?"

"Yeah." Tasha sighed. "I do feel kind of sorry for her. From what I could gather, her husband passed away a few months ago. So she's lost both parents and her husband."

"Gosh. And she's estranged from her stepbrother?"

"Yes. Anthony definitely doesn't have anything to do with her. It looks like she's got a couple of grown kids, but I couldn't really tell much about them. She just seems..."

"Like a grieving widow and daughter?"

"Yeah."

I passed off a nibble of catfish to Riley, who had settled at my feet.

"So what do you think of the place, really?" Tasha asked. "Do you think I stand a chance of competing against Clayton Henderson and his gorgeous rental home?"

"I think you'll attract a completely different clientele, and that's a good thing. Not everyone can afford several hundred dollars a night to rent a mansion by the lake. And his place doesn't have the great view that yours does."

"True."

"And, let's face it—the interior of your place is really homey. And I'm not just saying that because you got most of the furniture from our store. It's quaint and sweet. It's very. . ." I paused to choose my words carefully. "Comfortable. Inviting. But not snooty."

"Snooty is highly overrated."

"Right?" I laughed. "But I don't think Clayton is going to keep renting out his place anyway. I heard that his wife—ex-wife—moved in when they separated."

"Really?" She paused. "That's kind of. . .bittersweet."

"Yeah, but if anyone deserves a lovely home, Nadine does. That poor woman has been through so much already. That house is gorgeous, the perfect place to recover from trauma."

"She's definitely been through trauma." Tasha reached for her glass of tea. "And I guess I'm a little relieved to hear that Clayton's home is no longer on the market. That should draw more attention to mine."

"Exactly." I wiped the condensation from my tea glass before taking another sip.

Tasha gestured toward the house. "I'm still trying to think of a name for the place. I have to settle on that before I list it."

"True. What are you thinking?"

"How about Romantic Ripples Lagoon?"

I laughed so hard I almost dropped the slippery glass of tea. Probably not the response she was hoping for.

"Okay, then." She paused. "Moonlight Harbor?"

"I mean, that's nice. It gives off a peaceful vibe, for sure. But you're not really on a harbor, are you?"

"No. I'm not. I'll keep thinking about it." She brushed her fingertips against the paper towel in her lap. "Right now, the way that master bedroom toilet is leaking, I'll have to settle for The Leaky Tiki."

I laughed out loud. "Good grief."

We wrapped up our meal, but I still had a special treat waiting for our dessert. "Now, what do you say? Ready for some cobbler?"

"I sure am." She sighed. "I just wish I had some Blue Bell vanilla ice cream to put on top."

"Me too. Why didn't I think of that?"

"Because you had your hands full, girl," she countered. "You've been amazing, by the way. I could never have done all of this without you."

Warm feelings flooded over me at her words. "You're the best possible investment of my time and energy, Tasha. I hope you know that."

"Thank you for that. I really mean it."

I knew she did.

We ate our dessert and spent another half hour or so chatting about the home's potential.

Tasha was a list-maker and spent several minutes going over all of the lists in her head of things yet undone.

"Dallas has been really helpful. And he won't let me pay him a penny."

"It's probably a nice diversion from working on our ranch. And he's got some really great handyman skills. He and Gage really helped my dad out a lot when it came time to build the new barn. And he's great with repairs. He's got a real knack for those sorts of things."

"I've noticed. He seems pretty interested in my house."

Should I tell her that he was interested in more than that? Had she really not figured it out yet?

"He suggested the name Cedar Creek Retreat."

"I like it."

"Me too, but it sounds like church camp." She laughed. "Not sure that's the vibe we need."

This led to a great trip down memory lane about our years together at church camp as teens.

From the balcony, the sound of our laughter and quiet conversation drifted on the breeze, mingling with the gentle lapping of the water against the shore.

The whole thing was incredibly peaceful. Off in the distance the faint sound of crickets chirping served as a gentle backdrop, coupled with the rustling of leaves on the chinaberry tree nearest the balcony.

"Cabin by the Cove?" Tasha's words broke through the silence.

"It's a big house, not a cabin, though," I countered.

"Mm-hmm. True. I'll keep thinking."

After a while, I found myself drifting off. All of that hard work was getting to me.

"So what do you think?" Tasha asked after watching me stifle another yawn. "Sleep outside?"

"Sure. I brought the air mattress. It's in the back of my truck with my overnight bag. I'll go get it." I rose and stretched.

"Good call. I need to clean up this mess." She started tidying up our dinner mess, and we both headed downstairs.

It didn't take long to get the mattress set up and some fresh sheets on it. I grabbed a couple of pillows from the master bedroom, and before long we were both settling down for the night. Riley curled up at the foot of the mattress, her tail gently tap-tap-tapping against it as she snuggled into place. I took my spot, closest to the balcony railing, and before long was stretched out, enjoying the evening breeze.

"Hope we don't regret this," Tasha said as she lay down in the spot beside me.

I paused, reflecting on our earlier concerns. "Are you worried about that homeless guy coming back?"

"Not really worried, per se. Are you?"

"Nah. I think we're safe out here."

"Yeah. Me too."

A lovely silence grew between us. I shifted my gaze to the skies, where I noticed twinkling stars and that soft haze of the golden moon. Cicadas sang their nighttime song, their voices harmonizing with the occasional lapping of water from the lake against the shore. The whole thing was perfect, the loveliest backdrop for sleeping I'd ever experienced.

Or maybe I was just exhausted.

I must have dozed off shortly thereafter. I found myself in the middle of an amazing dream about a boat on the lake, bobbing up and down on gentle waters. Suddenly, I jolted awake as the sound of music filled the air. I sat up and tried to figure out what was happening.

Riley shot up and let out a bark, her ears now pointed in full attention.

"Tasha." I spoke in a hoarse whisper.

She never stirred.

"Tasha," I tried again.

When she didn't respond, I jabbed her with my elbow.

"Hmm? What?" Her eyes squinted open and then closed again.

"Tasha, do you hear that?"

"Hear what?"

Riley barked again.

"You mean the dog?" She groaned. "Yeah, I hear her. What's got her worked up?"

"The music."

I strained to make out the melody, which was now familiar. "Let Me Call You Sweetheart."

"Music?" She sat up and rubbed her eyes. "I thought I was dreaming that."

"No, you're not. It's the player piano."

I reached for my phone and whispered, "I'm calling the police."

"And tell them what?" Tasha countered. "That a player piano is making music?"

"Well then, let's go check it out."

We tiptoed into the house and I took hold of Riley's collar as she tried to bolt ahead of me. "Whoa, girl."

"You should let her go," Tasha whispered. "She'll protect us."

I wasn't as sure, but I did release my hold on the dog as we entered the hallway outside of the master bedroom. She bolted down the stairs ahead of us.

"Who's there?" I called out, doing my best to keep my voice steady as Tasha and I approached the top step.

Off in the distance, the music continued to play. By now, Riley was barking like a maniac from below. We tiptoed down the stairs into the parlor, and I flipped on the light. The keys on the piano moved up and down with eerie precision.

And then, suddenly, the music stopped.

Before I could say, "I think your piano is possessed," the front door slammed, and I saw a flicker of light outside of the glass window panes.

I wasn't sure what emboldened me, but I rushed to the front door and swung it open. Off in the distance the light flickered again—a flashlight, maybe? Seconds later, it disappeared. A shadowy figure darted off, away from the house and toward the road. Off in the distance I could almost make out the outline of a car. A small car. But my feet refused to budge.

Riley went into action, chasing after the person, only stopping when the car's engine kicked on and the vehicle pulled away. My exhausted pup returned moments later with a something I couldn't quite distinguish in her mouth.

"What have you got, girl?"

She dropped it onto the front porch, and I called out for Tasha to turn on the porch light. My gaze shifted down, and I groaned when I saw some sort of spray can. Weird.

"Really? I send you after the bad guys, and you come back with an empty can?"

Tasha joined me but let out a cry as soon as she stepped out onto the porch.

I turned back to see what had her so upset, and that's when I saw it...the real reason our nighttime visitor had come.

The front door was spray-painted with expletives and other graffiti, along with two very ominous words: Go Away, in bold black letters.

CHAPTER FIVE

It probably wasn't my wisest move, but I grabbed my keys and climbed into Tilly with Riley at my side.

"What do you think you're doing?" Tasha called out.

"Trying to get the license number from that car." I pulled out onto the road, tires squealing. I noticed the neighbor's porch light was on. Had we awakened him? If so, he probably wouldn't be happy.

I tore off down the road, praying I could find the vehicle. At one point I thought I had, but it turned out to be a mirage—just shadows in the darkness. I circled the tiny neighborhood a couple of times but finally gave up and returned back to her house.

"I can't believe you did that." Tasha slugged me in the arm as I entered the parlor. "Are you trying to give me a heart attack?"

"Sorry! I really thought I could get the license plate number."

She planted her hands on her hips, the pitch of her voice more animated than before. "Well, at least take me with you next time."

"Okay, okay." Only, I hoped there wouldn't be a next time.

We waited another hour or so until the sun peeked over the horizon to call the police, but I don't think either of us actually fell back asleep during that hour. Tension hung thick in the air between us as we huddled together on the leather sofa in the parlor. Even Riley seemed anxious as she paced the room and peered out the front window. My gaze shifted to the spray paint can, now on the coffee table. Evidence left behind. Maybe that would come in handy.

I simply couldn't make sense out of what had happened. Who would bust into her house in the middle of the night to deliberately scare us? And how did they know we'd be staying overnight? This was a first for us, after all. And why leave such a rude message?

Once we had the assurance the police were on their way, I placed a call to Mason. I'd heard concern in his voice before, but not like this. He insisted on coming over right away, and I told him that would be fine.

A few minutes later a patrol car pulled into the driveway. Tasha and I watched from the front porch, where Riley started yapping at the officer.

I recognized Deputy Shawn Warren from the Henderson County Sheriff's Office. We'd met several months back, when my beloved red truck, Tilly, had gone missing.

The handsome deputy was decked out in his usual uniform, which only seemed to accentuate his height and broad shoulders. He looked like a made-for-TV cop, ready to solve crimes and conquer the world.

As Riley bounded his way, Deputy Warren put his hands up.

"It's okay," I called out. "She won't hurt—"

I didn't get to finish because Riley almost knocked the man backward as she leaped up to put her front paws on his chest. He stumbled back and then caught himself just in time before going down. Whew!

I called her off then told Riley to sit, and—like the obedient dog she sometimes pretended to be—she sat.

"Did you ladies call the sheriff's department?" He made several long strides toward us on the front porch.

"Yes!" Tasha dove into an animated discussion about why we had called.

After listening for a couple of minutes he whipped out a notepad and pen. "You did the right thing in calling. Just let me take a few notes."

"You okay to come inside?" Tasha asked.

"Sure." His face lit in a gentle smile. "I've been dying to see the inside of this place ever since I heard it was being renovated."

"Well, c'mon in, then!" She opened the front door and gestured for him to join us inside.

We stepped into the spacious parlor—the coziest and most inviting space in the house.

Deputy Warren looked around and then said, "Wow. I've only been in here once before—the elderly woman who lived here was having some family issues, as I recall."

"Yes," I said. "We heard about that."

He continued to gaze around the room. "It definitely didn't look like this. In fact, it was more like a Hoarder's episode, as I recall."

"We've been working hard to clean it up and get it fixed for guests," Tasha said with a bashful smile. "What do you think of the wall color?"

He glanced up at the buttery yellow walls. I found them cheerful—the perfect complement to the rich hardwood floors—but wondered what a guy would think.

"Looks great. I don't have any decorating skills. My wife always took care of all of that. But I would say it's very calming, and that's a good thing for a house by the lake, right?"

"Right. That's the idea. And we had so much fun picking out the decor. My favorite is the rug." Tasha pointed down at the ornate vintage rug, which was adorned with all sorts of delicate floral patterns. I felt like it tied the room together perfectly.

"Looks good," he said.

My favorite part of this room was the stream of colors coming from the tiny stained-glass window above the front door. The morning sun set off a lovely array of colors shimmering across the room, reflecting all the way to the oversized coffee table, which we'd loaded up with books and magazines for future guests. Bessie Mae always said, "You never get a second chance to make a first impression" and this room made the very best one imaginable—filled with a mix of antique charm and modern comfort.

Deputy Warren paused and ran his hand over the keys of the player piano. "Wow. Haven't seen one of these in years."

I thought it was exquisite too. The polished mahogany casing gleamed under the shimmer of early morning sunlight peeking in through the windows. I felt the old piano added a bit of whimsy and nostalgia to the room.

"It came with the house," Tasha explained. "It's one of the few things we decided to hang onto after we purged the hoard."

Warren looked Tasha's way with a grin. "I thought you were going to tell me you were a concert pianist."

"Hey, with a player piano, *anyone* can be a concert pianist." She laughed, and then told him about her attempts to play the violin as a teenager. He countered with a story about bass guitar, and they somehow ended up in a full-blown conversation about musical theater. Go figure.

About the time they landed on their thoughts about *Les Miserables*, Mason arrived. He seemed confused to be walking in on a conversation about musical theater instead of the obvious.

I cleared my throat, knowing he was probably in a hurry to get to work. Then I gestured to the plush armchairs and the well-worn leather sofa, hoping someone would follow my lead as I took a seat.

"So tell me more about what happened." Warren looked back and forth between us then opened his notepad.

Tasha dove into another animated explanation of what had happened a few hours prior, but her story wasn't 100% accurate. She'd slept through the first part, after all, and it showed in her lack of details.

I raised my hand like a kid in a classroom, waiting to be called on.

Warren looked my way.

"I woke up first," I explained. "And I heard music coming from downstairs."

"Then what?" He looked up from his notepad.

"Then I tried to wake Tasha up, but she was out like a light."

"I'm a sound sleeper," she explained. "Melatonin. Works like a charm."

"You were taking medication?" He suddenly looked concerned. "That might interfere with your recollection, so we'll need to keep that in mind."

"It's just a supplement, but it does work to knock me out most nights," she explained. "But it's perfectly legal, I promise. If you ever have trouble sleeping, melatonin does the trick."

"I do have a hard time unwinding after long days." He sighed. "Since my wife passed a couple years back I—" He cleared his throat then looked my way. "Sorry. Then what?"

"I'm sorry about your wife," I interjected. "I remember meeting Carla at church a couple of times."

"Yeah, we had only been in the area a year or so when she was diagnosed. The whole thing was. . .awful. But the folks up at the church were really helpful."

Mason gave him a compassionate look, and before long the two of them were knee-deep into a conversation about the church.

"I've only been back in the Mabank area a few months," Mason explained. "I was away for several years. But going back to church feels like going home again. You should come back, Shawn. I'll save a place for you."

"Maybe I will."

This was one thing I loved about Mason. He always seemed to direct folks to the one place in town where they were most likely to find healing and a sense of community. Our little church really was like family.

The two guys went on for a while, until I glanced up at the wall clock and noticed the time: 10:42. I needed to get back home soon to help out at the shop.

Deputy Warren looked my way. "Sorry. It's kind of nice to have folks to talk to. Gets kind of quiet around my place." He paused and then rolled his pen in his fingers. "Then what happened?"

"Riley started barking, and I finally got Tasha to wake up," I said. "We followed the sound of the music, and when we got to the top of the stairs it stopped. Then I heard the front door slam."

"Someone was actually *in* the house?" Mason's jaw flinched.

"Yes." I hated to worry him but had no choice. "And I saw a flicker of light through the windows."

"I was still too freaked out by what the player piano had been doing," Tasha added. "I didn't notice the lights."

"So strange." Mason still looked troubled, and a little confused. "Are you really saying it was playing all by its lonesome?"

"Yep," Tasha and I spoke in unison.

We all shifted our gaze to the piano at the same time, as if expecting it to spring into action before our very eyes. It didn't.

"What do you know about the piano?" Warren asked. "Anything of consequence?"

Tasha shrugged. "Anthony—the former owner's son—said it was probably ninety years old, or more."

"It does seem to be a little wonky," I explained. "I bumped into it earlier in the evening and it started playing on its own, so I guess it has a glitch."

"Some sort of mechanical malfunction?" Warren asked.

I wasn't exactly sure. "Maybe, but the fact that it actually played the melody makes me wonder if the foot pedal got stuck in place or something. But I haven't had a chance to check it out yet, so I don't know for sure."

"You're just saying that when it went off in the night it wasn't the first time. Right?" Warren gave it a closer look.

I nodded. "That's right. Could be some problem with the piano."

"Or. . .it could be the angels playing it," Tasha said. "I saw something like that in a movie once."

I gave her a funny look. "Then the angels have interesting taste in music, because 'Let Me Call You Sweetheart' is still the only song I've heard it play."

"Did anyone ever consider taking the roller out?" Mason asked. "These old pianos only play whatever happens to be on the song roller. Right?"

"Sure. State the obvious." I elbowed him.

"I'm wondering if someone deliberately sabotaged the piano to do this," Tasha suggested. "To scare us, I mean."

I had to admit, that was a creepy thought.

"I'm thinking it would have to be someone with player piano experience," Warren said. "Otherwise, how would they know to manipulate it?"

"Our suspect list just went *way* down." Mason laughed. "I don't know anyone with player piano experience."

A look of concern passed over Tasha's face. "I'm guessing Belinda knows something about player pianos, since this was the house she grew up in."

"Wait. Who's Belinda again?" Warren asked.

"The daughter of the former owner. She was estranged from her family, but she's been harassing me since I bought the place."

"Tell me more about her."

So Tasha dove right in, giving animated detail after animated detail. "I think she lives in Tyler now, but she grew up here. From what I heard, she had a falling-out with the family. Now she wants the house for herself."

"You think she's the one who showed up in the night?" Mason asked.

"No idea," Tasha countered. "But I wouldn't put it past her."

"If so, she scared us to death," I added. "I wouldn't want to meet up with her in a dark alley."

"I, for one, thought we were very brave in the moment," Tasha said. "One never knows how one might respond in a crisis, but I think we did really well. Don't you, RaeLyn?"

I nodded. "Yep. I was kind of proud of us."

"So you rushed downstairs. . .and then what?" Warren asked.

"When I found the living room empty, I went out on the front porch to see if someone was out there," I said.

Mason's jaw flinched. "You shouldn't have done that, RaeLyn."

I appreciated his concern, but what could I do about it now? "I know. I should have waited, but I thought I might see who it was. But after I saw the flash of lights through the glass panes in the front door, I knew I only had that moment in time to catch the guy."

"What did the light look like?" Deputy Warren asked.

"Just a flicker, like someone with a flashlight running off," I said.

"And you thought that was the perfect time to risk your own life by going outside?" Mason gave me a "We're going to talk about this later" look, and I shrugged.

"Anyway, by the time I got out there, Riley was already chasing after the guy."

"Wait, who's Riley again?" the officer asked.

"My dog." I pointed to the sleeping dog at my feet.

"Oh, right. The one who almost knocked me over earlier."

"You're sure it was a guy?" Mason gave me a pensive look. "How could you tell?"

"Well, whoever. . . Riley was chasing after the person. But before I could do anything about it, he—or she—took off in what appeared to be a small car."

"Any guesses on make and model?" Warren asked.

"No, they were parked quite a distance off, past Bob Reeves' house. But Riley made it all the way down there. She came back very winded and carrying something in her mouth."

"What did she have?" Mason asked.

"This spray paint canister." I picked it up from the coffee table and handed it to him. "Riley's not much of a cattle dog, but at least she's got some hunting capabilities. That gives me hope."

"Okay." Warren looked it over then scribbled a few more notes. He glanced Tasha's way. "Anything else?"

"Other than the part where RaeLyn jumped in her truck and took off after them, hoping to get the license plate number?" Tasha asked. "Because I thought that was a little risky."

I jabbed her.

"RaeLyn!" Mason slapped himself on his forehead. "You *chased* them?"

"Only for a minute. Or five. But I had Riley with me. I was perfectly safe."

"You don't know that," he countered, his eyes riveted on mine. "They could have been armed."

"Oh." I hadn't thought of that.

Warren diverted his attention to Tasha. "Is there anyone who might be upset at you?"

Tasha's brow wrinkled. "Well, actually, I got this certified letter—"

"Other than your neighbor, I mean." Warren interrupted her.

"My neighbor?" Tasha looked perplexed. "Bob Reeves?"

"Yes. I heard about the petition. We all did."

"Petition?" Tasha, Mason, and I spoke the word in unison.

"Someone started a petition…against me?" Tasha looked flabbergasted by this news.

"Well, against the idea of a vacation rental in the neighborhood," Warren explained. "Only reason I heard about it is because I live a couple of streets over on Lakeside Court, and he came to my door a few days back with a clipboard in hand, spouting some nonsense about property values in the neighborhood dropping once the vacation rental opens for business. He put together a petition to present to the county, as I understood it."

"No way." Tasha looked like she might be sick. I kind of felt that way too. Was it hot in here?

"I wouldn't worry too much," the deputy said. "As of then he only had three signatures, and two of them confided in me that they felt pressured to sign to get him to go away."

"The third?" I asked.

"Was his own signature." Warren closed the notepad and tucked it under his arm. "I wouldn't worry about Bob. I don't think he's behind this. He's cranky, but I don't see him as a real threat. He's just set in his ways and doesn't want to be bothered with new neighbors."

"Well, I wouldn't have thought of him at all, until you said all of that." Tasha plopped down onto the sofa, looking more upset than before. "I can't believe someone actually started a petition against me. Wow."

"What about Conner?" Mason turned his attention to Warren. "When RaeLyn told me she was spending the night here, I checked in with your sergeant, and he assured me you guys were keeping a close eye on Conner."

"Yeah, he's been on our radar for a while now," Warren said. "One of our other deputies caught him squatting here a few weeks back when the place was vacated. But I haven't really noticed him hanging around recently. Have you?" Warren glanced Tasha's way.

"No." She shook her head. "But I don't trust him. I never did."

"Understood." Warren squared his shoulders. "Tell you what—I can keep closer tabs if you like."

"That would be great." Tasha flashed him a warm smile. "Since you're a neighbor and all."

"Happy to." He grinned right back at her.

I cleared my throat, hoping to get this train back on track.

"Now, what were you saying about a letter?" Deputy Warren asked.

"Hang on a second and I'll show you." Tasha disappeared into the kitchen and came back out moments later with the certified letter. "I just got this yesterday morning. It's from the previous owner's daughter. She believes she's the rightful owner of the property."

"Is she?" Deputy Warren gave Tasha a pensive look.

"No. I have the deed. I closed on the property weeks ago. I can show you all the paperwork."

"There's no need for that. If you closed on the house, you closed on the house. It's a done deal."

"Exactly!" She gave him an admiring smile. "There were no red flags during the purchase, and I'm the rightful owner."

We wrapped up with a bit more conversation, and then Warren went on his way. Convinced we were okay, Mason also headed out to work. Speaking of which, I needed to get back home soon to help Mom in the shop, but one lingering thing wouldn't leave me alone, something I wanted to take care of before leaving.

"I say we do more digging on social media to learn more about Belinda," I suggested.

"I already did that."

"I know, but let's dig deeper. Go back further. Check out her family members." I signed onto Facebook on my phone and typed in Belinda's name. It didn't take long to find her account, since Tasha had already located it earlier. I couldn't see much of her page since we weren't friends, but what I did see made my skin crawl.

"Gosh, some people are just angry, aren't they?" I pointed to one of her posts, filled with vile language and anger.

"Sure looks that way." Tasha's nose wrinkled. "Nasty."

"I wonder about people like her, filled with so much bitterness." It broke my heart, really. To live with that much angst? Must be awful. A lot of Belinda's posts sounded almost threatening.

It didn't take long to see that many of her posts were pointed—against her stepbrother, Anthony, and his son, Jimmy. She actually called them by name and accused them of a variety of crimes against her. Yikes.

"Did Anthony respond to any of these?" Tasha asked.

"There's nothing from him in the comments that I can see," I countered. "Let me see if I can find his account."

I did a bit of searching but came up lacking. Unless he went by another name, there was no account listing him.

"He's probably avoiding her at all costs," Tasha said. "I would."

I glanced down at my watch and did my best not to groan aloud. By now, Mom and Bessie Mae had already opened the antique store and customers were, no doubt, flooding in. Saturday was our busiest day. I'd promised to be back no later than eleven, but we were coming up on that now and I couldn't possibly leave. Could I?

Judging from the look of panic in my best friend's eyes, no. I'd better text my mother to give her a heads-up.

So that's what I did.

She didn't respond. No doubt she was up to her eyeballs in customers. I'd hear about it later, but what could I do? Tasha needed me.

CHAPTER SIX

I arrived at the antique shop around eleven thirty to find my mom and Bessie Mae juggling dozens of customers. Many—like Mom's friend Dot—were there to place items on consignment. Still others were there to shop.

And shop they did! By one fifteen we'd sold the old cast iron stove, an item I'd worried we'd be stuck with forever. And by two thirty we had a buyer for the Noritake china set. I was thrilled it found a good home. Some things were harder to get rid of than others, and that was often the case with china patterns from the 1980s.

A text came through at three from Mason, reminding me of our date tonight.

"Cajun food okay? I was thinking we could try out that new place in Athens."

"Sure. Sounds good. I like it spicy."

"Me too."

"I just need to get home in time to write my article for *Mabank Happenings*."

"I thought you usually turned your articles in on Tuesday nights."

"Yes, but this is a special piece to promote the Fourth of July celebration, so we need to time it perfectly to give folks enough time to make plans."

"Got it. I'll get Cinderella home before the clock strikes twelve, I promise."

Okay, that made me laugh. But I really did need to write that article, or my editor would have my head.

I wrapped up my work in the shop around five and headed inside to prep for my date. After a shower, I changed into a cute new outfit I'd gotten from a new boutique in Gun Barrel City. By six, my makeup was on, and I was working to make some sort of sense of my long, dark hair. I decided to wear it up, in part because of the extreme heat.

As I worked, the luscious scent of Bessie Mae's chicken fried steak had me second-guessing the Cajun food idea. I'd never turned down her steak before, but I didn't want to ruin my meal.

When Mason arrived a short while later, I said my goodbyes and we headed out. Always the perfect gentleman, he opened the passenger door of his truck for me and I climbed inside.

On the way to the restaurant, a call came through from Tasha. I glanced down at my phone, ready to silence it.

Mason glanced my way. "Something important?"

"No. Just Tasha. I'll call her back later."

"No, go ahead," he said. "I don't mind."

So I took the call. But before I could even say, "Hey, I'm on a date with Mason," she dove right in.

"As soon as the house passes the inspection on Monday, I have to list it online on the rental site. The longer I wait, the less time I have to come up with my next mortgage payment."

Right. There it was again, the mortgage payment conversation.

"Anyway, I still don't have a name for the place," Tasha said. "So I'm calling for help."

"I'm with Mason. I'll put the call on speaker so he can help too. He's better at this sort of thing than I am."

"Hi, Mason!" she called out. "Sorry to interrupt."

"It's no problem." He put on the turn signal and eased into the left lane to pass a slow-moving truck.

"What about something really peaceful?" I suggested. "Like Serenity Shores."

"Like the rehab center by the hospital?" Mason eased his way past the truck.

"There's a rehab facility named Serenity Shores?" This surprised me.

Mason nodded. "Yeah, I just called them a few days ago, asking for information."

"About. . ." Tasha and I spoke in unison.

"Oh, just trying to get information for a. . .friend." His gaze shifted to the window. "Is it going to rain?"

I glanced up at the gray skies, suddenly concerned. "The sky has that weird color to it. Kind of a yellow-gray. That's never good."

"Never thought to check my phone, but we've had a lot of unexpected storms of late," Tasha said. "What's up with this crazy weather!" She dove into a panicked conversation about her house—something about making sure the shutters were in place—then ended the call.

"I guess we'll just figure out a name for the house some other day," I said as I tucked my phone into my purse.

A few moments later, Mason and I arrived at the restaurant. I couldn't help but laugh as I saw the exterior decor. We had watched this old Pizza Hut building transform over the past fifteen years—first to a Mexican restaurant, then southern-style cooking, and now a Cajun restaurant with a giant crab affixed to the roof. If we held on long enough, it would be a pizza joint once again.

We entered the place and I chuckled at their ingenuity. The new owners had used some of the same leftover decor from the restaurant before, only changing it up a bit to make it transition from southern to Cajun. I found myself distracted by the walls adorned with purple and green Mardi Gras masks and the framed poster of jazz musicians.

But, man! The aroma of spice in this place was definitely different. My nostrils started flaring the moment we walked in the door. And the rousing zydeco music playing overhead definitely added to the ambient feel of the place.

The young hostess seated us at a table with a red and white checked cloth, which I recognized from the restaurant's Pizza Hut days. She passed off colorful menus then headed back to welcome another guest.

A couple of minutes later, soft drinks in hand, we made our choices. I opted for the red beans and rice with smoked ham hock. Mason ordered the crab cakes with seafood étouffée, along with a bowl of shrimp and sausage gumbo. We also ordered two appetizers: fried pickles and shrimp firecrackers. Spicy shrimp with cream cheese, wrapped in a wonton and deep fried? Yes, please!

Okay, so maybe our eyes were bigger than our stomachs. By the time my entrée arrived I wasn't terribly hungry anymore, but I didn't let that stop me. I dove right in to the red beans and rice, making quite the production out of my eating experience. At this point, I really didn't care what anyone else thought. They were all enjoying their food too, so what did it matter if I made a goober of myself?

After just a few bites—just about the time the lights inside the restaurant started flickering—the door swung open and Clayton Henderson walked in.

Suddenly I didn't feel like eating…anything. I'd never been a huge fan of the man. He always made such a splash about being the most successful guy in the county, after all. But his recent rendezvous with Meredith Reed had turned my stomach. His poor wife, Nadine, didn't deserve that. And there was little nice that could be said of his new arm candy.

And here they were—the infamous duo—arm in arm at the local Pizza-Hut-turned-Cajun-joint, looking as unassuming as could be. Unless you counted the fancy clothes. They were a little out of place in such a casual setting.

"Wonder where Nadine is tonight," Mason muttered under his breath as he caught a glimpse of the overdressed couple, now chatting it up with the hostess.

"Last I heard, she was living in their big house on the lake," I whispered. "That's what Dot told Mom, anyway."

"He's not renting it out anymore?"

"Nope." I shook my head. "From what I understand, it's now Nadine's place until the divorce is final. Then I'm not sure how the dust will settle.

Maybe they'll sell it. I guess we'll see. But for now I'm happy to hear he's not renting it out."

"Well, that's good news for Tasha, I guess." He took a sip of his drink then shifted his gaze to Clayton once again. "One less rental property for her to compete with."

"I guess, but it's kind of sad to think about Nadine rattling around in that monstrous house all by herself. I've been feeling really sorry for her lately. I rarely see her anymore, do you?"

"Nope." He shook his head. "I'm guessing she's tucked herself away on purpose. Can't blame her for wanting her privacy."

"True." My gaze shifted to Meredith. She ran her fingers through her bleach-blond hair and giggled in an over-the-top sort of way at something Clayton said.

"Nadine deserves that big house and so much more," Mason said, his voice lowered to a hoarse whisper. "But I'm guessing this one's not happy about it. She probably wanted the B&B for herself."

My gaze followed Meredith as they took a seat in a booth not far from us.

"I heard these two are in the in-town house," I explained. "She's living there with Clayton."

Mason gasped out loud at that revelation. "I can't imagine they would be brazen enough to shack up together, what with Clayton being on the deacon board at church."

"He stepped down last week," I explained. "Heard it from my dad after a special meeting was called last Sunday after church."

"You sure know the goings-on around here, RaeLyn." Mason gave me an admiring look. "You're almost as good as Dot, and that's really saying something."

"I just pay attention. That's all. Maybe it's the writer in me."

We watched as Meredith pulled off her sweater, revealing a low-cut blouse in canary yellow. Ugh. Awkward. Clayton glanced my way and nodded, as if greeting an old friend. I nodded in response, unsure of what else to do.

Looked like we would have to change the conversation. We'd been spotted. And they were definitely within earshot now.

Lightning flashed across the sky, that shocking bright kind that felt like it might hit the building. It was followed by a loud clap of thunder that caused me to jump.

I reached for my phone and scrolled through it for the weather app. I gasped after opening it and turned the phone Mason's way. "Did you realize we're under a tornado warning?"

"No way." His gaze shot to the window just as another shock of lightning streaked the sky.

The restaurant's door swung open, and a familiar man stepped inside. Conner Griffin.

I dabbed some of the spicy sauce off my lips with my napkin but kept my eyes on the man as he entered the restaurant, his clothes covered in raindrops.

Mason looked up from his plate and watched as the manager came out to greet Conner then led him to a table, where they sat down across from each other with some sort of paperwork between them.

"Hey, looks like Conner decided to apply for that job after all." Mason brushed his napkin over his lips too. "Told him he should."

"Can't fault a man for looking for work," I countered.

But after what had happened last night, I still had to wonder if Conner was the one who had paid us a visit. It wouldn't be the first time he was caught on Tasha's property.

Mason didn't appear to share my concerns. He excused himself then rose and walked over to the other table to greet Conner. I watched as the two of them engaged in a lively conversation. A couple of minutes into it, they shook hands. Then Mason headed back my way, all smiles.

"Everything okay?" I asked as he settled into his chair and reached for his fork.

"Yeah, I was just asking if he needed a ride back."

I laughed. "Only you would invite a potential suspect on a date."

"Potential suspect? You really think he's the one who broke in last night?"

"Well, sure. He was living in the place just a few weeks ago. It just makes sense."

"Not to me." Mason shrugged.

"You're very trusting."

"Not really. I just thought he might need a ride. But he said he's got a car now. An older VW Bug. Pastor Burchfield gave it to him."

"Pastor Burchfield gave him a car?" This surprised me.

"Yeah. They've actually been spending quite a bit of time together."

"Well, they need to tread carefully. That's all I'm saying."

"I guess I don't really understand why you're so suspicious of him," Mason said. "Yes, he was staying on the property, but what if that's all there is to the story?"

"Nope. I don't buy that," I responded. "He's my key suspect, in fact."

CHAPTER SEVEN

"Conner Griffin is your key suspect?" Mason asked.

"Yes," I countered. "He has motive, opportunity, and desperation."

"Please. Do elaborate." Mason leaned back in his chair.

I lowered my voice to avoid being overheard. "Motive: he was kicked out of the house by the police, which probably has him feeling resentful and bitter, thereby thinking about revenge."

"I don't know about that."

"Opportunity: He's familiar with the house, the property, the whole neighborhood. He knows the lay of the land. He knows when and where to strike."

"Okay, I'll give you that, but—"

"Desperation." My volume rose as I grew more animated. "His lack of resources and friends to mooch off of. I suspect he had no place else to turn, so he resorted to an act of sabotage, if for no other reason than to draw attention to his plight. Or, to find a place to sleep. He's homeless, so. . ."

"You can nix that last part." Mason lowered his volume to a hoarse whisper. "He doesn't need a place to sleep. He's not homeless."

"What do you mean?"

"The church offered Conner the old parsonage, since it's not in use anymore. When he starts earning an income they'll let him pay a little rent, but for now they're giving him a chance to stay there in exchange for working on it."

"Wow. That old house is really run down. I'm surprised anyone could stay in it."

"I know." Mason sighed. "But he's pretty handy, so he's already tackled that sagging porch. And he's scraping the peeling paint from the exterior. After years of neglect, that house is finally getting the update it deserves. From some very skilled hands, I might add."

"Well, that's nice," I acknowledged. "I guess you could say he's earning his keep then?"

"Yes. And I'm really relieved—for him and for the church," Mason said. "I've been worried about him for a while. Remember what he was like in high school? Always a loner."

"Yeah." I paused to try to remember more about him. "I just remember his parents were always in and out of jail and he stayed with his grandmother a lot. I think he ended up in CPS custody for a couple of years when he was in junior high, right?"

"Right." Mason gave him another glance. "Then he dropped out of school during our junior year and left town for a while. I think he did some time in jail too."

I gave Mason a thoughtful look. "I guess it's good the church is helping. Sounds like he needs it. But I hope they don't live to regret it." I paused to think through my next words. "The guy can be hard on houses."

"We don't know that," Mason countered. "It's possible he had nothing to do with the break-in."

"Well, whoever it was disappeared in a small car. And you said he drives a VW Bug, so. . ."

"You told Deputy Warren you couldn't make out the type of car, though. Right? It could have been anyone."

"Except that he was spending nights in the house until the police told him he couldn't. I'm guessing he's not happy about being booted."

"The parsonage is a great option for him." Mason took a sip of his sweet tea and then jabbed his fork into one of his crab cakes. "I have a feeling Pastor Burchfield will be checking in on him frequently. And if he falls off the wagon, they'll get in touch with his AA sponsor."

"He has one of those?" I suddenly felt like a heel for suspecting him.

"Yeah. He's been sober for several weeks now, but just hasn't had much luck finding a job. Hopefully that will change tonight." Mason glanced over at the table where Conner continued his conversation with the manager. "I put in a good word for him."

"You're an amazing man, Mason Fredericks." I took a bite of my red beans and rice and stared into his eyes. He always saw the good in people, even when others didn't.

"Nah. I just know what it feels like to have life throw curveballs your way, so I try to extend a little empathy."

He did, for sure. After his father's tragic death last year, Mason had worked hard to make the best of things. No wonder he had such compassion for others.

A loud clap of thunder interrupted our conversation. I glanced out the window to my right and gasped when I saw how close the streak of lightning appeared. Another round of thunder shook the pane of glass to my right, and I felt my nerves kick in. We'd been having a lot of these strange storms lately.

We continued to eat, and the storm continued to rage overhead. Out of the corner of my eye I saw the restaurant manager rise and head to the kitchen. Moments later he returned with a plate of food for Conner, who stared at it like a pup seeing a bone for the first time.

Just then, another clap of thunder shook the building and the lights flickered off and on. A collective gasp went up from all of the patrons at once.

"I feel like this is how it always is with summer storms." Mason took a swig of his drink.

"How what is?"

"One minute the skies are bright and normal, and then the next. . .bam. Black as midnight and winds howling. Trees tipping over. Dumpsters flying."

"Dumpsters?" I shot a glance out the window, hoping I wouldn't see one flying my way.

"I witnessed it personally in the Walmart parking lot a few weeks ago. Crazy. A big green dumpster took out a couple of smaller cars, but the Ford F250 held up pretty well."

"It's a good truck," I said.

"It is."

We both paused for a moment to offer homage to one of Texas' favorite trucks.

Of course, I was partial to Tilly, Grandpa's 1952 Chevy 3100. But everyone already knew that.

Outside, the storm continued to pelt the building, and the lights did their off-on thing multiple times in a row. At one point, the glass in the window next to me rattled loudly. At least, I thought it was the glass. It might've been my nerves. They were pretty shot too.

"Let's move to an interior table." Mason rose and started grabbing cups and utensils.

Good move.

Less than a minute later we were situated at a table in the center of the restaurant, along with most of the other patrons, who all decided in tandem that sitting near the windows wasn't the best option.

Well, all but Clayton and Meredith. They seemed oblivious as they sat across from each other—hands clasped—staring at each other all dreamy-eyed next to one of the east windows. Ugh.

Mason and I sat, hunkered down, as the winds howled overhead. Could this day possibly get any worse?

Apparently so. Seconds later the lights flickered again. . .and then went out. Just as the waiter appeared at our table with our drink refills. He left them and then returned a couple of minutes later with some emergency candles.

A few minutes later, we sat by flickering candlelight, finishing up the last of our spicy meal.

"Did you have stuck-in-a-Cajun-themed-Pizza-Hut-during-a-tornado on your Bingo card for this summer?" I asked. "'Cause I sure didn't."

Another clap of thunder served to accentuate my point.

"Hey, I actually planned all of this," Mason countered. "I thought it would be romantic to eat by candlelight."

"Sure you did." I couldn't help but laugh at that idea. Still, there *was* something rather romantic about being in a dimly lit room, seated across from the man I. . .

Hmm. We hadn't said the *L* word yet, had we?

Before I could give that notion any more thought, the waiter happened by to refill our drinks. He and Mason lit into a conversation about the weather and a loud clap of thunder caused us all to let out a collective cry.

"A friend of mine once got trapped in a liquor store during a bad storm," the waiter said. "He was never the same after that." The young man moved on to the next table, still talking as he went.

We wrapped up the meal just as the storm settled down, and we decided to make a run for it while the running was good. The parking lot was slick and dangerous, and I was happy to make it to Mason's truck in one piece without falling. Once inside I breathed a sigh of relief.

I couldn't make out the moon or stars through the thick, murky clouds, but at least the road lights were still shining bright. We drove toward my house, talking all the way.

When we parked in my driveway Mason got out of the driver's seat and came around to open my door, his usual MO. I slid out—*slid* being the key word in such a tall truck—and landed straight in his arms.

Talk about a happy problem. He held onto me and didn't let go. Until my brother Logan pulled up in his car. He got out with a bag from Brookshire Brothers grocery store in his hands.

"Don't mind me." Logan held up the bag. "They sent me on a Blue Bell run. In the middle of a storm. Go figure."

"What flavor?" Mason asked.

"Cookies and Cream. You staying?"

"You bet."

Logan headed into the house, and I turned back to Mason.

"Hey, before we go in, I have a question."

"What's that?" He planted a little kiss on my forehead.

"The friend, the one you were calling the rehab about. Was it Conner?"

He took a little step back. "Look, I've been spending some time with him. I think he just needs someone to take an interest in him. You know? I'd want that, if I were in his shoes."

"You're a good man, Mason. But please be careful. I still don't trust him."

"I know you don't." He pulled me closer and gave me a tender kiss on the cheek. "But I also know you make me want to be a better man, so

I can't promise I won't talk to Conner."

"You're already the best. Tasha told me that you hired an AC guy to work on the unit at her house today while she was busy at the restaurant, and you wouldn't let her pay for it."

"She wasn't supposed to tell anyone that."

"It slipped out. She also said you personally got rid of the mess on the front of the house—all of those threatening messages. You painted over them?"

"In a lovely shade of soft yellow," he said.

"You're a good man. You're always looking out for others, and I really love that about you."

There it was—the *L* word. Sort of.

Before I had a chance to give it any more thought, he had me wrapped in his arms, lips pressed against mine.

Just as quickly, he pulled away and murmured those words I'd been waiting so long to hear:

"Cookies and Cream."

CHAPTER EIGHT

Okay, so Cookies and Cream wasn't what I'd been waiting to hear. But those words definitely held a special place in my heart. And by the time I'd finished a big bowl of that delectable Blue Bell favorite, I felt loved. And content. Ice cream and "I love you" weren't exactly the same thing, but they were mighty close, at least in my neck of the woods.

Thank goodness the storms passed overnight, though I spent the first couple of hours in my room writing a comprehensive article for *Mabank Happenings*. I managed to promote all of the pertinent upcoming events I could in just under twelve hundred words—the parade, the air show, the patriotic sing-along, the bake sale, and even the quilt show. Hopefully my editor wouldn't be too put off by the fact that so many of my recommendations were for events my loved ones had a hand in. They were, after all, community favorites.

At one in the morning I hit the SEND button on the article and crawled into bed, exhausted. By the time I awoke on Sunday morning, the skies overhead were bright and clear. Good thing too, because our Sunday school class had big things scheduled after church. When the service ended, we all planned to head to Tasha's house en masse to finish up the last-minute items on her to-do list. As Bessie Mae always said,

"Many hands make for light work." Or something like that.

I was the first to walk into our Sunday school classroom that morning. It felt weird to see the room empty. I settled into a chair on the front row and fussed with the sleeves on my blouse, which were a bit off-kilter. Mason joined me moments later, followed by Tasha and Dallas.

It was so fun to see Tasha in her usual colorful, sparkly attire instead of a T-shirt, shorts, and perspiration. Her ensemble for today included a bright red sparkling top and black capris, complete with shiny red sandals. She wore her gorgeous red hair in an updo that made her look both sophisticated and quirky, especially when you factored in the huge red clip holding it all up. Not everyone could pull off this look, but she could. My simple white blouse and jeans looked plain in comparison.

Tasha and Dallas settled in next to each other, as they'd been doing for weeks now. I wasn't sure if she read too much into that, but I knew Dallas did. He had staked his claim, if in no other way than Sunday school seating arrangements.

The other class members joined us in the moments that followed, and I was thrilled to see Shawn Warren come through the door. He was greeted by several of the regulars, who seemed thrilled to see him. Mason made room for him, and before long it was time to make some announcements. My BFF went first. She rose with gusto to share about this afternoon's get-together at her place.

"We'll provide food and fun, but I need y'all's help with some of the last-minute things that need doin'," Tasha explained to the group. "I *have* to get past tomorrow's inspection, and then I can list the place online. After that, I'm good to go. So even if you can't come out today, please keep me in your prayers. I need 'em!"

The conversation that followed assured her—and me—that everyone would definitely rally around her, in person and in prayer.

I knew that temperatures would be approaching one hundred degrees this afternoon, so I was mighty glad Mason had already taken care of the AC at her place. That was one less thing we needed to worry about. And Tasha seemed to be hopeful, now that she had a whole crew of friends coming in for the final push.

After that announcement, I shared some details about our church's role in the upcoming Fourth of July celebration. I'd spent last night writing about it, after all, so the event was definitely on my mind.

According to my weather app, the Fourth was going to be a scorcher, and there wouldn't be any air conditioning for the outdoor events, but many of the town's festivities would be held at the various churches, including a cake walk at the nearby Methodist church and a patriotic music celebration in our own church sanctuary, which would pay tribute to our area's veterans. My dad was particularly excited about that one, and had volunteered to help. I shared as many details as I could in the time allotted to me then wrapped up with a "Hope to see you all there. If you want any more details, look for my upcoming piece in the *Mabank Happenings*. You'll find everything you need there."

By now they were probably all used to hearing me carry on about my newspaper column. Writing those weekly articles was one of my favorite ways to stay on top of the town's activities, and I always tried to include things that my friends and loved ones would enjoy, especially at this time of year.

It was also a fun way to keep my writing skills sharp. Not that writing about bake auctions was exactly award-winning material, but at least it kept my pencil sharpened and my imagination intact.

After my spiel, our teacher, Landon James, dove into a great lesson, one that really hit home, about how God places the lonely in families. His wife, Annie, chimed in with a few thoughts about how God had played this out in her own life by bringing children for them to adopt.

I paused to think that through. Bessie Mae, in particular, jumped out at me. My sweet elderly aunt had never married, but she had always found a home with us. We adored her. She was a permanent fixture—both in our home and our hearts. Had we adopted her, or was it the other way around? Regardless, I was awfully glad God placed her in our family. She certainly brought joy—and a lot of good food—into our lives.

Just a few minutes into the lesson the door opened, and a shiver ran down my spine as Conner Griffin slipped inside. He gave Mason a nod then took a spot in the back row, away from the crowd. I brushed my palms against my thighs. Was it getting warm in here, or did the guy just make me feel uncomfortable?

Seeing Conner at church might make Mason feel like a good Samaritan, but I wasn't ready to trust the guy yet. In fact, I planned to keep a close eye on him—not just today but in the days to come. He'd better not show back up at my friend's property, today or ever.

I found myself distracted thinking about him and missed a big chunk of Landon's lesson. When the class ended, I headed into the sanctuary and took my usual spot in the pew behind my parents. Mason sat next to me. Warren eased his way into the spot next to Tasha and Dallas. And Conner?

I cranked my head to see if I could find him. Ah. There he was, in the back row, right by the doors. Maybe he planned to make a quick exit. I could almost imagine what he was plotting as he sat there. For once, I wished I was in the choir. Never mind the fact that I couldn't sing a note. Not a choir-worthy one, anyway. But sleuthing would be a lot easier from the front of the sanctuary. From the choir loft I could keep a better eye on him.

The service seemed to whiz by. I knew that Mom and Dad would be staying at the church to help set up for this week's big events. The rest of us—including our fearless Sunday school leaders—headed over to Tasha's place for a very full afternoon. Warren had to work the afternoon shift at the sheriff's department, so he couldn't join us. And Conner wasn't planning to come, thank goodness. I would have spent the whole afternoon looking over my shoulder. I'd already allowed distractions to steal my morning. I wouldn't let them take my afternoon too.

When I arrived at Tasha's place I changed out of my church clothes and into more comfortable shorts, T-shirt, and tennis shoes. I also pulled my unruly hair into a ponytail, knowing the heat and humidity would have me looking like a French poodle, otherwise.

Before we could dive in to our work, my brother Logan showed up with his girlfriend, Meghan. Aunt Bessie Mae showed up a few moments later with food for the whole crew—her homemade chicken salad and some croissants and a fruit platter. She'd also brought a huge foil pan of peach cobbler. My friends' eyes bugged the moment they saw it. I didn't blame them. Bessie Mae's chicken salad was the stuff dreams were made of. And that cobbler. . .wow!

Mason arrived with a couple of gallons of sweet tea and some sodas, as well as cups and ice. Then Dallas came in with a variety of chips and dips. Looked like we were all set. Time to fuel up for the work ahead.

Bessie Mae paused from her work and gestured around the kitchen with a smile. "Tasha, this is my dream kitchen."

Tasha's smile brightened. "Thank you, Bessie Mae. That means a lot, especially coming from you."

"I know a good kitchen layout when I see it. And just think of all of the family memories that are going to take place in this beautiful house! Families on vacation. Husbands and wives on honeymoons."

"I was thinking it would be a great place for a women's retreat," Annie added. "What would you think of that?"

"Oh, I like that idea." Tasha reached for her phone and began to jot down the ideas as we gave them to her. "What else?"

"It's right on the lake, so it'd be good for a fishing weekend for the guys," Mason said.

"Or, the perfect place for a bride and her attendants to prep before the wedding," Meghan chimed in. I had to wonder if, perhaps, she was referring to her own potential wedding. Was there something she and Logan weren't telling us?

"Why didn't I think of any of these things?" Tasha kept typing into her phone. "I only thought about the obvious—families coming here on vacation."

This led to a lengthy and fun discussion about all of the other possibilities for the place. Before long, Landon was offering to pray over both the food and the house, and we all joined hands around the kitchen island to do just that.

Afterward, Tasha dabbed at her eyes as she thanked us all. "This has been a hard process," she said. "Especially with events of late. But I'm grateful for all of you. I really mean that."

Bessie Mae reached over and took her hand. "You hang in there, kiddo."

"I will." Tasha offered a forced smile. "Even when it's not easy, I promise."

"You know what John Wayne always said, right?" Bessie Mae's gaze traveled from Tasha to the rest of us. "Life is getting up one more time than you've been knocked down."

"Thank you, Bessie Mae. I needed that."

"There are plenty of amazing roads ahead for you. God's got big plans for you, and I suspect He's going to use this wonderful home to help accomplish many of them."

My stomach rumbled, and suddenly I could hardly wait to get started on our lunch. Just as we loaded up our paper plates, a rap at the door interrupted us. Mason offered to get it. He returned moments later with a very testy Bob Reeves. The elderly man looked back and forth between us all, his brow wrinkled in concern as he took in various members of the group.

"Is this how it's going to be?"

"How *what's* going to be?" Tasha reached for a napkin and dabbed her lips. "Friends eating sandwiches?"

"No." He rolled his eyes. "A row of cars up and down the street and a crowd of people making noise right next door to my house. This is a residential neighborhood, you know."

"Well, sure." Tasha reached for a chip and dunked it into some bean dip. "And I'm your neighbor." She made a production out of biting into the chip, and then she grabbed another.

"And a mite sure better neighbor than the folks who lived here before." Bessie Mae turned from her spot at the kitchen sink and gave him a pensive look. "The Kellers let this place fall down around them, and you know that's a fact, Bob Reeves. You should be happy at what Tasha has done."

His gaze shifted to Bessie Mae, and for a moment I thought I saw a hint of something in his eyes I couldn't quite describe. Surprise? Happiness? Just as quickly, he frowned.

"That might be the case, but for weeks now all I've heard are hammers and saws and such. It's enough to give a man a headache."

"But look at how nice the place turned out." Bessie Mae offered a broad smile as she gestured to the new cabinets and island. "They've fixed this place up, and it's lovely. So why don't you stop your fussing, Bob? You get grumpier every time I see you, and that's not a good look on you."

Worry lines furrowed his brow. "Well, that was unnecessary, Bessie Mae."

"Just stating the obvious." She walked over to the island and began to fix another chicken salad sandwich, loading up her croissant until it overflowed.

"You always did." He paused and gave her a passive look. "State the obvious, I mean."

I couldn't seem to take my eyes off the pair. Their banter was fascinating to me.

"I'm reminded of a time, back when we were in high school, when you told me that my new haircut looked like a sheep after shearing." These words came from Bob, who never took his gaze off of her.

"Did I?" Bessie Mae's cheeks flashed pink as she looked up from the plate she was fixing. "That sounds like something I would say. I always did have a way with words, didn't I?"

"Yes, you did."

The rest of us stood in silence, as if watching an old black-and-white movie play out in front of us. Only, my aunt was definitely in full color today, especially as she slapped the paper plate down in front of him with a playful smile. And I had a feeling she was just getting started.

CHAPTER NINE

"I'm just saying, you could be nicer to these kids." Bessie Mae gave the cranky Mr. Reeves a pensive look. "They've been working mighty hard to make this a place to be proud of."

His gaze shifted to the chicken salad sandwich then back up to her.

"Now, what's all this I hear about you getting the neighborhood stirred up with some sort of silly petition?" my aunt added. "Did I hear that right?"

Oh boy.

"Well, I..." He ran his hand along the top of the sandwich, as if toying with the idea of eating it.

"Pitting folks against each other." She clucked her tongue and then reached for a cup, which she filled with ice. "Rallying support against these godly young people. It's just wrong, Bob, and you know it. All you're doing is alienating yourself from some mighty fine people. If only you would take the time to get to know them, I think you would fall in love with them, as I have. There's the answer to your problem right there."

"What problem?" Now he gazed at her with a new intensity. "I have a problem?"

"Yes, you do. Loneliness."

Bob muttered something under his breath, and his gaze drifted to the floor. "I never asked for a hotel to go in next door to my place," he countered. "All these people coming and going? It's going to wear on my last nerve."

"Only if you let it." She poured sweet tea over the ice in the cup and passed it to him. "You can choose not to. Besides, having people around will do you good. God designed us to live in community."

He grunted. "Wouldn't expect you to understand."

"What's that supposed to mean?" Bessie Mae planted her hands on her hips.

I wondered for a moment if the two might end up at fisticuffs. Only, his gaze was still fixed firmly on her eyes. Well, that, and the food on the plate in front of him.

"Just saying, you're surrounded by family all the time. You're used to the noise. The chaos. I've been alone since Soo-Min died, and this is a quiet little cul-de-sac, now that the Keller family is gone. I like it that way."

"I'm sure things won't get out of hand with the guests. And you can learn to like anything you put your mind to." Bessie Mae gave him a pensive look. "We just need to get you out more. And this is a good start. You're staying for lunch, Bob."

"I. . . Well, I've got work to do. And then I planned to make a bologna sandwich, not that it's anyone's business."

She flashed a warm smile as she gestured to an empty chair at the nearby breakfast table. "Now you don't have to. Enjoy that chicken salad, and then I'll give you a tour of the house. You're going to love what the kids have done with it. I dare say the renovations have brought property values up for the whole neighborhood! Isn't that wonderful?"

I wasn't sure how she managed it, but she coaxed that old coot into a chair at the table, where he downed a sandwich, chips, fruit, and two glasses of sweet tea.

Moments later she was offering him the grand tour, with Tasha and Dallas serving as tour guides. They went from room to room, finally landing back in the parlor, where the afternoon sunlight rippled in past the stained-glass window above the front door, adding a variety of colors to an already beautiful space.

"I haven't been in this house for years," Bob said. "Doesn't look a thing like it used to."

"The only item that remains is the player piano." Tasha gestured toward the beautiful piece. "Any idea why it got left behind when the family took the rest of the things?"

He gave it a closer look, and then walked over and ran his index finger along the keys. "There's a long story behind this piano, but I'm not of a mind to tell it, at least not today." His expression seemed to darken, if only for a moment.

"Ever known it to play by itself?" Tasha asked.

He glanced up, wrinkles framing out his brow. "Of course not. Player pianos require human interaction. Except the digital ones. They've got those now, you know."

He lit into a discussion about digital self-playing pianos, and for the first time I saw a spark of life in his eye. Bessie Mae must've noticed it too because she hung on his every word.

A short while later the conversation shifted to Tasha's to-do list. At that point it was all hands on deck. Tasha was pretty serious about that list, and thank goodness we had plenty of people to cover the various tasks. Most were menial, but no one seemed to mind.

Bessie Mae packed up the leftover food, tucked it away into the fridge, then asked Bob if he wanted to go for a walk around the lake.

He put his hands up and took a step back. "Definitely not. I've got to draw the line somewhere. It's 98 degrees out there."

"Have it your way, but just know you're welcome to join me." She turned abruptly and gave him a look that could almost be described as compassionate. "You always were, Bob."

Okay then. Maybe there was more to this story than met the eye. I'd have to ask my aunt about it later, when the dust settled. She headed out the back door, and he eventually tagged along behind her. Before long the rest of us watched through the windows as they walked along the water's edge.

And that's how I discovered the windows needed to be cleaned. They were pretty streaky. By the time Bessie Mae and Bob headed to their respective homes, Mason and I had already taken care of that task and I'd had my first workout of the day.

The next several hours were spent detailing all of the remaining areas of the house. We scrubbed baseboards, cleaned cobwebs, and swept up all sorts of mess some of the workers had left behind. As we went from room to room, I happened to notice some things we'd overlooked before. The master bedroom could use a few more art pieces on the wall. And a lamp on the bedside table.

The master bath was missing a few key items too. I made a list and compared it to the inventory of what we had on hand at the antique store. My parents would probably be open to offering Tasha a handful of items as a housewarming gift. I hoped.

Around three, the guys decided the kitchen cabinets needed a fresh coat of paint. And by four thirty, the ladies were hard at work rearranging the furniture in the living room. By early evening we had almost finished our work, and most of our friends had headed home for the day.

Only Dallas and Mason lingered. I was at that "If I sit down, I'm never going to be able to stand up again" point, so I watched—upright—through the upstairs master bedroom window as Tasha and Dallas watered the plants out back. She teased him with the hose, turning the water on him—just for a second—and he let out a holler. Then he grabbed the hose and returned the favor. Before long, they were both soaked.

Okay then.

"Those two are something else." Mason's voice sounded from behind me, and I turned to face him.

He pulled me close, but I pushed him away. "Dude. Do you smell me? I reek!"

He nuzzled his nose into my neck. "You smell like a good, honest day's work."

I pulled away and shook him off, more embarrassed than anything. "More like three days."

We both laughed, and then I followed behind him as he opened the door leading outside. We settled onto the chairs on the back balcony to watch the sun set off in the distance.

Before long, Tasha and Dallas joined us, both still damp. No one spoke for a few moments as we watched the sky come alive with color over the rippling waters of Cedar Creek Lake.

"Moments like these really make me want to live here full-time." Tasha's words broke the silence. "And then I remember that I have—"

"A mortgage!" we all said in unison.

"Yeah." She sighed. "That pesky little thing. So I have to rent it out." She looked back and forth between us. "Right?"

"Right," I said. "But you could stay here whenever the house is empty, you know. It's the perfect setup, as long as your parents are okay with you going back and forth."

My brother cleared his throat, and I wondered what he might be thinking.

"I don't know why you're worried, anyway," he said. "This house is great."

"It is, isn't it?" She sighed and then reached to rest her hand on his. "I'm so glad you discovered it, Dallas."

"I still can't figure out the whole story about the former owner." Mason glanced my brother's way. "Who owned it again?"

"My friend's grandmother lived here until last year," Dallas explained. "She was something of a hoarder."

"Something of?" Tasha laughed. "The woman was a hoarder, plain and simple."

"After her husband died, the place fell apart around her," Dallas explained. "Especially during that final year when she got really sick. The family tried to intervene, but they were so busy caring for her medical issues that there wasn't time."

"It's all coming together in my mind now," Tasha said. "So your friend is Anthony's son, Jimmy."

Dallas nodded. "Yep. Jimmy and I were friends from fifth grade on."

"Jimmy must be the nephew of the woman who's been such a thorn in my flesh," Tasha interjected.

"Do you mean his aunt Belinda?" Dallas's eyes widened. "You know her?"

"She's the one threatening to file the lawsuit against Tasha," I explained. "Tasha knows her, all right."

Dallas jerked around to look at Tasha. "Someone's filing a lawsuit against you?"

Oops. Guess she hadn't told him yet.

With the wave of a hand she appeared to dismiss his concern. "Yeah, but I'm trying not to worry about it. I've got a call in to my dad's lawyer to see what I should do, but I think she's just bluffing. I guess we'll see."

"Want me to ask Jimmy about it?" Dallas asked. "He might have some input."

Tasha grew silent for a moment, but then said, "Sure, if you think he has some sway with his aunt."

"I doubt it. From what Jimmy said, his aunt Belinda was estranged from the family even before his grandfather passed. That whole side of the family was. . ." His words drifted away. "I don't want to sound rude, but they were a piece of work, especially Belinda's son. I think he's Jimmy's age. The two never got along."

"Hey, look on the bright side," Tasha said. "Maybe Bob Reeves will sue me too. Then I'll officially be the most sued woman in town."

"Good grief," I countered. "Let's not go down that road."

"Sometimes we have to laugh to keep from crying," she said, and then turned to face the sunset. "Maybe we'd better change the subject. The skies are too pretty to ruin them with chatter about people who hate me."

"They don't hate you," Dallas said. "They don't even know you. No one who ever took the time to get to know you could have a bad thought about you, Tasha."

"Aw, that's sweet, Dallas." She gave him a little wink. "You know how to make a gal feel better."

We grew silent again and turned our attention back to the sun, which dipped low over the horizon, changing the colors from bright pink and gold to a more subdued amber.

"The views of the lake are amazing from this angle," Dallas observed. "No matter who rents this place—or what they use it for—they're all going to see that this house is the perfect hideaway, especially at sunset."

"That's it!" Tasha slugged him on the arm.

"Ow!" He turned and gave her a stunned look.

"You've just named her, Dallas!"

"I have?"

"Yep." She smiled and leaned back in her chair, a contented look on her face. "Sunset Hideaway."

CHAPTER TEN

On Monday morning, less than half an hour after I opened up our antique store for the day, a text came through from Tasha: "Pray for me. The home inspector's here right now. I need this to go well so I can get the house listed."

I responded with a quick "Praying! I'm sure it will."

I hoped so, anyway. We'd sure poured a lot of time and effort into the place, and yesterday's work-a-thon had taken care of the remaining issues, as far as we knew.

"Something else happened with Belinda Keller," she wrote back. "I'll have to fill you in later."

I responded with two words: "I'm praying."

Then I turned my attention to my customer, Mrs. Oberdeen, who lit into a story about her cousin's gallbladder operation. Unfortunately—or fortunately—I had to pass her off to Mom so that I could wait on the next customer, an impatient redhead with a thick New York accent who informed me that the wait was entirely too long.

I muttered a quick, "I'm sorry," and gave her a discount on the antique wall clock she was purchasing, which seemed to calm her down. I wasn't sure how they did things on the upper east coast, but here in the south we didn't rush folks through. We took the time to get to know them. And their cousins' gallbladders.

The morning flew by, and I found myself overwhelmed with folks buying. . .and placing items on consignment. Apparently, Trinkets and Treasures was garnering quite the reputation. We now had folks coming all the way from Canton to visit.

Lots of these customers tried to talk me into opening up a shop over there. I'd been tempted. Canton was the location of one of the world's largest monthly flea markets and outdoor vendor areas, after all. But the idea of facing that crowd, even once a month, was too overwhelming to me. Besides, Trinkets and Treasures was doing fine, even making money. Most businesses didn't turn a profit for the first year, but we were already sailing.

Okay, that might have a little something to do with the fact that we didn't pay actual salaries, not the kind you could brag about, anyway. This was a family-run business.

Family.

My thoughts shifted for a moment to Tasha's comment about Belinda. How awful would it be, to be estranged from your own flesh and blood? Man. I thought about Landon's Sunday school lesson, about how God chose to place the lonely in families. Not everyone had that, did they? Maybe the point was to include others, to make them feel like part of the collective family. If nothing else, I could do that with the folks who came through our shop.

After working for three hours or so, I traded off with Gage, who took my spot at the register so I could head back to the house to eat an early lunch. I heard the familiar strains of western music from the TV and glanced into the living room to find Bessie Mae dozing in her recliner as a John Wayne movie blasted from the television. She deserved a rest after all the work she'd done on our behalf, so I did my best not to wake her.

I quietly fixed a turkey sandwich, grabbed a soda from the fridge, then headed to sit in the recliner opposite my aunt. After I set my food down on the small end table between us, she stirred awake and then looked my way with an impish smile.

"Just resting my eyes a bit." As a gunfight ensued in the movie, she reached for the remote to turn down the volume.

"I don't mean to disturb you." I picked up my sandwich and took a bite. "Just needed to put my feet up. I'm still wiped out from this weekend's activities."

"Me too. And you're not disturbing me." She sat up in the chair and reached for her tea glass on the little end table. "How's it going out there?"

"Busy but good." I paused and my gaze shifted to the television. "Can I ask you a couple of questions?"

My aunt muted the TV entirely. "Sure, honey. What's up?"

I put the sandwich back on the plate. "It's about Bob Reeves."

"O-oh?" She fidgeted with the remote, her gaze shifted toward our family's piano, situated in front of the big picture window to our right. "What about him?"

"I can see that you know him better than we do, so I'm wondering about his. . .character."

"His character?" Deep creases formed between her brows. "Who said anything about his character? Who have you been talking to?"

"No one. I was just wondering—"

"Folks around these parts have been quick to judge his character for years, and that's why he's become such an old fart. If people would've left him alone, he might have softened over the years instead of growing harder. But gossips have pushed him into a corner and turned him into a hermit. If they knew his true story, they might not be so hard on him."

My goodness. I certainly hadn't expected that sort of defensive reaction. I nibbled on my sandwich, deep in thought. Perhaps I shouldn't move forward with my questions after all.

"Now, I'm not saying he gives a good impression." She released a lingering sigh. "Just the opposite, in fact. But he's not the same sweet guy I used to know years ago."

"Which is why I want to ask you my next question." I leaned in a little closer. "Do you think there's any chance he's the one who broke into Tasha's house the other night and spray painted the front door?"

She released a long sigh. "The Bob Reeves I knew would never have considered such a thing. But now that he's holed up by himself most of the time, who can say? Loneliness and bitterness can turn even the kindest heart hard."

I had a lot of questions about what she'd just said but didn't ask them. Instead, I got right to the point.

"I'm nervous it might've been him, since he seems to have a real problem with Tasha taking over the house and turning it into a vacation rental. I was sound asleep when the intruder broke in, but it scared me half to death."

"Well, I'm sure it did, honey. Which makes me even more doubtful that it might have been Bob. I just can't picture him doing that."

"He wants to shut her place down. Deputy Warren told us as much."

"I addressed that petition pretty well, I think."

"You did. And I'm grateful. I know Tasha is too."

She shook her head. "He can be a pill. But to go to such lengths? I just can't see it. That's not in his nature."

"I'd sure love to find out. Would you be willing to do a little sleuthing?" I took another bite of my sandwich.

"Me?" She laughed. "I can barely remember my name from one minute to the next. You think I can help you figure out who sabotaged the inn?"

I brushed the crumbs from my lips. "First of all, you're the one who helped me figure out who stole Tilly a few months back. And you've got the sharpest mind of anyone I know. You can quote lines from every John Wayne movie ever made, and you've got a thousand recipes filed away in your brain."

"True." She nodded and pointed to her head. "I do seem to have a rather organized filing system in my noggin."

"We're the Hadley Sleuthers, remember?"

The edges of her lips turned up. "Yes, I remember. So what would I need to do?"

"Just. . .spend time with him. Get to know him. Maybe he'll open up to you." I grabbed a chip and ate it. Then I reached for my sandwich again.

Her cheeks flushed pink. "I don't know about that, kiddo."

"Why?" I spoke around a full mouth.

She shook her head, and for a moment I thought I saw tears glistening in her eyes. "Let's just say he might not be willing."

"But you could try?" I set the sandwich down. "Maybe take him some cookies or something. Get him talking."

"He always loved my oatmeal craisin cookies." Her thoughts seemed to take her somewhere else for a moment. "He once bid high dollar at a bake auction for them. Of course, that was a million years ago, when dinosaurs roamed the earth."

"Hahaha."

"The man loved my sweets. That's sure and certain."

"Perfect. Oatmeal craisin it is. I'll leave the rest up to you."

She yawned and kicked back the footrest on the recliner. "I'll go ahead and bake them now and take them over later this afternoon." Moments later, she was on her way back into the kitchen, a woman on a mission.

I finished my sandwich just as the first batch went into the oven. "Promise you'll save some for us?" I said.

"Duh." She laughed. "I wasn't born yesterday, kid."

CHAPTER ELEVEN

"One more thing?" I asked my aunt before heading back out to the shop. "Could you try to get a look at Bob's car? The person who broke in was driving a small car."

"Why would he need to drive a car to the house next door?" She grabbed the flour bin and set it on the countertop. "That makes no sense at all."

"Unless he was doing it deliberately, to throw us off track? You know? Just check out his car, pretty please?"

"I'll do my best, honey," she said. "But I make no promises."

I made my way back across the field to the shop and found Gage waiting on a young blond woman with a lovely, thick southern drawl. She didn't look familiar to me but definitely sounded Texan, through and through. He seemed to be deeply engaged in conversation with her, so I didn't disturb him. Instead, I headed to the back room to do some sorting.

A short while later, Tasha stopped by to do a bit of browsing for those last-minute items I had offered as a housewarming gift.

"I come bearing gifts!" She held up a bag from Fish Tales, her family's restaurant. "You hungry?"

I opened the bag and, in spite of my big lunch, almost swooned when

I saw the fried shrimp inside.

"Well, it's lunchtime. So I took a chance and brought some lunch to offer in exchange for the goodies you're passing my way."

Should I tell her that I just ate a sandwich? Nah. Instead, I popped one of the shrimp in my mouth and almost swooned as I bit into it. "Delicious!"

"My dad does make the best fried shrimp in town," she said. "Fries too. Did you see those?"

I dug around in the bag, finally coming out with the container of French fries.

As I took a bite, Dallas brushed through the door, claiming he had to pick up something for my dad. Mm-hmm. Sure he did. His gaze shifted at once to Tasha, who flashed him a broad smile.

"Hey, you," she said.

"Hey, back."

"I brought fried shrimp." She gestured to the bag in my hand, and I realized she'd meant it to be shared. I grabbed another shrimp then passed the bag his way.

"Thanks." He reached inside and grabbed one. As he bit into it, that delirious look appeared on his face. I was pretty sure it was the shrimp. Or, maybe it was the girl. He gave her the sweetest smile ever, but she seemed distracted by a vase on a nearby shelf.

"Oh, this is new!"

"Sure is," I said. "It's yours, if you want it. If you're ready to look around, we've got a bunch of other new items in the storeroom. We haven't put them out for the customers yet. Just pick out what you like."

"You sure?" she asked.

"Of course," Dallas chimed in. "Our gift to you."

"That's sweet." She batted her eyelashes in his general direction.

I cleared my throat. "But before you go back, tell me. . .what happened with the inspector?"

"Oh my." She giggled and her cheeks flushed the prettiest shade of pink. "He was something else. Super nice. Handsome. Lives in Kaufman. I think he's new to the area."

My brother's ears seemed to perk up at this news.

"He had some questions about the electrical. He suggested I get a new panel installed. But he went ahead and passed the house, so we're safe to let guests stay. I'm breathing a lot easier now that that's done."

"I'm sure."

"That's great news, Tasha." Dallas offered a heartfelt nod.

"I know. First thing I did was go online and list the house at a vacation rental site." She laughed. "Well, I'd actually already uploaded everything days ago. I just had to press the button to set it live. But Sunset Hideaway is officially listed for daily or weekly rental, effective immediately. I do hope the weather will cooperate. It's supposed to rain again tonight. Ugh!"

She went on to talk about the inspector at length, giving us his name—Cody—and his backstory. Apparently, his family moved down to Texas a couple years back when the real estate market was so hot. "His parents have their own realty company. And he started doing inspections not long after that."

"Sounds great."

"He's an only child," she added. "I heard all about that. But y'all, he's got the cutest accent. They're from New Jersey." She stressed the words New *Joy*-sey with a thick, fat Jersey accent.

I laughed. And then stopped when I heard Dallas clear his throat.

Okay, so he wasn't keen on hearing about Mr. Inspector.

"You still need me to come and help with the loose slat on the back porch steps?" he asked. "I could look at that panel while I'm there."

"You're the best, Dallas!" Tasha slipped her hand through the crook in his arm and leaned in to give him a peck on the cheek. "I couldn't have done any of this without you." She shifted her gaze my way. "*All* of you."

My brother's face turned beet red. He decided to head out, not picking up anything for our father before leaving. I led the way to the back room to help Tasha pick out some last-minute items for her place. Before long we were up to our eyeballs in lamps, rugs, and several other items that were perfect for her place. I could hardly wait to see them in their respective rooms.

A short while later, as I helped her load her car, I finally had a chance to ask the question that had been bugging me all day. "Okay, now tell me what happened with Belinda. You said there was more trouble?"

Tasha's smile faded at once. "Yeah. Big trouble. She's legit suing me.

Some strange guy served me papers this morning."

"Do you have them with you?"

"No." She shook her head. "Left them at the house."

"But, suing you for what?"

"She claims to have found a different will, one that names her as a beneficiary, as well as her stepbrother."

"Dated when, though? If it was written years ago, there's probably a more recent one."

"Yep. And the letter acknowledged that. But she's claiming her stepbrother manipulated her stepmother with the later version to rob Belinda of her inheritance."

"Do you think that's true?"

"No. My dad's attorney knows the lawyer who helped Mrs. Keller draw up her final will. Anthony wasn't even with her on the day it was written. And this lawyer specializes in estate law. He says she was in her right mind and that we have nothing to worry about."

"Well, good." That made me feel better.

"But that hasn't stopped her from claiming the other will is invalid due to. . ."Tasha paused and appeared to be thinking. "Undue influence, lack of capacity, or fraud. Pretty sure that's what the letter said. She believes the probate court should reconsider the distribution of assets, house included."

"Do you think she will officially contest the new will in court?" I nibbled on a French fry as I pondered the problems this could potentially cause for my friend.

Tasha shook her head. "The attorney said he doesn't think she would dare. He thinks she's just blowing hot air."

"Well, good."

"So in theory, I have nothing to worry about. Belinda would have to prove fraud, and that would be hard to do, since Anthony wasn't even there with his mom when the will was drawn up."

"Right."

"The attorney told me to relax. I own the property. She has no claims to it. And like I said, I've already opened it up to vacationers, so hopefully someone will rent it soon. Did I mention I have a—"

"Mortgage." I completed her sentence. "Yeah. Well, you do what you need to do, and I'll pray, I promise. If she has no claim, she has no claim. You have nothing to worry about. This is just a scare tactic, I would say. She's trying to psychologically manipulate you."

"She's going over the top. You won't believe what else she's done."

I was almost afraid to ask.

"She found my Facebook account. You wouldn't believe what she posted on my page. I took a screenshot before deleting it." Tasha turned her phone around, and I gasped as I read the inflammatory words written there about Tasha being a thief and a liar. "That's awful."

"I know. I reported her."

"But you're not Facebook friends. How did she manage to post to your page?"

"My page was set to public before, in part so that I could promote the property and the restaurant." She sighed. "But now I've had to change that. Which stinks."

"It sure does."

"I'm not going to let her get to me," Tasha said. "I'll set my mind on things above, just like the Bible says."

"Good girl."

Tasha arranged the items in the back of her little truck then turned to face me. "Hey, I almost forgot to tell you something important."

"About Belinda?"

"Nope. Clayton Henderson."

"What about him?" I asked.

"This is the craziest thing ever, but he approached my dad about buying our restaurant."

"What?" I could hardly believe it. "Why would he do that?"

"I have no idea, but he seems determined to own every profitable business in town. Can you believe that?"

"Surely he knows your family would never sell Fish Tales." I paused to think this through, an idea occurring to me in that moment. "Do you think it might've been Clayton who showed up at your place the other night?"

"I thought about that too." She leaned against the truck. "He's definitely the type to want to scare me."

"And he owns a small sports car," I said. "A Corvette."

"Meaning?"

"It was a small vehicle that drove away from your house the other night. I'm just saying it could've been his."

"Ugh." She groaned. "I don't think my dad is seriously considering Clayton's offer to buy Fish Tales—at least I hope not—but I'm going to tell him our suspicions, regardless. If he thinks for one minute that Clayton broke in to his daughter's house, he's more likely to come out with a shotgun than a sales contract."

I knew her dad pretty well, and she wasn't kidding about that. He would protect his daughter at all costs.

Tasha pulled away a couple minutes later, and Dallas reappeared with worry lines creasing his brow. He stopped me as I turned to head back inside the shop.

"Hang on a second. I want to ask you a question."

"What's that?" I squinted to avoid the glare from the blazing sun overhead.

"You know Tasha better than I do." He kicked the gravel from the parking lot with the toe of his boot.

"Right."

He squinted as he looked my way. "Do you think she's interested in this Cody guy?"

"Dallas Hadley, are you jealous?" I punched him in the arm.

"I didn't say that. I'm just asking because. . ." He raked his fingers through his hair. "Anyway, never mind. Just wondered if she said anything else to you about him. Besides all that stuff just now."

"If you want the honest truth, most of her conversation these days is about her house. And the few moments apart from that conversation are actually about how great you've been to help out so much. So I don't think you need to worry about some new flash-in-the-pan inspector, cute or not."

"You think?"

"I know. But if I were in your shoes, I'd go ahead and let her know how you feel."

"I'm not so good with words." His gaze shifted to his feet.

"Then don't use words. Send flowers. Women love that. Have some roses delivered to the restaurant when she's working so that she—and everyone else—can see how serious you are."

"You think?"

"Is that your new phrase? Yes, I think. And by the way, she's crazy about yellow roses. I'm not sure if you knew that, but she is."

"I've never ordered flowers before. Wouldn't even know how."

"It's easy-peasy. You can do it online. That way you don't even have to go into a florist's shop in person. And you can personalize a note to say whatever you like. Be creative. Sweet."

"That helps." He released a slow breath. "Okay, I'll do it. Yellow roses. You're sure?"

"Sure and certain. They're her fave."

"Okay, thanks." He offered a warm smile. "I appreciate your help, RaeLyn. I'm navigating new waters here."

"You won't drown. I promise."

Still, gauging from the look on my brother's face, he was already looking for a life preserver.

CHAPTER TWELVE

Monday evening, just an hour or so before suppertime, Bessie Mae disappeared on us, claiming she needed to make a run to the grocery store. I knew where she was also headed but didn't tell the others. She could reveal it later, if she chose to.

My aunt asked me to keep an eye on the two King Ranch Chicken casseroles in the oven, and I agreed to do so. She also instructed me to put her peach pie into the oven as soon as the casseroles were done, and I agreed to that too.

Around six fifteen Mom put together a beautiful big salad to go with our meal. Gage came in from working in the barn about five minutes later. He was covered in sweat and dirt—not an unusual look around these parts.

"Where's Bessie Mae?" Gage asked as he plopped into one of the kitchen chairs.

"Off on an errand," Mom said. "But we're going to wait on her. Supper will be a little late tonight. And don't you dare sit on my chairs looking like that!"

He stood up with a grunt. "Bummer. It's been a long day out in this heat, and I'm wiped out. With Dallas at Tasha's so much I've had to cover his workload." Gage grabbed an oatmeal cookie and shoveled it into his mouth. "You can't blame a guy for looking like he's worked hard all day."

"True, but you smell as bad as you look," Mom said. "So go take a shower before we all pass out. You've got plenty of time, since Bessie Mae's not here yet. Now, get."

When our mother said "get" we all got. So out of the room he went. I peeked in the oven at the King Ranch Chicken and noticed it had finally started to bubble around the edges.

A couple of minutes later, my brother Logan arrived, looking fresh as a daisy in a clean button-up and slacks. His hair was styled—not a strand out of place—and he smelled of aftershave. Quite a contrast to Gage. Such was the difference between a bank job and working the ranch.

Logan walked over and gave Mom a kiss on the cheek before reaching for a cookie.

"How were things at the work today?" she asked.

"Good. They're moving me up to manager." He offered a confident smile. "Comes with a nice pay raise, which is timely."

"Timely?" Her eyes narrowed. "How so?"

"Does this mean you're going to start paying rent?" These words came from my father, who entered the kitchen from the hallway.

"Now, Chuck, we've talked about this." Mom clucked her tongue at him. "As long as the boys are helping out around the place, there's no need for all that nonsense. This is a family home, and everyone earns their keep in their own way. Logan does more than his fair share."

She wasn't wrong about that. Logan helped out with finances—both for the ranch and the store. He definitely earned his keep and then some.

"And I'm family." Logan grabbed another cookie. "Speaking of, where's Bessie Mae?"

"At the store," Mom and I said in unison.

"Hope she gets here soon." My father rubbed his oversized belly in exaggerated fashion. "I'm starving."

"You could live off the fat of the land for a few days, at the very least." Mom jabbed him in the gut with her index finger. "If you know what I mean."

"I wouldn't last a day." He reached for an oatmeal cookie.

"Honestly!" Mom opened the oven to check on the casseroles inside.

"You guys act like we couldn't survive without Bessie Mae."

"We couldn't," Dad countered. "She keeps us alive."

"What am I?" My mother looked up from the oven. "Chopped liver?"

"Never cared much for liver," my dad said. "I'd say you're more like a top sirloin steak, Flora Hadley!" He swept her into his arms and planted kisses on her face, nearly causing her to lose her grip on the oven door.

My mother's cheeks flamed red and she swatted him with the hot pad. "Chuck! I could've burned myself."

"Nah, I had you in my grip. And what's a little fire between friends?" Oh my.

Still, I had to give it to him. In spite of their occasional snippy exchanges, my parents were the best example of a marital relationship I'd ever seen. I could only hope and pray to end up as happy and committed as they were, when the time came in my own life.

My thoughts drifted to Mason. Without even second-guessing myself, the words *He's my better half* flitted through my brain.

He was. And I knew it. Surely he did too.

As if to punctuate my point, a text came through from Mason: "Just thinking about you. Can I call later?"

I responded with the words "Of course! Any time after dinner is fine."

We often ended our days with a lengthy phone chat, swapping stories about all that had taken place. Tonight would be no different.

By six thirty, Gage was done with his shower. Minutes later, Jake and Carrie arrived with the baby. On their heels, Dallas arrived, looking beat.

"I got the busted window on that old shed fixed over at Tasha's place," he said. "It was no small feat. I still have to tackle the door handle, but it can wait." He headed off to take a shower.

Mom and I pulled the King Ranch Chicken from the oven when the timer dinged, and I popped the peach pie in to bake.

Bessie Mae arrived back home around 6:40, all smiles, with a Brookshire Brothers bag in her hand.

"I bought more Blue Bell," she proclaimed. "I needed more Golden Vanilla ice cream to go with that peach pie. How's it coming along? It smells mighty good in here." She opened the oven door, peeked inside, then offered a nod. "Looks great!"

I took the ice cream from her and placed it into the freezer alongside the other cartons in various flavors.

She headed over to give the casseroles a look and nodded. "These turned out nice too."

"Just pulled them out of the oven a little while ago," I told her. "So they're still nice and hot."

"Well, I timed that little outing just right, didn't I?" She gave me a wink then called all of us to the table to eat.

The meal was passed in usual fashion, with only one exception: Dallas never showed up at the table. I peeked in on him and found him sound asleep in his bed, so I saved him a plate with a large serving of King Ranch Chicken. No doubt he would be hungry when he woke up.

After dinner I offered to help Bessie Mae clean the kitchen. No one else objected. Even Mom seemed relieved as she ventured off into the living room to put her feet up.

I started clearing the table and then sidled up next to Aunt Bessie Mae at the kitchen sink.

"Well?" I asked, my voice lowered.

She seemed a bit aloof in her response: "I gave him the cookies."

"And?"

"He said thank you."

"That's it?"

A little smile turned up the edges of her lips. "I think he was happy to get them, but there were no big conversations, if that's what you're hoping for."

"And the car?" I asked.

She shrugged. "Must've been in the garage. I didn't see one in the driveway, so I can't help you there, girlie. But I did see someone else hanging out down the street."

"Who's that?" I asked.

"Pretty sure I saw that young man—the one who was squatting on the property for a while."

"Conner? Where?"

"When I first turned into the neighborhood. There's a little side street to the right, a dead end. He was out there, standing next to a little car."

"A Volkswagen?"

She nodded. "Yes, that's it."

"Could just be a coincidence," I said. "But it makes me nervous that he's hanging around the neighborhood."

"I thought you would want to know. I don't know if he's a potential threat, but my antennae went up when I saw him. I think he's your key suspect, honey. Not Bob Reeves."

I sighed. Loudly. Would I ever figure this out?

"Bob is kind of a closed book," Bessie Mae explained. "It's going to take a while to crack that cover open."

Turned out, it wasn't going to take as much time as she thought. Bob Reeves showed up at our family's antique store the following day, just before noon. I was startled when I saw him amble in, and even more surprised when he reached for a basket. Was the man actually planning to shop?

Bob looked a bit. . .spiffier. . .today. He wore a plaid button-up and a nice pair of slacks, and he'd done something different with his soft white hair. Combed it a different way, maybe? And he smelled of after-shave. I wasn't a huge fan, but it smelled familiar, like something Papaw would've worn.

Mom greeted him with a warm welcome and I did the same, and then he began to browse the store, looking genuinely interested in the items on our shelves. For the first time, I noticed the slightly hunched gait.

"Let me know if I can help you find anything," I called out as I watched him pick up a small hand shovel and place it in his basket.

He grunted "Yup!" in response but kept his back to me.

Bessie Mae must've seen him coming from the house, because she showed up breathless a few moments later, still wearing her apron. Unlike Bob, she didn't look as well put together. My usually impeccable aunt had messy hair, and her apron was covered in blobs of batter. Or dough. Or something.

"Bob." My aunt's cheeks flamed pink as she took quick steps in his direction. "What brings you this way?"

His face lit in a smile when he saw her, but he quickly tried to suppress it, from the looks of things. "You gave this place such a big build-up last night when you stopped by with the cookies. I just thought I'd better check it out for myself."

Mom glanced my way and mouthed the words, "She took him cookies?"

I nodded then strained to make out the rest of their conversation from my place at the register.

"How did you enjoy them?" Bessie Mae asked, offering a coy smile as she spoke.

"Just as good as I remembered. You loaded 'em up with pecans. Pecans are my favorite."

"I know. Remember we used to shuck them for hours on the back porch when we were young?"

"How could I forget? That pecan tree still out there?" He shifted his gaze out the front windows of the shop and toward our house. I knew he couldn't make out the pecan tree from here, but kudos to him for trying.

She nodded. "You won't recognize it, it's so big. But it's still dropping pecans on our heads every year, just like it always did. We've been blessed with an overabundance this season, for sure."

"If you like pecans, we've got a freezer filled with bags of them from that tree," Mom interjected from her spot beside me at the register. "Bessie Mae, give him a bag before he goes, will you? I can hardly squeeze anything into that freezer without worrying a bag of nuts will fall on my head."

Her words provided a much-needed bit of levity to the conversation.

"I would never turn down pecans." Bob's gaze never left my aunt's face.

"Well good. I'll give them to you on one condition." Bessie Mae planted her hands on her hips.

"What's that?"

"Where's that petition you started?"

"Why?" He gave her an inquisitive look. "You want to sign it?"

"I most certainly do not. I want to tear it up and toss it in the trash can. And when I do, you can have two bags of pecans and all the peach pie you can stomach."

"You can't just step into a man's world and start tearing things up, Bessie Mae."

Bessie Mae's brows elevated mischievously as she kicked back with, "Well, you can't blame a gal for trying, now can you?"

CHAPTER THIRTEEN

I had a sneaking suspicion Bessie Mae and Bob were no longer talking about petitions.

"I'll think about it." He reached into a bin filled with old DVDs. "But I really did come by to shop. I wondered if you might have any old 33 1/3s."

"Sure do," I said. "We've got a great collection, in fact."

Bessie Mae seemed intrigued by his question. "You still have that old record player?" she asked. "The big one that looked like a piece of furniture?"

He nodded. "Yep. Still have my vinyl collection too. They're in mint condition."

"Are you wanting to sell them?" I asked. "Because those are going like hotcakes right now, and some are worth a pretty penny."

"Absolutely not." He put his hands up. "I could never do that. I just want to add to my collection, not take away from it. If you'd had them as long as I have you would understand."

All righty then.

"You still have that Hank Williams album?" Bessie Mae asked, her lips turning up in a smile.

Bob's eyes twinkled as he glanced her way. "Well, of course!"

"Remember, we used to listen to 'Jambalaya' over and over again."

She seemed to lose herself to her thoughts. "It was always a favorite. So fun!"

"Wore out a lot of needles on that album, didn't we?" He offered her a tender smile and a moment of what felt like reverent silence settled between the two of them.

In that moment, I thought I saw a shimmer of tears in her eyes. Or maybe it was just perspiration. It was warm in here today.

"That song kept me going when I was in Korea." He paused and seemed to drift off in his thoughts. "Every day, all I wanted was to get back home to Texas and play my records with the gal I..." His eyes grew moist.

Bessie Mae reached over to squeeze his hand. "It's funny how a song can take you back in time, isn't it?"

"Sure is." He seemed to disappear on us again but finally sprang back to life. "The only thing that saved me was the guys in my unit. We were like brothers. Especially Billy Landers. He was from the Dallas area, so we had that in common. He was a Hank Williams fan too."

"I remember you telling me about him in your letters," Bessie Mae said.

They wrote letters? I did my best not to look like I was eavesdropping, but this was too good to miss.

A smile lit Bob's face. "We would sit and talk about Texas for hours. It kept us sane."

I found that really sweet. But this conversation also raised a lot of questions.

It didn't look like I was going to get answers anytime soon. Before giving away any more clues, my aunt was showing him around the shop and talking a hundred miles a minute about our inventory. A short while later—after he paid for half a dozen records and the other items in his basket—she coaxed him up to the house with the promise of an early lunch—leftover chicken salad sandwiches and chips.

He turned her down...until she mentioned the peach pie and Blue Bell Golden Vanilla ice cream.

I watched, amazed, as Bob agreed, and then countered with an invitation to come to his place one day soon to listen to some of their favorite albums on his old record player.

Bessie Mae agreed right away, with eyes sparkling.

Then they disappeared, arm in arm, out the door of the shop, across our property to the house.

Mom looked after them, mouth agape. "Um. . ."

"I know." I shrugged as I kept a watchful eye on them through the front window. "That was fast."

"What do you mean?"

"Bessie Mae and I were working on a plan. Looks like it was a success."

"A plan?" Wrinkles creased my mom's forehead.

"She baked up those oatmeal cookies yesterday to take over to his place."

"Is that where she went last night? I thought she was at Brookshire Brothers." Mom paused to greet a group of older ladies who entered the shop together.

"Oh, she stopped by the store on her way back to cover her tracks. But she definitely took a bunch of the cookies to him. They were an ice-breaker. We're trying to see if she can get him to talk." I reached under the register to drop a couple of receipts into the box we kept there.

"About what?" Mom asked.

"I'm trying to figure out if he's the one behind the break-in the other night. He started that petition to get Tasha's place shut down, and he hasn't been shy in telling everyone how he feels about it. So Tasha and I suspected he might've been the one to bust in on us and vandalize the place."

"Oh, I see." Mom's gaze drifted out the window. "The man I saw just now doesn't seem capable of such a thing."

"I agree. But maybe he's hiding something. You know?" I followed her gaze and noticed my aunt and Bob had stopped at the gate leading to the field that separated our house from the shop. They appeared to be deep in conversation.

"I'm guessing Bessie Mae's not going to have to work hard to get him to talk. Those two seem like—"

"Old friends?" I tried.

"Yeah." My mother's gaze followed them as they walked across the field toward the house. "Or more."

My imagination went into overdrive as I thought it through. "Do you suppose Bessie Mae has a past?"

"I have no idea," Mom countered. "Even if she did, I wouldn't have guessed Bob Reeves to be part of it. I'll confess, I've never really known much about the man, other than the obvious. He's kind of brusque."

"For sure." My gaze shifted to the women, who were carrying on about several of our antique salt and pepper shakers.

"I've always wondered how Soo-Min put up with him, to be honest." Mom lowered her voice. "Though, she was different too."

"I don't remember her at all," I admitted. "What was she like?"

"A loner. She kept to herself. And she's been gone a few years now. He's been a Grumpy Gus ever since."

"Grumpy Gus is a nice way of putting it. He hasn't exactly welcomed Tasha to the neighborhood and that's problematic. She's going through so much already, what with the lawsuits and all."

"Lawsuits?"

"Yes, she just got served, in fact. Said the guy came by in person." I paused to explain what was going on with Belinda Keller, and then I added, "Tasha definitely doesn't need an irritated neighbor too."

"That makes me so sad." Mom fussed with the items on the counter, straightening them. "I can't imagine why anyone would go to such lengths to shut down another person's business. Poor Tasha."

"Me either, but whoever showed up at the house the other night wasn't playing around. They were dead serious." I gave my aunt and Bob Reeves another look. They were standing pretty close together. He certainly didn't appear intimidating, at least not to Bessie Mae, apparently.

"Based on how he was acting just now, I can't imagine it was Bob," Mom's gaze shifted out the front windows once again. "But looks can be deceiving."

"Right?" I shivered, remembering Wyatt Jackson, our elderly neighbor who had stolen my beloved truck, Tilly, just a few short months back. "They certainly can."

We took a break from our conversation to wait on the women as they approached the register with items for purchase.

After they disappeared from view, I added their receipts to our collection then turned back to Mom. "Where were we?"

"Actually, I was just thinking about Soo-Min." Mom turned her attention to straightening up a stack of brochures for the Fourth of July event near the register. "She was always a little. . .aloof. Didn't really give many of us a chance to get to know her."

"I wonder why?"

"Maybe she felt like she didn't fit in," Mom said. "I don't know. We really did try. I remember Bessie Mae invited her for lunch once, but she didn't show up."

"Strange."

"And when she was sick with breast cancer, the ladies at the church all kicked in and helped with meals and cleaning and such. Like I said, we made every effort. But she seemed to shut us all out. We never knew why. She was a closed book."

"That's the same phrase Bessie Mae used to describe Bob." I looked out the window at them and watched as he reached to take her hand.

Maybe that book was opening as we spoke.

"Ever since Soo-Min passed away, Bob has become more of a hermit." My mother's words interrupted my ponderings. "We hardly ever see him at church anymore, and I can't remember the last time he showed up for any type of city gathering, either."

"Sad."

Only, he didn't look sad now, did he? As he and Bessie Mae made their way across the field and toward the back door of our house, the man almost had a skip in his step. Crazy.

CHAPTER FOURTEEN

As soon as Bessie Mae and Bob Reeves disappeared into our house, I made a quick run out to the parking lot to check out Bob's car. Mom followed on my heels, probably worried because I took off so fast without an explanation.

"What are you doing?" she asked.

"Just looking for his. . ." My gaze landed on the tiny red car. "Whoa."

Mom's eyes widened. "I haven't seen one of these little MG Midgets for years. This thing is a classic."

"It's so. . .small." I gave the vehicle a closer look.

"They were really popular back in the day." Mom sighed. "I always wanted one."

She carried on and on about it as we made our way back inside the shop to take care of incoming shoppers. Was that the car I'd chased after in the night? The idea made no sense. Bob lived next door, after all. Why would he be out driving?

Right now, it seemed like I'd never know. I dove back in to my work and tried to put it out of my mind.

I managed to slip away from the shop just before we closed up for that afternoon. With plans to attend the Cedar Creek Chamber of Commerce meeting at seven that evening, I needed to head into town, but I left a couple of hours early in search of my mom's best friend, Dot. I needed her input on something. If anyone might be able to answer the questions tumbling around in my brain, Dot could.

I called Tasha to see if she could join me, and she agreed, but said she could only give me a few minutes.

"I'm supposed to be at the restaurant by six to help out," she explained. "Summer called in sick."

"Summer?"

"Our new server. From what I understand, her little boy has strep throat."

"I don't think I've met her yet," I said. "You'll have to introduce me when I come in on Sunday."

"She just moved here from Rockwall," Tasha said. "Her husband passed away a couple years ago, right after their baby was born. She came here to be near her parents. They live in Gun Barrel City."

"Oh, I see." Even though I didn't know Summer, I suddenly felt very sorry for her.

"Why are you going to the chamber meeting so early?" Tasha words interrupted my thoughts.

"To talk to Dot. I'm dying to know the backstory about Bessie Mae and Bob Reeves."

"Do you think there's a backstory?" Tasha asked.

"Yep. I forgot to tell you that he stopped by earlier today and bought some vinyls. Then she invited him into the house for lunch."

"Oh, wow."

"I know. And I suspect there's more to this story, but there's only one way to find out."

"Agreed. If anyone would know, Dot would."

"Yep." My Mom's BFF was the head of the Chamber of Commerce. If she couldn't help me, she would figure out who could.

We both paused for a moment to pay silent tribute to Mabank's most knowledgeable historian and all-around woman-of-influence. We were lucky to have Dot. No doubt about that.

I headed out minutes later, up to my eyeballs in speculations about Bessie Mae and Bob Reeves.

Unfortunately, the skies decided to open up—just as Tasha had predicted—as I pulled into town. Before long, rain was pelting the windshield of my truck. I turned on the wipers right away. These summer storms were about to wear me out.

Tasha met me at the Chamber office a few minutes later, umbrella in hand. Unfortunately, the office was closed, but I knew where we'd find Dot—at the Mabank library, where she served as head librarian.

Mom's BFF was just closing the library to the public as we arrived, but she opened the door and ushered us inside with a broad smile.

"Well, this is an unexpected pleasure." She led the way through the foyer and into the heart of the library to her oversized desk. "Here to pick up a book?"

"Here on a research dig," I explained as we pulled up chairs next to her desk.

"What's up?" Dot pushed her bifocals onto the top of her head with a pensive expression on her face. "I know that look. Is this about the Fourth of July event? I saw your article this morning. Well done."

"Thanks, but no. It's about Bob Reeves," I explained. "Do you know him?"

Dot leaned back in her chair, arms crossed at her chest. "Of course. Poor old curmudgeon. He hasn't been the same since Soo-Min passed."

"Yeah." I nodded. "I don't know him well, but he's Tasha's neighbor now and—"

Dot fussed with a stack of books on her desk, straightening them as she interrupted me. "Oh, I've heard all about it. He started the petition to get her to shut down her rental property."

I gave her an admiring look. "Man, you *are* good."

Dot laughed. "Well, people tell me things. We'll leave it at that. What's he done now?"

"It's not so much what he's done recently. . ." I lowered my voice and leaned forward. "This is more about Bessie Mae and Bob Reeves, back in the day."

Dot's eyes widened. "Do tell."

"Actually, we were hoping you could tell us," I said.

"Yes, we got the feeling there was more to their story when they were younger," Tasha chimed in. "He stopped by my place when Bessie Mae was visiting, and their whole interaction was very. . ."

"Familiar," I said. "And he came by our shop today, and it was the same thing."

"Like they were old friends or something," Tasha interjected. "Or. . .more." She batted her eyelashes in playful fashion.

"Really?" Dot looked stunned by this notion, and it really took a lot to get Dot stunned.

"Yeah." I sighed. "But she's not saying much, and I don't get the feeling Mom knows anything about the two of them."

"Is that what you're thinking?" Dot gave me an inquisitive look. "That the two of them were actually, well, the two of them at one time?"

Tasha nodded, as if she had it all figured out.

I simply shrugged in response. "I don't know. She just said something to make me wonder. All I've ever known about Bessie Mae is that she never married. I know she had her heart broken once upon a time, but no one ever shared that story with me."

Dot's eyes widened. "And now you think the one who broke her heart might have been Bob Reeves?"

I paused to think through my response. "Crazy, I know. Until a few days ago I would never have given it a moment's thought. Now I can't stop wondering."

Dot pushed her chair back and stood. "I say we start in the obvious place. Follow me."

Like her dutiful students, we did just that. She led us back to the county's historical section, honing in on the small area dedicated to Mabank's history.

"Did you know we have every yearbook Mabank High has ever put out?" She began to thumb through a copy of one before putting it back into place. She finally pulled out one with the year 1952 on it. "I say we start here. I'm not sure what year Bessie Mae graduated from high school. Several years ahead of me, for sure. But your grandfather graduated in '52, and she was quite a few years younger, so I'm guessing we can safely start here."

"How did you remember Papaw graduated in '52?" I asked.

"Because you drive a '52 Chevy 3100—the Advanced Design series—that he won his senior year. Remember?"

"Man." I gave her an admiring look. "Your brain is like a finely oiled machine."

She laughed and gestured to the library shelves. "Well, it should be, after forty years of working here. Now, where were we?" She grabbed a couple more yearbooks and gestured for us to join her at a nearby conference table, where she had plenty of room to spread them out.

Moments later she pressed an open yearbook in my direction. Tasha reached for another. Before long we were all on the prowl for photos of the young Bessie Mae.

It didn't take long, thumbing through them, to find pictures of my aunt in her late teens. The school was much smaller back in the '50s, and apparently Bessie Mae was quite the star of the show.

Literally. She starred in the 1959 senior show, *Annie Get Your Gun*, dressed in an Annie Oakley costume. And from what we could gather, she was head of the 4-H that same year. And the president of the home economics club. I wasn't surprised by that last one, but the theater stuff threw me a little.

"Wow, she was a real go-getter," Tasha said. "Looks like she's always had a lot of energy."

"Still does." I paused and looked at her senior photo—a lovely black-and-white photo featuring a vintage hair style. "Check this out. Most likely to. . ." I squinted to read the words written down. "Win a blue ribbon in a pie baking contest."

"That makes sense," Tasha said. "She's the best cook in the county." A pause followed. "Please don't tell my family I said that."

"I won't. But you're right. She's an amazing cook."

"I think it's funny that she played the role of Annie Oakley," Dot said.

"Why?" Tasha looked her way.

"Annie was this defiant, stubborn sharpshooter who could hold her own around the menfolk. But of course, in the end, she fell head over heels with her archnemesis."

"Oh, wow." That was interesting.

"Speaking of the archnemesis, any pictures of Bob yet?" Tasha asked.

A little more digging revealed a picture of him in uniform. "Oh, look!" I turned the yearbook around for the other ladies to see. "He was in the ROTC."

Dot pursed her lips. "That makes me wonder..." She rose and disappeared for a couple minutes before returning with her iPad. "I know he served in Korea, but I don't know what branch of the military he was in."

Moments later, we had our answer.

"So he was in the army," I said as I stared at a photo of him in uniform in the Mabank newspaper.

"Yes, and this was post-Korean War era," Dot explained. "Lots of the boys in your Papaw's age group were drafted. But I'm guessing Bob enlisted before being drafted. A lot of the ROTC boys did."

"I thought the war ended earlier in the '50s," I said.

"It did, but we still have troops in South Korea to this day. The war might have ended, but the ideological war between North and South Korea never did, so we've always had a presence there."

"Interesting." Tasha gave one of the pictures a closer look.

Dot managed to pull up some pictures from newspapers on the computer, and I was startled to see just how handsome Bob used to be as a younger man. Especially in that army uniform. Wow! He looked every bit as stylish as Bessie Mae did with that fancy do.

Tasha's eyes bugged as she took in the photographs. "I can't believe it's the same man. Look at those gorgeous eyes. And that hair. He was..."

"A James Dean look-alike," Dot said.

"James...who?" Tasha asked.

Dot simply shook her head in response. "Look him up. You'll see."

Tasha grabbed her phone and started scrolling. Before long, she was bug-eyed, showing off pictures of James Dean.

"So tell me again, what year did Bessie Mae graduate?" I asked.

"Looks like she graduated in '59," Dot said.

"Let's check out the senior prom pictures from that year," I suggested. "I have a sneaking suspicion we might find some answers there."

We located the pictures moments later, and I gasped when I saw that my very own Bessie Mae had been prom queen in 1959. And a very handsome Bob Reeves, her king.

"Well, that explains a lot!" Tasha said. "I knew I was right about the two of them."

"Looks like they dated, and then he went off to the military," Dot said.

"But they didn't marry." That made me sad. They certainly looked like the perfect duo, but something must have happened to break them up.

"Let me see if I can find a marriage license for him to know when he married Soo-Min," Dot said.

Tasha seemed astounded by this. "You can do that?" she asked.

Dot looked up from her iPad. "Well, of course, silly. Public records for the win!"

It took some effort, but she finally found a record of Bob Reeves marrying Soo-Min on June 9, 1962, in the Henderson County Courthouse.

"That's what I thought," Dot said. "He was just home from serving."

"Makes me wonder what Bessie Mae was up to in 1962," I countered. "It's kind of sad that he came back and married someone else."

"As I recall, the whole thing was shrouded in mystery." Dot turned to face us. "I believe he brought Soo-Min back with him when he returned from Korea."

"Oh, I see." That must've really upset Bessie Mae.

"Quite the story, if I'm remembering right." A thoughtful look passed over Dot's face. "I believe she was expecting before they got married. So they moved here and she had the baby—a little boy—about four or five months later."

"Oh my." So that explained why he and Bessie Mae never married. How sad for my poor aunt, to have the man of her dreams get some other girl in trouble.

"I always felt a little sorry for Soo-Min," Dot said. "I was a lot younger than they were—probably ten years behind them, age-wise—but I remember folks talking, and it wasn't nice. Folks can be so cruel with their gossip."

"What were they gossiping about?" Tasha asked.

"The situation. Soo-Min settled in as best as she could here, but I always felt like she was pining for home."

I paused to give this some thought before chiming in. "Mom said the ladies at the church tried to befriend Soo-Min, but she was. . .aloof."

"That's the right word." Dot closed the laptop. "And I always wondered if Bob was really happy in the marriage. He didn't put off that vibe." A moment of silence followed, and Dot appeared to be thinking. "Then again, men in the '50s and '60s weren't always terribly vocal about their feelings for their wives. You know?"

I didn't, but didn't say so.

"She didn't come to church with him?" I asked.

"In those first few years, I think she did." Dot scooped up the year-books and stacked them on top of each other. "But they lost their little boy at some point early on in the marriage. Billy drowned in the lake as a toddler. From what I heard, nothing was ever the same after that. They never had any other children, and she became something of a hermit."

"Oh, that's horrible." Suddenly my heart really went out to Bob. "Wait a minute. Did you say Billy?"

"I did."

"He told us that his best friend in his unit was named Billy. He must've named the baby after him to honor him."

"Another story worth investigating," Dot said. "But probably not today. I've got to get over to the Chamber soon to prep for the meeting."

Tasha's lips curled down in a frown. "I'm starting to feel really sorry for Bob Reeves."

"Me too," I admitted.

"But it still doesn't answer the question of what happened to the 1959 prom king and queen," Tasha said. "Were they *really* a duo in real life, or just on page in the Mabank High yearbook? You know? Was it all an act, do you think?"

Dot shook her head. "I suspect the queen was diligently waiting for her king, but he came back with a wife and a child on the way."

Man. My heart sank right away. If true, this gave me a newfound compassion for Aunt Bessie Mae.

CHAPTER FIFTEEN

I knew that Bessie Mae had never married. In fact, I couldn't even remember her talking about being interested in a man—short of carrying on about John Wayne all the time.

Was it, perhaps, because she still carried a torch for her king?

This would definitely be a question worth pursuing, though I wasn't sure how to broach the subject. There might be raw and tender feelings underneath my aunt's stalwart exterior.

Before I could give it any more thought, Tasha glanced at her watch and gasped. "I'm going to be late. Gotta go."

I walked her to the door, but she turned back to fill me in on something before leaving. "Hey, I forgot to tell you—I talked to my dad about Clayton Henderson. I asked if he was seriously considering letting Clayton buy Fish Tales."

This certainly piqued my interest. "And?"

"Dad said he's getting older, and he's tired of always being on his feet. I guess he always thought I would eventually take it over, but he can see that I'm more interested in the vacation rental."

"Gosh. Are you saying he's actually considering it?" This caught me by surprise.

"Well, he was. . .until I told him about our suspicions. Once he heard that Clayton might've been the one behind sabotaging the inn, he changed his tune in a hurry. Just as I predicted he would."

"Still, I feel kind of bad for your dad. If he's really looking at retiring. . ."

"He's only fifty-seven," she countered. "And Mom says he's just trying to make me feel bad for having other interests. But I thought you'd want to know that Fish Tales is going to stay in the family."

"Gotcha. I'm glad about that. I can't even imagine what the Hadley family would do on Sundays after church if Fish Tales ever disappeared on us."

"Hopefully that will never happen." She paused, a reflective look on her face. "Who knows? Maybe one day I'll own Fish Tales *and* the vacation rental. And other businesses, besides." A smile tipped up the edges of her lips. "Maybe I'll be the next Clayton Henderson."

"Minus the bad parts," I said.

To which she responded, "Duh," and then headed out the door.

I returned to Dot's desk and found her digging through old newspaper files. She eventually found an article about the death of Bob's young son and read it aloud to me.

I couldn't help but sigh after listening to the sobering details of the little one's passing. "This is just so tragic."

"Very." She turned the computer screen to show me a picture of Billy playing with a jack-in-the-box, all smiles.

My heart twisted as I imagined what it must feel like to lose such a precious, innocent child.

"I believe Bob was at work when it happened," Dot explained. "And there was a rumor that Soo-Min was napping when the little one slipped out. But that was never confirmed and no one ever asked, to my knowledge. There was certainly no police investigation or anything like that. We all just assumed it was a terrible accident."

"Oh, I'm sure it was. Was there a service for him?"

"Probably, but I have no memory of attending."

I skimmed the article to see, but found only found the words "private graveside service" written there.

Dot shrugged. "It's kind of strange that I've tucked away so much of this and don't remember."

"Very strange," I said. "You remember everything, Dot."

"Not so much these days." She laughed. "The other day I went to the fridge to get some butter and came out with sliced cheese."

"Could've happened to anyone." I paused. "Can you check one more thing for me, Dot?"

She glanced at her watch. "If it's quick."

"Bob drives an MG Midget. Red. I'm wondering if he's a member of the antique car club, the one that has the big shows."

"I'll have to check the Chamber records for that. Let's head that way now."

Moments later Dot locked up the library and we headed down the street to the chamber office. I tagged along behind her and was surprised to see a couple of our members already there ahead of us. Dot greeted them and then unlocked the door to usher us inside.

She went off to search the records for the car club and came back to report that Bob had never been a member.

By seven o'clock the room was full of folks ready to talk about the upcoming Fourth of July celebration. We were there to finalize plans for the big day with Dot leading the charge. Mason came early and jumped into gear, ready to help her with whatever she needed to set up the room.

Outside the thunder shook the building, and the rain pelted so hard against the windows I thought they might shatter.

That didn't stop folks from showing up, though. It took a lot more than a summer storm to keep the folks of Mabank from doing their civic duty. In fact, the room was a lot fuller than usual. With so many people around the county playing a role in the event, we had our hands full. But Dot went down the line, letting everyone ask their questions and share their plans for the upcoming day.

Things got a little awkward when Clayton Henderson came in. Thank goodness he didn't invite Meredith along. That would've been incredibly uncomfortable, especially because Nadine had opted out this year. She usually headed up the refreshments committee, and I knew she would be missed. But I didn't blame her for not wanting to participate.

It was obvious the community still adored Nadine. But it was also clear from the exchanges happening in this room tonight that they no longer adored Clayton. Many gave him the side-eye. And a couple even got into heated arguments with him. So much for being the head honcho in town. It seemed folks had lost their respect for the man, and I didn't blame them.

Still, I had to give it to Mason. Whenever things would get heated, he seemed to have the uncanny ability to naturally jump right in and calm them down. He was a bridge, of sorts, between the townspeople.

I'd always known this about him, of course. He had this ability from the time he was young. Some folks just knew how to foster open communication and cooperation. He also seemed to know how to address concerns and dispel problems. Kind of like how the storm was now easing up outside, he got the people calmed down and talking sensibly about the topic at hand.

More than anything, he managed to get us all unified and excited about the event. And, to be honest, we needed that.

By the time the meeting ended, Dot was asking Mason to consider a larger role in the Chamber. He hemmed and hawed about it, but I knew he would eventually say yes. And I happened to think he would be very good at it. Should I tell him so?

Later, as he walked me to my car, I took the opportunity to share my thoughts.

"Hey, you were really good in there."

He slipped his arms around my waist and drew me close. "What do you mean?"

"I mean, with the people. You have a natural way about you. You know how to win friends and influence people, and not in a shady way but with genuine kindness."

"Thanks." He shrugged. "It's not so hard. Just be yourself."

"Not everyone has your gift," I countered. An idea hit me all at once. "Did you ever think about going into politics?"

He snorted. "Um, no. Never met a politician who didn't make me want to wash my hand after shaking his."

"They're not all like that."

"The ones I've met are. They're like the oil in my car."

"Meaning?"

"They need to be changed. Often."

Okay, that got a laugh out of me. "Just promise you'll pray about it. I could see you running for mayor one day. Maybe even senator. Wouldn't that be fun?"

He pressed a little kiss on my forehead. "Well, if that ever happens, you'll have to be my campaign manager. Promise?"

"Of course."

"And you'll have to write my speeches. You're going to be a famous writer someday, you know."

Now it was my time to snort.

"Hey, I see your gifts too." He kissed me soundly, as if to prove the point.

"Whatever. But I'd say you're a shoo-in for mayor already. You won't even need my help. Your speeches come naturally."

He pulled me a little closer and spoke so softly I could barely make out his words. But I was pretty sure he said, "Oh, I'll *always* need your help."

Unfortunately, I couldn't make out the rest, because his lips got in the way.

CHAPTER SIXTEEN

The storm passed quickly, and Wednesday morning dawned bright and beautiful. I, for one, was grateful. With tomorrow's Fourth of July celebration coming up, we needed clear skies and dry pavement. According to the weather app, we would have just that. Thank goodness.

In spite of the lovely weather, the traffic at the store was slow this morning. Not unusual for a weekday morning, especially midweek. When a call came through on my cell phone from Tasha, I had plenty of time to take it.

Her opening line piqued my interest. "You'll never believe what happened after we parted ways yesterday."

"What's that?"

"A delivery guy showed up at the restaurant with two dozen yellow roses. . .for me!"

"Oh?" I did my best to play it cool.

"Yes!" She released a girlish giggle. "My mom flipped out. My dad was more curious than anything. But here's the crazy part. . .whoever sent them didn't sign the card. It just said, 'In case you haven't figured it out, I think you're amazing.'"

"Well, obviously they're from—"

"Cody must've decided to surprise me. We had the best conversation about yellow roses when I told him I was thinking of planting some in my front flower boxes. He told me that his mother specializes in roses and offered to put me in touch with her. I guess she's quite the gardener."

"Cody?"

"The inspector. Remember? I told you all about him. His family is in real estate. Apparently they're gardeners too."

"Well, yes, but how did he know where you work?"

"Oh, I told him. He's planning to stop by the restaurant to try out our gumbo. He was bragging about that new place in Athens, but I told him theirs couldn't hold a candle to ours."

Should I tell her the gumbo in Athens was pretty amazing? Nah, maybe not.

"Anyway, those yellow roses were a brilliant move on his part. Talk about making a great first impression, not just on me but my parents. Can you believe he would go to such efforts?"

Ack.

"I mean, that would be a bold move on his part, but at least I know he's genuinely interested. Why else would he send flowers?"

"Well, if you really want to know who—"

"Maybe I'm getting the cart ahead of the horse." She paused for breath. "Oh, gotta go. Dallas is here to work on the loose boards on the deck off the pier. We'll talk more later."

"Right. Later." And at that, we ended the call.

My poor brother.

I didn't have time to worry about him for long because my father came in with my oldest brother. Jake had baby Annalisa with him. I took her into my arms to play with her. Not that one could play with a three-month-old, exactly, but I oohed and aahed over her in playful fashion.

"Look!" I squealed. "She's smiling at me!"

"Pretty sure she's gassy." Jake spoke through an exaggerated yawn. "She's been like that ever since Carrie left."

"Where is Carrie?" I asked.

"She has a lunch date with a friend from college. It's the first time she's left the baby with me." His nose wrinkled. "I'm not saying I don't know what I'm doing, but I thought it would be good to kill some time before Annalisa's nap by visiting the family. You don't mind, do you?"

"Of course not! You can bring her to us any time." Mom reached to take the little one from my arms. "You know that."

"Yeah." Jake yawned once again. "I thought about bringing her at four in the morning when she wouldn't fall back asleep. Carrie was in a deep sleep, and I was trying to play the role of super-dad. But apparently I need some work."

"You'll be fine," Mom said. "And you know you can bring her to me at any time, day or night."

I knew she meant it.

"Three nights in a row the thunder has kept her awake," he explained. "I mean, I'm happy to see all of this rain. I was afraid we were going to end up in another drought, like last summer. But even I have my limits."

"It's passed now," I said. "I checked my weather app, and we're in for clear skies for the rest of the week."

"Thank goodness. Maybe I'll finally get some sleep."

Mom managed to keep the baby calm, and we had a wonderful time visiting with her. Jake finally headed back to the little house to put her down for a nap.

By noon the trickle of customers had slowed to a stop. We'd been toying with the idea of closing up shop, and this seemed like the perfect opportunity.

Mom and I made our way back to the house, where we found Bessie Mae in a tizzy, all worked up over her baking for tomorrow's big event.

I loved a good pie baking day, especially during peach season. Today the house smelled of peaches. And blackberries. And a host of other yummy pie offerings. I could hardly believe my eyes when I saw all of the goodies.

"Are you making a coconut cream?" I asked as I made my way from pie to pie, examining them closely.

"Nope. It would melt in the sun. I'm sticking to a mostly patriotic theme, anyway. Blackberries. Strawberries. Raspberries."

I pointed to the peach pie.

"Peaches are in season, and we had them in abundance."

Still, the blueberry pie was my favorite. It would go for top dollar in the bake auction, no doubt. I marveled at how she decorated the crust to look like an American flag. I honestly had no idea how she did all of this, but my hat was off to her.

I'd seen Bessie Mae in workhorse mode a thousand times, but the efforts she was pouring into her baked goods today really took the cake, pun intended. Over the next couple of hours, with our help, she baked half a dozen cakes for the bake auction, and more patriotic cupcakes than I could count for the cupcake walk.

The whole kitchen counter was awash in red, white, and blue buttercream and tiny cupcake picks that looked like the American flag.

My dad summed it all up in one word as he came in from tending to the horses: "Wow."

He spoke for all of us.

I would offer to help, but I'd already promised Tasha I would come by with a final load of antiques to finish decorating her place for the big Fourth of July open house tomorrow afternoon, so I needed to do that before the day slipped away from me.

As I headed out the door, Bessie Mae stopped me. "I almost forgot to tell you something, honey."

"What's that?"

"I asked Bob for more details about the player piano, and he said it used to belong to his family when he was a boy."

"You're kidding."

"No. His father sold it to the Kellers when Bob was younger. Happened during a time when Bob's dad was hard up for money. But Bob never really forgave his parents for that, from what I could gather."

"Wow. He's a pianist?" I knew the answer, of course, having seen the yearbook photos. But I would play dumb.

"Oh my, yes. I'm telling you, he was quite the showman back in the day." A smile lit her face. "My stars, that young man could play a merry tune on the piano. I used to just sit in awe, watching his fingers move across the keys. Not everyone has that kind of skill. I don't know anyone else, in fact."

"I see." Still, it made me wonder if he wanted it back badly enough to sabotage Tasha's home to get it. Surely not.

"Yep." Bessie Mae seemed to lose herself to her thoughts for a moment. "He accompanied us many times when we put on shows at the high school. His piano skills were far better than the other musicians, but he never bragged about it."

I continued to play dumb as I posed the other question that made sense. "So you were a theater kid?"

"Sure. Did lots of shows over the years. Not sure I could even count them all, but my, did I have fun! I even played Annie Oakley my senior year."

Should I confess that I already knew that?

"Is that why you love John Wayne movies so much?" Mom's words interrupted my thoughts.

"Nah. The Duke was always my first love." Her smile faded for a moment, and I thought I saw a hint of pain in her eyes. Just as quickly, she smiled again. "Well, maybe not my first but the only one that lasted."

And the only one that hadn't broken her heart, from what I could tell.

"We used to have some old reels of my childhood," my aunt explained. "I'm not sure what ever happened to them. My daddy was the first man in town with a home movie camera. I think he called it a Super 8 or a Dual 8 or something like that."

"Do we still have it?" I asked.

"Probably. And I think those movie reels are still hiding out somewhere too. Probably in the attic over at the little house. But I don't plan to crawl up there anytime soon. My attic-crawling days are behind me, I'm afraid."

I didn't blame her. But that didn't mean I couldn't climb into the attic. It wouldn't be the first time. Perhaps one day soon I would do that.

I headed out to Tasha's place and was surprised to see so many people out and about. Bunting was going up at the churches in Payne Springs, where I made the turn to Tasha's place. And all along the lake, folks were enjoying the day. I saw everything from tiny fishing boats to luxurious charter boats. There were even a couple of smaller airboats out on the water. Yes, the people around Cedar Creek Lake were certainly getting into the holiday spirit.

When I walked into her house a few minutes later, I called out to Tasha and she hollered back, "In the kitchen! Come on in!"

I made my way inside and my eye was immediately drawn to the vase filled with gorgeous, large yellow roses on the kitchen island.

"Aren't they exquisite?" She gestured to them with her head as she continued to load the dishwasher.

"Yes, they're amazing."

"I guess Cody's trying to be coy. I haven't heard from him, but I suppose that's just his way. You know?"

"Actually, I wanted to talk to you—"

Her phone dinged and she reached for it, putting a finger up to ask me to wait.

"Oh!" Tasha's mouth rounded as she read whatever message she'd found on her phone. "Oh, oh, oh!"

"What is it?"

She turned the phone around, all smiles. "Someone is interested in renting Sunset Hideaway!"

"Who? When?"

"Let me check." She took a seat and fumbled with her phone until she finally found the email.

"Looks like they want it for a full week. That's good."

"Starting when?"

She squinted as she looked at the phone a little closer. "Oh, wow. They want it right away."

"Right away?" I looked around the messy room. "As in, right now?"

Tasha shrugged. "They're asking for a phone call to explain."

"Is it a family?"

She squinted and appeared to be reading. "Looks like it's just one person. A woman."

"Interesting."

"Wait a minute." She looked up at me, eyes wide. "You're never going to believe this, RaeLyn."

"What?"

"It's Nadine Henderson. Clayton's ex-wife!"

CHAPTER SEVENTEEN

"Clayton and Nadine aren't divorced yet," I countered. "Though I think he's filed." I grabbed Tasha's phone and looked over the email, my gaze finally falling on the name: Nadine Henderson. With a 903 area code in the phone number. "Wow. Definitely her."

"Why in the world would Nadine Henderson want to rent my house when she lives in that gorgeous home on the lake?" Tasha brushed her messy hair off her face. "It makes no sense."

"I have no idea. But you should call her and put it on speaker so I can hear every word."

Tasha quickly made the call, and I soon heard Nadine's voice on the other end of the line.

"I hate to catch you off guard with such a sudden request," Nadine explained. "There's some sort of major electrical problem at my place—the whole panel has to be replaced, as well as a lot of the wiring. They say it's going to take days and will be quite the mess."

"Oh, no!"

"Well, we can thank Clayton. He hires the cheapest folks in town to do these projects. I'm not surprised at all."

She might not be, but I was.

"Like I said, they're saying it's going to take several days to fix it all, and the power will be off most of that time. So I need a place to stay. I've got workers coming tomorrow morning, so I need a plan as quickly as possible." She paused. "I'm already miserable enough these days without factoring in the Texas heat."

"I understand." Tasha dove into a conversation about the heat. "But there's one little teensy-tiny problem. I'm supposed to have an open house tomorrow afternoon after the Fourth of July celebration and the whole town is likely to turn up."

"I don't mind. I can skedaddle for a few hours, and I'll make sure the place is presentable."

"Are you sure?" Tasha said. "It's only for three hours, from four to seven."

"Don't mind a bit." Nadine paused. "Would you mind terribly if I bring my shih tzu, Coco? I could board her, but she's tiny and won't cause any problems. I can pay a pet deposit if you like."

"I don't mind at all," Tasha said. "Sunset Hideaway is pet friendly. But. . ." For a moment I thought I saw a flicker of pain in her eyes. "Just giving you a heads-up, Nadine. This house is so sweet and quaint, but it's nothing like the house you're accustomed to. You've got quite the castle over there."

"Castle?" Nadine grunted. "More like a prison. Your place will be a breath of fresh air, trust me. So please don't apologize."

"Okay, sounds good." Tasha went on to give Nadine a few instructions about how to fill out the online application, and then she looked at me with panic registering on her face. "Oh. Help."

"What can I do?"

We flew into gear, sweeping, vacuuming, and dusting. We'd just finished brushing the last of the cobwebs out of the corners when the doorbell rang.

Tasha drew in a deep breath and then answered it, acting calm, cool, and collected. Should I tell her that her hair looked like it had been through a hurricane?

Nadine stood on the front porch, shih tzu curled up in her arms, and an exquisite Louis Vuitton suitcase at her side.

"I think it's absolutely adorable, Tasha." She gestured with her free hand to the front of the house. "This darling porch is everything. And so is the wraparound balcony."

Tasha reached for the bag. "You'll get to enjoy it all for a full week. And longer, if you need it. You're our first guest, and I want you to feel at home."

"I'm sure I will."

We led her inside and she set the puppy down. The little shih tzu was a bundle of fluff, his soft silky coat tumbling down over his tiny frame in waves of white and caramel. The pup proceeded to sniff every square inch of the room.

"Don't worry about him," Nadine said. "He's potty-trained."

The little dog's dark eyes sparkled with curiosity as he made his way from one piece of furniture to another. Perhaps *pranced* would have been a better word. The sweet little thing was irresistible. He melted my heart right away.

We spent the next several minutes walking Nadine through the house, starting with the parlor. She fussed over the room and the decor choices then honed in on the player piano. "I haven't seen one of these since I was a kid."

"You, too, can be a piano aficionado in no time." Tasha laughed. "I'll show you how to use it, if you like."

"Um, no." Nadine laughed. "No one has ever called me musical, and I'm thinking this isn't a good time to start down that road."

She ran her fingers along the delicate lace curtains we'd hung in the windows on the far side of the room and peered through them.

"This is a completely different view of the lake. It's gorgeous."

"Isn't it?" I looked out at the sunlight rippling off the water. It almost looked like a picture postcard, just the image to draw someone in.

She took a couple of steps toward the fireplace—a grand old thing, mantle adorned with all sorts of quaint knick-knacks.

I tried to envision all of this through Nadine's eyes. Yes, it was simple in comparison to her home, but we had filled this place with thoughtful details and personal touches—from the vase of wildflowers on the side table in the parlor to the vintage clock that sat on the oversized mantle. I loved every square inch of this home and hoped others would too.

"I wanted the parlor to feel like you'd stepped back in time," Tasha explained. "It's the true heart of the place."

"It's lovely. And very relaxing." Nadine ran her hand along the back of the plush leather sofa.

Tasha blushed and said, "Thanks. That means a lot coming from you."

We then took her on a tour of the rest of the house. Tasha described every room with great enthusiasm, her animated words sounding more like a realtor's pitch.

We finally reached the beautiful master bedroom.

Nadine gasped as she saw the view through the windows. "It's beautiful. I'm going to love waking up with these views. And I love these French doors leading out to the balcony."

"We slept on the back balcony the other night," I said. "It was so peaceful."

Well, if you didn't count the part where an intruder had awakened us, anyway.

"Yeah, that was the night—"

Tasha stopped short of explaining, thank goodness. Nadine would probably run for the hills if she knew we'd been vandalized.

"If you're staying for a full week—" I interrupted. "I think you could take turns, sleeping in the different bedrooms. Try all four of them out!"

"What a fun idea." She giggled. "You know, I feel like a kid on a vacation. I'm sure Coco and I are going to have the most relaxing week here."

I certainly hoped that turned out to be true.

"If you need anything, please let me know." Tasha was suddenly all business again.

"I will, but please don't hurry off," Nadine said. "I'm really enjoying our conversation. I don't get that much these days. I've become something of a loner since Clayton and I—well, you know."

"Of course." Tasha led the way back down to the kitchen, where she prepped three glasses of sweet tea for us. Then we settled onto the barstools at the island.

"Maybe I should confess the whole truth," Nadine said as she put Coco down on the floor. "I picked your place on purpose because I knew it would irritate Clayton."

"No way." Tasha's eyes widened at this news.

"Yeah." Nadine's nose wrinkled. "Can I be completely honest?"

Tasha nodded. "Of course."

"He was furious when he heard you were opening a vacation home."

Oh boy. This should be good.

"Wait. . .what?" Tasha shook her head. "Whenever I saw him, he would smile and ask me how it was going. He never gave me any indicator he was upset."

"Honey, he's as fake as the day is long, kind of like that bleach blond he's spending time with."

"But. . ." Tears sprang to Tasha's eyes. "I don't understand."

"He even went so far as to try to have the bank stop you from getting the loan."

Tasha gasped. "Thank God he didn't succeed at that. But I don't understand. Why would he want me to fail?"

"Because. . ." Nadine reached for the tea glass. "If Clayton Henderson can't succeed, no one can."

"But he's been successful at everything he puts his hand to," I argued. "He pretty much owns everything in town."

"Like the B&B that's now mine?" Nadine said. "And the Italian restaurant that had to close its doors because of mold? And the vintage cars that he lost money on? Behind closed doors, he's not as impressive as you might think."

I got her point. Clearly he didn't succeed at everything.

"What you see with Clayton Henderson is an illusion," she said. "It's a perfectly painted self-portrait, an image he wants to present to a town that reveres him. But that image is cracking, and he's struggling with the emotional side of that. When the king of the hill takes a tumble, he gets a little more bruised than most on the way down, due to the size of his ego."

"Wow."

"You don't think he would try any shenanigans while you're here, do you?" I asked. "Because, if you do, I could ask Deputy Warren to check in. He lives nearby."

"I honestly don't know what Clayton is capable of." She released an exaggerated sigh. "But I suppose I would feel better knowing an officer was stopping by."

"I'll make sure that happens," I said.

Minutes later—while Tasha and Nadine chatted at length about the house's design choices—I stepped out onto the front porch to give Shawn Warren a call. He answered right away with a chipper, "Deputy Warren!"

I countered with, "This is RaeLyn Hadley."

"Hey, RaeLyn. How can I help you?"

"Tasha has her first customer. Or, client. Or, whatever you call it."

"Guest? I'm thinking a vacation rental is more like a hotel, right?"

"Right. Tasha has her first guest and it's someone we know. Nadine Henderson."

"Oh, interesting." He paused. "That's a family name I know."

"Yeah." We all did. "Anyway, Nadine's been going through some personal stuff lately and is a little nervous about being alone in the house. So we were hoping. . ." My words drifted off.

"I'll be glad to."

"Thank you so much."

"Does she have a restraining order against anyone?" Warren asked.

"If by anyone you mean her ex-husband, I don't think so. She didn't mention one. But maybe you could check?"

"I'll do that. Should be in the system, if so. But I'll keep an eye on the house as I come and go from the neighborhood. Don't mind a bit."

That certainly made me feel better.

"Give her my cell number, will you?" he said. "Tell her to call if she needs anything at all."

"Thank you." I was overwhelmed with gratitude and knew Tasha would be too.

"No problem," he countered. "And while I've got you. . ."

"Yes?" I shifted the phone to my other hand and pressed it against my ear.

"Your friend Tasha. . ." A definitive pause followed. "Is she seeing anyone?"

CHAPTER EIGHTEEN

Did everyone in the county want to date my best friend? Really?

"I, well. . ."

My hesitation must've caused him to rethink the question. "Sorry, that was probably out of line. I shouldn't have asked you that." A nervous laugh followed on his end. "Not very professional of me."

"No, it's okay. I think she's interested in someone, but there's nothing solid there." I stopped short before going into my brother's interest in her. That was no one's business.

"Well, we are neighbors," he said. "Maybe I could borrow a cup of sugar?"

"She's not actually going to live in the house most of the time," I reminded him. "Only when it's not rented out to vacationers. Er, guests."

"Right." He paused. "I'll just have to up my visits to her family's restaurant. I'm already a regular at Fish Tales. I think her family likes me. I've been trying to make a good impression on them, anyway. Her dad seems like a great guy."

Good grief. This guy was seriously interested in Tasha. Did she have any idea? If so, she'd never mentioned it, and Tasha mentioned everything. That girl spilled the tea on a regular basis. I could only guess that she had no clue. Which meant my brother wasn't the only one unable to convey his feelings.

We ended the call, and I thanked Deputy Warren once again for his willingness to keep an eye on the place while Nadine was staying there. Then I headed back inside.

"What did he say?" Tasha asked as I made my way back into the kitchen.

"He's happy to swing by. You should be perfectly safe, Nadine." I decided to leave it at that, at least for now. Maybe later, apart from company, I could fill Tasha in on Shawn Warren's interests in her.

"Wonderful! Now, if you ladies don't mind, I'm going to take my bag up to the master bedroom and unpack." Nadine reached down to swoop the tiny pup into her arms. "Come on, Coco. Let's get settled in our new digs."

She turned and headed toward the stairs, pausing only long enough to grab the designer suitcase from the parlor on her way up.

"I could carry that for you," Tasha called out.

"No thanks!" Nadine hollered in response. "I'm an independent woman now. I need to learn to take care of things myself." Her suitcase thump-thump-thumped up the stairs.

When Nadine was out of earshot, Tasha and I dove into a quiet but lively conversation about all that had just transpired.

"I'm so glad she's staying here," Tasha said. "Folks will really follow her lead, don't you think? I mean, she's still very influential in the community."

"Yes. And she's really nice too." I paused to think through my next words. "I confess, I never really took the time to get to know Nadine before. Maybe it was the age difference. She's closer to my mom's age. Or maybe because I just don't care for her husband."

"Almost ex-husband."

"Yeah." My phone dinged, and I fished it out of my purse. "Oh, man. Speaking of my mom, she and Bessie Mae are really needing my help back at the house. I should probably go now."

"Thanks for coming by. That last-minute cleaning spree was just what we needed. I'm so glad you were here when Nadine called."

"Me too. Always happy to help."

I led the way to the front door, pausing only long enough to pet Coco, who had taken up residence on the parlor sofa. The little doll rolled over to expose her tummy, and I gave it a tickle.

As we stepped out onto the porch, the roar of a car engine came tearing up the road. Tasha and I both stopped, shocked, as a tiny green sedan pulled into her driveway and screeched to a halt.

The small car looked like it had seen better days, but that wasn't really what concerned me. The driver's side door opened and a slightly rounded woman in a rough ponytail came barreling toward us, as if ready for a fight. Only, she stopped short of the front porch, probably when she saw tiny Coco begin to growl.

Tasha planted her hands firmly on her hips. "You need to leave my property right now, Belinda, or I'm going to call the police."

"Don't you mean *my* property?"

"No." Tasha voice grew more strained. "I mean the property I closed on, the property I have the mortgage for, the property I've renovated. Mine."

Belinda's jaw line tensed. "We both know the will Anthony showed up with was fraudulent, and I'm going to prove it in court. In the meantime, you need to do the right thing and give up possession of the house. I need a place to stay. ASAP. I have no other options, and since this is my family home—"

"I'm sorry. I hope you figure something out, but you can't stay here. This is no longer your family home."

"We'll see about that." Belinda reached for her phone and mumbled something about calling the police, but by then I'd already punched in Shawn Warren's number.

I whispered into the phone, "Can you come right now? We have an emergency."

Things escalated as the woman's voice rose to a higher pitch. Before long Nadine had joined us. She scooped up Coco and stood in the doorway, eyes wide, listening to Belinda carry on.

Deputy Warren showed up within minutes. Like Belinda, he came barreling onto the property. Only, at his presence, the tension in Tasha's face immediately softened.

He bounded from his patrol car and headed our way, calling out, "What's going on here?" as he looked back and forth between us.

"This is the lady I told you about," Tasha said. "The one who keeps harassing me, saying the house is hers. But it's not."

Warren turned to face Belinda. "Ma'am, you're going to have to stop showing up here unannounced. I'm going to have to arrest you if you do it again."

"Why wait until she does it again?" Tasha asked. "Why not arrest her right now?"

"If she cooperates and leaves, there's no reason to," he countered. Then he turned to face Belinda. "I'm giving you the opportunity to do that, ma'am."

She stormed toward her car, hollering, "You'll be hearing from my attorney."

"I've already heard from her attorney," Tasha muttered. "And my attorney says there's nothing to her claims."

Nadine stood in the doorway, holding Coco. The edges of her lips curled up in a smile as she said, "Well, that was fun."

It didn't feel like much fun to me. And I had to confess—if to no one other than myself—that I felt nervous leaving Nadine alone in the house. Tasha must've felt it too, because she lingered on the front porch after the deputy left, a bewildered look on her face. I felt just awful for her.

"Do you really suppose she has no place else to stay?" I asked once we got back inside.

Tasha shrugged. "Maybe. From what I could gather from her Facebook page, she's struggling on multiple levels. She was pretty vocal about her financial woes. I saw that someone started a fundraiser for her after her husband died to help pay for the funeral."

"Oh, wow." That certainly changed things. "She must really be in a dire place. Maybe she does need a place to stay after all."

"Badly enough that she would vandalize my property?" Tasha asked.

"I don't think she can. I think she's bluffing, to see what you'll do."

"I don't know if I have legal recourse to keep her away, though. You know?"

"You will, if you file a restraining order against her."

Tasha groaned and dropped into her seat. "Has it really come to that? I'm filing restraining orders now?"

It did seem a bit extreme but would certainly serve its purpose, keeping Belinda away.

All the way home I thought about Tasha's plight. None of this seemed fair. The snippy neighbor. The homeless guy. Clayton Henderson. Belinda Keller. All Tasha ever wanted to do was create a lovely place by the lake where folks could come and relax. Instead, she'd ended up with more drama than a scene from *Annie Get Your Gun*. Minus the song and dance numbers, of course.

I rushed home and dove right in, helping Mom and Bessie Mae finish up the baking for the Fourth of July event. Afterward, we made a quick run to the church to drop off all of the goodies so that we wouldn't have as much to do in the morning. Then I checked in with Mason, who asked if he could come by for a while.

By five thirty, Mason and I were side-by-side on the porch swing. He gestured to the kitchen window, directly in our view from the porch swing. Through the window, we could make out my mother and Bessie Mae, deep in conversation while they worked to make dinner. I couldn't believe they were still going. I was pooped.

"They've worked hard today," I said.

Mason gave me a compassionate look. "I'm guessing you have too."

"Yes, for sure." I then filled him in on the goings-on over at Tasha's place.

"Wait." He sat up straight and looked me in the eye. "You're saying that Nadine Henderson is staying at Tasha's place right now?"

"Yep. And she's specifically staying there to irritate Clayton, from what she told us. Though, she did seem pretty smitten with the house."

"Wow. And you had to call the police because the former owner's daughter showed up?"

"Looking pretty rough, I might add. She said she needed a place to stay, so I have to wonder if she's lost her home. Maybe I can do a little research to figure that out."

"If she's lost her home, that's her issue, not Tasha's."

"Right." I paused. "But we still involved the sheriff's department, so they can keep an eye on the place."

"Great idea."

I pinched my eyes shut, feeling the weight of sleep drifting over me.

Just as quickly, they popped back open. "Speaking of Deputy Warren, he's got the hots for Tasha."

Mason's eyes bugged. "I beg your pardon?"

"He asked if she was dating anyone."

"Ah." Mason leaned back against the swing. "What did you say?"

"I said, 'Sort of.' I mean, she and Dallas aren't technically dating. And she's got a crush on the home inspector guy. So I wasn't really sure how to respond, to be honest. Did I tell you about the yellow roses?"

"Yellow roses?"

"Yeah. She has no idea who really sent them. Poor Dallas."

"This story is sounding like one of those soap operas my mom used to watch when I was little."

"Isn't it, though?" I swatted at a mosquito. "Let's just hope it doesn't end with anyone coming down with a case of amnesia."

"Might make for a great plot twist."

"True." And if there was anything we Hadleys loved, it was a great plot twist.

CHAPTER NINETEEN

The back door of the house opened, and Logan and his girlfriend, Meghan, walked out. They waved at us but then took seats at the patio table, out of ear shot.

"Those two are seeing more and more of each other," Mason observed.

"Yeah. Mom's afraid he'll pop the question."

"Would that be such a bad thing?"

"She never got over the fact that Meghan was married once before, to Meredith's ex."

Mason gave the duo another glance. "That was a long time ago, and she admitted it was a huge mistake. Personally, I think Meghan's a good match for Logan. They seem to have a lot in common."

"Very different occupations. She's a nurse at the hospital in Athens."

"If your family ever needs medical help, she'll be close by." He smiled, as if that settled the whole thing.

"Tell that to Mom. If he did marry her, it would change the dynamic of the ranch, for sure. It might be weird if they end up living in his tiny trailer, though." I couldn't quite picture it.

"No weirder than Jake and Carrie living in the little house next door." Mason gestured to the house just a few yards from where we were sitting.

"That's where Bessie Mae grew up, right?"

"Right. And I guess you have a point. We've always been flexible, moving folks around as the need arose. But Logan's place is a tiny little trailer, not exactly big enough for two. I wonder if Meghan would be content with such a small space? I sure wouldn't. Talk about claustrophobic."

My thoughts shifted to the trailer. I'd only been inside a few times, but it felt cramped to me.

"When did Bessie Mae come to live with you?" Mason's words interrupted my pondering. "I don't remember."

"When I was young, she still lived in the little house. I think she came to some kind of an understanding with my parents when Jake was about to get married. She wanted to keep the family together, so she offered the house to them in exchange for a room at our place."

"That makes sense."

"She was always over at our place anyway. And this gave Jake and Carrie the privacy they needed. Mom and Dad converted our home's garage for Bessie Mae. Have I taken you on a tour?"

"You have not. You told me about it, but I haven't seen it."

"I guess all of that happened while you were off at college. That's why we have the carport and the shed now, since the garage is gone."

"Makes sense."

"Follow me. I'll show you." I led him inside the back door of our house, down the narrow hallway, and through the door that had once led to the garage but now led to a spacious master, complete with its own bath.

I found Aunt Bessie Mae snoozing in her chair, Bible in her lap. The quaint and homey room smelled of a mixture of muscle rub cream and rose-scented perfume—not the most pleasant combination. Mason rubbed at his nose as we approached.

I put my finger to my lips and we tiptoed into the room. I watched as Mason's gaze shifted to the various pieces of artwork on the walls. There were pictures of the family, of course. But there were at least two of the Duke for every one of us.

He mouthed the word "Wow" and I knew he'd probably have plenty of thoughts to share later.

I pointed to one of my favorite paintings, the one with a quote I'd come to love: *All battles are fought by scared men who'd rather be someplace else.* That was so true—of men and women.

We made our way back out into the kitchen. Sure enough, Mason dove right in, his words more animated than usual.

"I knew she loved John Wayne," he said, "but that was more than I expected. I've never seen so much memorabilia together like that before. She could open her own shop."

"She would never let any of that go, trust me." I laughed. "In fact, she's been collecting paintings of him for years. And we've been adding to her collection at every birthday. Or Christmas. Or whenever we find something perfect at a flea market. Trust me when I say we've got our Duke radar up at all times."

"Your aunt is something else." He paused and appeared to lose himself to his thoughts. "I wish I still had a family member in that age group."

"What about your aunt Lucy?" I asked.

"Mom's sister?" He shrugged. "We weren't very close before Dad died, and have drifted even more."

"You should reach out to her."

He grew silent but then responded with the words, "I will."

As we headed back outside, I was struck with an idea. "Hey, would you help me with something?"

"Sure. What's that?"

"Earlier Bessie Mae mentioned a camera that her dad had back in the '50s. A Super 8 or something like that?"

"I love those old home movie cameras. Haven't seen one in years, though."

"She said it's probably still up in the attic at the little house. I'm dying to find it, and the movie reels too."

"Are you thinking what I think you're thinking?"

"Maybe." I flashed him a bright smile. "But I'm not a mind reader."

"You're going to take your aunt on a trip down memory lane?"

"If I can find those movies, yes. I'll have to figure some things out, but I'd love to surprise her."

"I think that's a great idea." He gave me an admiring look.

"Is now a good time?"

"Sure." Mason laughed. "I love nothing more than climbing into a hot attic in 98-degree weather."

"Very funny."

I texted Carrie to make sure it was okay if we popped in. A couple of minutes later my sister-in-law ushered us inside her little house and pointed up to the pull-down ladder in the hallway, which led up to the attic.

"I feel like I saw that camera in a box with some of Bessie Mae's childhood belongings," Carrie explained.

"I'll look." Mason pulled down the ladder and then ascended it. His voice sounded muffled from above me, but I was pretty sure I made out, "Which box did she say again?"

I climbed a couple of steps and hollered out, "She wasn't specific."

"Perfect. That'll make it easier." The sound of items banging and clanging went on for a couple of minutes before I heard a groan.

"You okay?" I called up.

"Yeah. Just whacked my head on a beam. No worries. I've got plenty of brain cells to spare."

I couldn't help but laugh at that image. I took a couple more steps up until I had a visual of the attic. It was a treasure trove of items, many of which dated back half a century or more. I'd already discovered many of them, but this attic was the gift that kept on giving.

"This place could use some organization," I observed.

"You should think about dividing it by category," Mason suggested. "That's what I'd do."

"Of course that's what you'd do." I laughed. "And when it's cooler we'll come back and do that. But for today I just need those movies."

It took a bit of scrounging, but I finally managed to locate the box in question. Buried underneath a bunch of metal tins I saw the edge of what looked like—

"The camera!" I held it up and then gave it a closer look.

Mason took several steps in my direction, the old floorboards creaking beneath him. "Wow. That definitely looks like something we'd find in your antique store."

"Only, I doubt we'll ever sell it. Too many memories were recorded with this."

"Agreed." He took it from me and examined it with great care. "This is really something else. And it looks like it's in great condition."

"Except for the dust." I pulled out the round tins with the movie reels inside. My heart skipped a beat as I held one of the small metal tins in my hands. "I've heard about these all of my life but have never seen them."

"Movies of your dad's life?"

"And Bessie Mae. And Papaw."

"Wow." He dug around until he came out with a projector. "This isn't in great shape. Not sure if you can get it to work or not. Want me to tinker around with it to find out?"

"Yes. Please."

We transferred them all to a smaller box, which Mason hefted onto his shoulder.

"Is that it?" he asked.

I looked around and was startled to see something familiar. "Check this out, Mason."

He drew close, nearly dropping the box off his shoulder. "What is it?"

"A player piano roll."

I ran my fingers along the strip of perforated paper, which was punched with meticulous tiny holes.

"You have a player piano?"

"No, just the regular one," I said. "And hardly anyone even plays it anymore. But I certainly know someone who owns a player piano."

And as soon as I could, I would figure out what this song was, and why someone had tucked it away in our attic.

CHAPTER TWENTY

No one in Texas did the Fourth of July better than the Cedar Creek Lake residents. Our combined efforts were something to behold. Collectively, we provided a plethora of activities for individuals and families alike. Celebrating our freedom was something we took very seriously in these parts, and I, for one, hoped that never changed.

My personal favorite was the Thunder over Cedar Creek Lake Airshow. This was a favorite with locals and folks all over the county too. In fact, people came from as far away as Dallas and Tyler to see this show, which featured aerial acrobatics by professional pilots, zipping in and out over the lake in civilian and military fighter crafts. I particularly enjoyed the dogfight simulations, which were breathtaking. Best of all, the local veterans' foundation put the event on, which made it even more special. We showed up in droves to support them.

Of course, our local churches got in on the patriotic celebrations too. There was a quilt show at the Methodist church, featuring red, white, and blue quilts. The Assembly of God church was hosting a vintage car show in the parking lot. I was so thrilled to have Tilly in the mix. The Baptists sponsored a patriotic sing-along. Local businesses sponsored snow cone trucks, food trucks, and even waterslides for the kids. And there was usually some sort of concert in the park on the Gun Barrel City side of the lake, featuring popular country western singers.

All of this was capped off with a terrific fireworks display in the evening. If one lasted that long. We had an open house planned at Tasha's new place at four but were hoping to be done in time to catch the fireworks after, if only from her side of the lake.

My whole family turned out midmorning for the annual parade, put on by the volunteer fire department. All four of my brothers participated in the volunteer fire department brigade, and I was giddy to join other vintage car owners, proudly driving Tilly along the route, fully decked out with American flags. I could barely hold back the tears in my eyes as I waved at the crowd. Papaw would've been so proud.

After the parade, I parked Tilly at the vintage car show and located my mother and Mason. We visited several of the booths where locals were selling their wares. I was particularly interested in the adorable red, white, and blue hand-crafted items. We had some amazing, talented people in the Mabank area.

After we wrapped up our shopping, I caught a glimpse of Clayton and Meredith on the far side of the street, just outside the Chamber of Commerce entrance. The audacious woman wore the same over-the-top Statue of Liberty costume she'd worn at last year's Pioneer Day event, the one featuring way too much cleavage. It did not have the desired effect. Most folks just diverted their attention away from her, even the menfolk. I didn't blame them. The woman might be begging for attention, but right now everyone just wanted to avoid her.

Still, this didn't stop Clayton—always a showboat—from making a big splash. He passed out business cards to anyone who would listen to him ramble on about all of his new business ventures. From what I could gather, he and Meredith were opening a new beauty salon in Mabank in the old barber shop. Well, lovely. Clayton was in the beauty biz now too?

My thoughts shifted to Nadine and all that she had told us about Clayton's feelings toward Tasha. My stomach churned as anger took hold.

Was Nadine here right now? I knew she planned to head out later in the afternoon with a friend, but I sure hoped she wasn't looking on, seeing what I was seeing. If so, how would she take this news?

I looked around the crowd but didn't see her. Hopefully she and Coco were curled up on the balcony at Tasha's place, overlooking the lake and completely avoiding her ex and his shenanigans.

We all decided to grab some food. I was surprised to see Conner Griffin working at the hot dog stand alongside the pastor's wife.

"Hot dogs, folks?" he called out as we passed by. "Just a buck."

We stepped into the line to get our hot dogs, the heat of the summer sun beating down on us relentlessly.

I had to admit, the aroma of sizzling hot dogs filled the air and mixed with the scent of perspiration and mustard. It made for quite the combination. Still, I could hardly wait to sink my teeth into that juicy hot dog with all the trimmings. If we ever made it through this ridiculous line. Oh well. The wait would be worthwhile. I convinced myself it only added to the festivities.

All was well until Tasha joined us. At first, she didn't seem to recognize Conner. I didn't blame her. He looked a lot different with his hair cut, face shaved, and wearing a patriotic T-shirt and jeans. In fact, he was downright handsome. Who knew?

Then, suddenly, she seemed to make the connection. She locked eyes with him, and his gaze shifted downward.

"I know you," she said. "You're—"

"Out of mustard. Sorry. Be right back." And at that, he took off, leaving the pastor's wife to tend to all of the customers alone.

"How can I help y'all?" Melody asked.

"You don't need to be out here, working in this heat." My mother's words sounded more like scolding.

I agreed. Melody was undergoing treatment for ongoing kidney issues. Someone else needed to give her a break.

"You just let me come back there and help you," Mom insisted. And next thing you knew, my mother was serving hot dogs and chips to passers-by.

I kept looking for Conner to come back, but he did not. Mason must've noticed too, because he excused himself to go in search of the man.

"He's a troubled soul." Melody kept her volume low as she stepped into the spot beside me. "But a nice man with a lot of potential. We've been putting a lot of time and effort into getting to know him. Did you know he served in Afghanistan? He was in the Air Force."

I did not, and I told her so. In spite of this news, Tasha still didn't look comfortable.

There was so much to do after finishing our hot dogs. We started with greeting guests for the patriotic sing-along. I stuck my head in the door to give a listen as the songs rang out.

Ordinarily I listened to worship songs and hymns in the sanctuary of our little Baptist church. But today the building was flooded with the joyful sounds of patriotic tunes. And boy, did people ever sing along!

The choir was decked out in red, white, and blue, and little children waved flags as "God Bless America" and "The Star-Spangled Banner" rang out. It did my heart good.

The brilliant colors of the stained-glass windows provided the perfect colorful backdrop for this special day. As laughter and applause erupted between each song, I felt an uncanny sense of unity with my fellow townspeople. The Fourth of July had that effect on me every year, but it seemed extra-special this summer.

Maybe it was the sound of Mason's voice next to mine, but my heart swelled with joy as he belted out the familiar words to the patriotic tunes we both loved.

After the sing-along, Tasha and I decided to take a peek at the bake auction. The Baptist church's fellowship hall buzzed with anticipation and excitement as long stretches of tables were on full display with the goodies.

Homemade cakes, pies, cookies. . .and much more, made my mouth water. Up front, Pastor Burchfield played the role of auctioneer, doing a terrific job making the items sound delectable. If the man ever gave up on ministry, he definitely had a future as an auctioneer. His charismatic, booming voice held us all spellbound. And the twinkle in his eye as he promoted his wife Melody's lemon pie? Priceless.

The energy remained high as enthusiastic bidders waved their paddles high, each one anxious to outbid the other so that they could take home their favorite sweet treats.

I found myself bidding on one of Aunt Bessie Mae's cakes but stopped short of winning. Truth be told, I just wanted to up the ante with my bid. The proceeds were going to charity, after all.

When the auction ended, we located Bessie Mae, hanging out with the Methodists at the quilt show. The Methodist church's fellowship hall had been beautifully transformed into a colorful gallery of quilts, with rows and rows of meticulously crafted beauties on display. If I thought the choir at the Baptist church was red, white, and blue, these quilts took that theme over the top. Each one told a different story of patriotic pride from a different quilter.

Tasha and I strolled through the room admiring the handiwork of the ladies who'd done all of this. I'd never seen such intricate stitching and creative designs.

After showing us around, my aunt glanced at her watch and gasped. "Oh my. I'm late for the cupcake walk."

"We just came from the bake auction," I explained. "They're already done. They've made a lot of money, for sure."

"The cupcake walk is separate," she said. "And I promised to help."

"After being on your feet all day yesterday?" I chided. "Bessie Mae, surely they can find someone else to stand out in this heat and help with a cupcake walk. You deserve to rest."

Her eyes sparkled with an unusual excitement. "It's in the fellowship hall at the Presbyterian church, and it starts in ten minutes. I've asked a friend to help. Maybe he's already there." She gave me a little wink.

The woman was definitely up to something.

We tagged along behind her until we reached the church where this particular event was being held. I was shocked to see Bob Reeves pressed up against the wall looking like a man who'd rather be anywhere else but here.

"Bessie Mae!" I gave her an admiring look. "How did you get him here?"

"Oh, easy." With the wave of a hand she acted as if it was no big deal. "I just promised to make him some banana pudding. The man was always infatuated with my banana pudding."

I had a feeling he was infatuated with more than that. He followed dutifully behind her and even allowed her to put a patriotic LET THEM EAT CAKE! apron on him before insisting that he run the music for the cupcake walk.

I watched him follow her lead as the cupcake walk began, his eyes never leaving her. There was an excitement in the air as children made the rounds, circling the numbered squares. Off in the distance, cupcakes filled a table. Winners would be able to take whatever they liked.

Bob ran the music from a cell phone that was hooked into a sound bar. He looked nervous but somehow kept things going. Okay, he caused the songs to stop and start a bit more abruptly than one might have expected, but I could tell he was doing his best. Whenever the music would stop, his eyes would scope the crowd, as if to make sure everyone was happy.

The kids seemed to have a blast, and so did some of the parents, who were just as eager to participate. I didn't blame them. There were a lot of great-looking cupcakes on that table, including Bessie Mae's delicious Italian cream cake flavored ones, my personal favorite, thanks to all of those chopped pecans. Yum!

Off in the distance I caught a glimpse of my sister-in-law, wearing three-month-old Annalisa in one of those little carrier things. She waved and then walked my way.

"What did I miss?" Carrie asked.

"Well, let's see." I gestured with my head to Bessie Mae. "Pretty sure someone has a new love interest."

Carrie's eyes widened. "Really? That would be amazing. As long as I've known Bessie Mae she's never shown interest in anyone."

"I suspect there's a reason for that. Turns out, she and Bob Reeves were sweethearts in high school."

"Do tell."

I would have, but the baby started fussing, and Carrie decided she needed to slip into the church nursery to feed her.

I went looking for Tasha and found her talking to Shawn Warren, who was stationed in the church foyer. He held her spellbound with some sort of conversation about gardening.

Off in the distance Dallas watched. He had that same sad puppy-eyed look that a dog in the shelter had when overlooked by passers-by.

I took several steps in his direction, determined to cheer him up.

"Before you say anything. . ." He put his hand up. "I sent the yellow roses like you suggested."

"I know."

"She never even acknowledged them."

Oh, she had acknowledged them, all right. She just thought they were from someone else. But how could I tell him that?

"Did you sign the card?" I asked.

His gaze shifted down. "Kind of. I left a cryptic message. But if she knows me, she'll get it."

"I wouldn't be so sure," I countered. "Because with Tasha you have to just put it out there. Otherwise. . ."

"Oh, I can see the otherwise part with my own eyes." His gaze shifted to Warren and Tasha. "How am I ever going to compete with a man in a uniform?"

"Or a guy in an inspector's uniform," I almost added. . .but didn't. My poor brother had enough to fret over today without finding out there were two other fish in the pond.

Though, from the looks of things, only one was swimming frantically. I watched as Warren handed Tasha some sort of business card. She responded by hugging him, which caused my brother to let out a grunt. Like, a loud, audible grunt.

Tasha came bounding our way. "Well, that was nice of him."

"What?" I asked.

"Shawn just gave me some amazing advice about the garden I want to put in the backyard. Apparently, he's really got quite the green thumb. He wrote down the name of a product he recommends for my roses. Would you believe, he grows them too?"

"Of course he does," Dallas said.

And at that, my brother decided to opt out of the conversation. He found someplace else to be.

Tasha looked after him as he walked away. "Dallas okay today? He's acting kind of weird."

"Maybe it's the heat," I said. "It's affecting everyone."

"Could be." She tugged at her collar. "It's messing me up too. I always tell folks I make very poor decisions when I'm overheated."

"Yesterday you told me that you make very poor decisions when you're tired."

"That's true."

"And last week you told me that you make very poor decisions when you're hungry."

"That's *absolutely* true." She giggled. "When you put all of those things together it looks like I make a *lot* of very poor decisions."

Hopefully not in the romance department. My brother would be devastated. Should I tell her that?

Tasha paused for breath. "Hey, speaking of the heat, I passed the snow cone booth on my way in and I'm dying for one. Come with?"

"Sure. Why not." The conversation about Dallas would have to wait for another day.

We headed out to the snow cone truck, and as we did we ran smack-dab into Conner Griffin. Literally. Tasha smashed right into him, obliterating the blue snow cone in his hand, which was now all over his white T-shirt.

"Oh, man." His eyes widened and he backed away, muttering something I couldn't quite make out. The guy was definitely nervous in her presence, but why? Because he had spray painted the front of her house, perhaps? Or because she'd just covered him in blue dye?

Seconds later, Mason appeared with my brother at his side. Dallas looked to be in better spirits, now that he was talking to Mason.

Mason really did have that effect on people. He managed to connect with Conner, and before long the three guys were chatting about something to do with cars. Were they wanting to head over to the Assembly of God church to look at the rows of vintage cars, perhaps?

No, this was something else, entirely. They lost me about the time Mason mentioned alternators. I wasn't sure what that had to do with the Fourth of July, but guys would be guys, regardless of the date.

I overhead Conner say something about not having enough money right now to take care of something, but Mason responded with, "Come by, anyway. We'll figure something out."

My big-hearted guy, at work again.

"I want to hear all about your new job," Mason added.

Conner dove into a conversation about the Cajun restaurant then lit into details about their gumbo.

"Why is everyone always talking about how good the gumbo is at that new place?" Tasha asked, and then took a nibble of her snow cone. "I guess I need to go see for myself so I can check out the competition."

"I'll take you." These words came from Dallas, who looked more than a little pleased with himself for thinking of it.

"That sounds good, Dallas. I'd like that."

A lovely little silence rose up between them. Of course, it was soon squelched with the laughter and conversation of the townspeople around us.

Still, I couldn't help but think this little trip to the Cajun restaurant was just what Tasha and Dallas needed. Maybe a real date would give him the courage to let her know he'd sent those yellow roses.

Or not.

Shawn Warren headed straight for us, all laughter and smiles as he shared an exciting story about the airshow.

Dallas stood quietly listening, but I could tell he was worried. And all the more when Warren convinced Tasha she should join him for a walk down Market Street to look at the various booths.

To her credit, she turned him down.

"I'm sorry, but I've got to get back to the house," she explained. "We've got a big open house at four, and I still need to pick up some things from Brookshire Brothers on the way. Sorry about that."

And just like that, both of the fellas pining over my BFF were rejected. They headed off together to get another hot dog, and she and I decided to pack it in.

Despite the heat, my heart was very full. Buoyed by the joy of those around me and the overwhelming sense of camaraderie, we made our way back to our vehicles. By the time I settled into the driver's seat in my scorching hot car, I was ready for a nap. However, that was out of the question. We still had way too much work to do.

CHAPTER TWENTY-ONE

On our way back to Sunset Hideaway, Tasha and I stopped off at Brookshire Brothers to pick up a couple of Texas charcuterie trays she had ordered. They were definitely a feast for the eyes. I'd seen some amazing charcuterie boards before, but these were piled high with gorgeous slices of brisket, jalapeño sausage, and what looked to be peppered turkey.

The trays were also loaded with a variety of cheeses—sharp cheddar, pepper jack, and creamy queso fresco, my personal favorite.

To add more variety, there was BBQ sauce, salsa, and a ton of Texas-shaped crackers, along with some roasted pecans.

In spite of the hot dogs and snow cones I'd eaten, my mouth watered at the very idea of nibbling on these goodies. It would be hard to save some for the guests.

Tasha's eyes bugged as she took them in, but probably more at the price. I half expected her to say, "Whelp, there goes my first mortgage payment!" But she did not.

While at the store, we also grabbed some tortilla chips, salsa, sweet tea, and lemonade. We would offer her guests a true Texas experience.

Upon arrival at the house, we found Nadine and Coco heading off to give us space.

"Don't worry about us," she said, as she set the little dog down. "We're going to Malakoff to have an early dinner with a friend." The tiny pup pranced across the parlor, showing of an adorable glittery red, white, and blue outfit.

The darling patriotic ensemble featured white stars on the sleeves and highlighted the pup's silky fur. Talk about charming! Coco's dark eyes shone with excitement and her tail wagged back and forth, as if to further entertain us.

"She would have fit right in with the celebration in town," I said. "That's an amazing getup!"

"Oh, thank you," Nadine said. "I'm one of those crazy dog owners who has a costume for every occasion. But thank goodness I've got a dog who seems to love it too."

"I think it's adorable." Tasha glanced my way. "You totally need to get one of those for Riley. She would be so cute in it."

"Um, no." My cattle dog would look—and probably feel—ridiculous in such a festive getup.

"Kind of glad I decided to stay in today," Nadine said as she opened the front door and stepped out onto the front porch. "It's blazing hot out here."

"Boy, don't we know it." I wished I had time to take a shower, but that wouldn't happen.

"Y'all have fun," Nadine said with the wave of a hand. "See you later." She headed toward her SUV, and a couple minutes later her shiny Lexus was rolling out of the driveway.

"I feel so bad she had to leave," Tasha said as we made our way inside the house. "But she seemed okay with it."

"Don't feel bad. You gave her a heads-up that you would be hosting an open house, and she agreed to it. So you've done nothing wrong."

We hauled everything inside and set up as quickly as possible in the kitchen. I was tickled to see that Nadine had left the place in spotless condition. The kitchen had the fresh aroma of cookies baking, and we were both surprised to find a platter of chocolate chip cookies on the island, with a note that read, "For your guests."

"Wow." Tasha stared at the platter, eyes wide. "I suppose I never really knew Nadine. I wouldn't have guessed her to be the baking type."

I had to agree with that. But Nadine was proving us both wrong in so many different ways. The more I got to know her, the more I liked her.

Tasha pulled out a stack of brochures with pertinent information about the house and set them on the island next to the platter of beautifully arranged cookies. "I'm going to ask folks to take pictures and post them on their social media accounts with my new hashtag."

I reached for the bag of tortilla chips. "You have a hashtag?" This was news.

"Yep! #sunsethideaway." She pointed at the brochure to show me. "Hopefully folks will see the pictures that friends and loved ones take today and want to visit."

"I think that's such a great idea." I paused from opening the bag of chips to give her an admiring look. "You're going to end up being a great marketer as well as business owner."

She laughed and then reached for a large bowl to pour the chips into. "Hey, what can I say? I studied marketing for a full year before I decided to change my major to business."

"It all works hand in hand."

"It does." She almost lost her grip on the bowl but caught it just in time. "And I do seem to enjoy it all. But remember when I thought I wanted to go to culinary school? And what about that one random summer I thought I wanted to be a vet tech."

"You always loved animals."

"Nope." She shook her head as the chips tumbled into the bowl. "You were the animal lover. I think I just wanted to be a vet tech because Michael Burchett was going to school to study to be a veterinarian. Remember the shameless crush I used to have on him?"

"Oh, funny. I haven't thought about him in ages."

"I think about him from time to time. He's probably married with a couple of kids by now." An exaggerated sigh followed.

"Your day will come, Tasha," I said. Probably sooner than she knew.

"I guess."

I strained to open the jar of salsa, finally passing it off to Tasha. "I remember a lot of crushes. But the truth is, you're the most versatile person I know. You really could've done any of those things and succeeded."

"Just call me Clayton Henderson." She popped open the jar of salsa, then reached for a glass bowl to pour it into.

"I will call you a great many things," I said. "Talented. Funny. Quirky. Faithful. Kind. But I will *never* call you Clayton Henderson."

"Okay, okay!" She rolled her eyes. "But can we just pretend for a moment that I have one-third of his success in this life?"

"There are ten thousand other people you should try to emulate before putting Clayton on the list," I said. "He's not the best role model."

"True. But I still want to know how to grow my business to be profitable, like he's done all these years."

Only, he wasn't always profitable, was he? This probably wouldn't be the time to remind her of that, though. We still had work to do.

We finished setting everything up on the island, and then she turned to give the room a closer look. Tasha smiled, clearly pleased with our effort. "Good! Now, let's check out the rest of this place to make sure it's ready to show off."

We did that and found everything to her liking. We were especially tickled that Nadine had gone over-the-top with the layout of the pillows on the bed in the master bedroom.

"I need to hire her," Tasha said. "She's got a flair for this."

"Well, she should have," I countered. "She's had years of decorating experience in those fancy houses of hers, after all."

About twenty minutes later, the first guests arrived. Tasha greeted Pastor Burchfield and his wife at the door, ushering them in with great fanfare.

"This is just darling, Tasha," Melody said. "You've outdone yourself!"

This, of course, caused my friend to blush. Or maybe it was just the heat coming from the front porch.

I led them on a tour, and just as we reached the stairway, the doorbell rang again and Tasha opened it to another round of guests.

Over the next couple of hours, people came and went, most of them offering flattery and praise for a job well done. If Tasha had any lingering doubts about how folks would feel about the place, she could lay them to rest now. Everyone commented on the decor, the layout, and the quaint feel of the gorgeous home. And many asked for her card so they could share her information with their loved ones. She countered by asking them to post pictures online to help with marketing.

Sometime around six, a familiar voice rang out. I turned to discover Clayton Henderson, his arm looped through Meredith's, as they stepped into the spacious parlor. Thank goodness Meredith had changed out of that ridiculous Statue of Liberty costume and was wearing normal clothes.

Well, a little over-the-top, but otherwise normal.

"This is *dah*-ling!" Meredith crooned with great animation as she spun to give the room a closer look. "Don't you think so, Clayton? It's almost as lovely as that beautiful hotel you love to take me to in Grapevine. What's it called again? The one with the amazing lobby?" She dove into an animated discussion about the beautiful room they'd stayed in on their last visit.

Clayton cleared his throat. No doubt talking about their escapades in Dallas hotels wasn't something he felt comfortable doing in front of a crowd.

"It's very nice." His face seemed to contradict his words. "If you like this sort of thing."

Okay, so Sunset Hideaway wasn't what he was used to, but did he have to be rude about it? Obviously, many people did appreciate Tasha's quaint and homey style. We'd already confirmed that.

I couldn't help but think about all that Nadine had told us—how Clayton didn't want to see Tasha succeed. Somehow, she managed to cover up whatever negative emotions she might be feeling as she led them through the parlor and into the kitchen.

"Feel free to help yourselves to some snacks," Tasha said with a strained smile. "Mi casa es su casa."

"I'm *die*-ing for a sweet tea, honey," Meredith said with dramatic flair. "These Texas heats are going to be the *death* of me."

I couldn't fault her there, but the woman was a little theatrical.

I led the way into the kitchen and pointed them toward the tea, and then I offered to give them a guided tour of the home. To be honest, I wanted to stick close because I had a hankering to listen in on any of Clayton's comments about the place. Plus, I had a flair for the dramatic too, so making each room sound like a showpiece would be easy, especially since I'd played a role in decorating them.

We covered the downstairs first, my descriptions of each room growing a bit more animated as I went long, particularly in the dining room with the spacious table that seated twelve guests. Then we headed upstairs.

I ran my hand along the railing of the curved stairway and pointed out the architecture of the place. "This house was built in 1907," I explained. "It was later owned by the Keller family. They left it to their son Anthony, who, in turn, sold it to Tasha."

"I remember the family well." Clayton paused. "Tried for years to get old lady Keller to sell me the place, but she wouldn't budge. Said she had other plans for it."

"*God* had other plans for it." I flashed a broad smile. "Now, let me show you the master. It's wonderful."

We stepped inside and everyone grew silent as we all took it in. There was a rustic elegance in this spacious room. Of course, the main feature was that gorgeous, oversized bed with its heavy carved headboard. Mom had let it go to Tasha for a fraction of what it was worth. But seeing it here now, especially through Clayton's eyes, made all of that worthwhile.

The bedding was pretty amazing too—crisp white linens and plush pillows in varying shades of blue. Very welcoming.

I gestured to the French doors leading out to the balcony. "This is my favorite part."

"I can see why," Meredith crooned. "It's lovely! I'd like to do something just like this when we build our new place!"

"Your new place?" I asked. How many homes did one man have to own?

Meredith clasped her hands together at her chest. "Oh, we've got all sorts of plans to build a—"

Clayton nudged her with his elbow as he cleared his throat. "Never mind all that. Let's take a look at the lake, shall we?"

And at that, he grabbed her by the arm and led her to the French doors.

CHAPTER TWENTY-TWO

We all stood gazing out the doors at those breathtaking views of Cedar Creek Lake. Its shimmering waters were visible from nearly every angle of the room, which made this space perfect for incoming guests.

"I just love these soft, gauzy curtains you've picked up." Meredith ran her fingertips along the edges of them. "I can just imagine how pretty everything is going to look when the morning sunlight comes peeking through."

Clayton let out a grunt.

We turned to leave the room, but as we did, Clayton's gaze shot down to the Louis Vuitton suitcase just inside the open closet door.

"Wait a minute..." He walked over and gave it a closer look. Then he glanced my way. "Is this my wife's?"

"*Ex*-wife's," Meredith corrected him.

Before I could answer, he caught a glimpse of the dog bed in the corner. Clayton turned to face me once again, jaw flinching.

"Why is Coco's bed here?"

"Nadine is my first guest." Tasha's voice sounded from the open bedroom door. "There's work going on at your—her—place, and she and Coco are staying here until it's done."

His fists clenched. "Why would she do that?"

"Oh, she *adores* this place," Tasha explained. "Said it's charming. A breath of fresh air."

"She would say that." He muttered something under his breath that I couldn't quite make out.

"She had *nothing* but kind words to say," Tasha added and then flung wide the French doors.

The blissful look on Meredith's face faded as he carried on about his ex-wife. Before long she disappeared onto the back balcony for a look at the lake. He joined her moments later, and we watched through the now-closed doors as they argued. Loudly.

"Trouble in paradise?" Mason's voice sounded, and I turned to face him.

"Looks that way. Clayton's not happy that Nadine is staying here."

Worry lines creased Mason's brow. "I'm just giving you a heads-up— Clayton's not happy about this place, period. Some of the locals have been talking about it. He's bitter about losing his place on the lake to Nadine, so I don't think he wants any of the other vacation rentals to succeed."

"Yeah, we heard all about it from Nadine," I told him.

"That's what bitterness will do to you, I suppose." Tasha walked over and fluffed up the pillows on the bed. "It's just so weird. Six months ago, I was the jealous one, wishing I had what Clayton had. Now the tables are turned. It feels. . .weird."

"To all of us," I said. "We're so used to seeing Clayton get whatever he wants. It's odd to see him struggling."

"We all have our struggles." Mason's gaze turned back to the couple on the balcony. "Some are just more visible than others."

We all watched as Clayton raised his voice to Meredith, who responded with a stunned look on her face. Yep, there was definitely trouble in paradise.

They didn't hang around much longer, but we found ourselves distracted by other guests anyway. Guests came and went for those first couple of hours, but things began to slow after that.

Around six thirty, Bessie Mae turned up with a large bowl in her arms, which she carried into the kitchen and placed in the refrigerator.

"What's that?" Tasha asked.

"Oh, I brought the banana pudding for Bob. He's going to be stopping by in a minute to pick it up. I hope you don't mind."

"Why didn't you drop it off at his place?" I asked.

"He's not there yet. The pastor at the Presbyterian church asked for his help with cleanup after the cupcake walk. That gave me just enough time to run home and snag this banana pudding from our fridge. He'll be along shortly."

True to her word, he showed up a few minutes later, just as the last of our guests headed out.

The poor man looked exhausted. Clearly, he didn't move at the same pace that Bessie Mae did. Then again, no one moved at the same pace Bessie Mae did. The woman could run circles around all of us.

Dallas came in just as we settled onto barstools at the island. My aunt dished up healthy servings of banana pudding. Not that I needed any more sugar. I'd been nibbling on the charcuterie tray goodies all afternoon long when no one was looking. My stomach was already stuffed. But that never seemed to stop me.

After we dove into our servings, I was pretty sure we all slipped off into some kind of sugar-induced coma. Bessie Mae's banana pudding was, after all, a southern culinary masterpiece—layers of creamy vanilla custard, delicious banana slices, and then my favorite part—those perfectly crisp vanilla wafers. Not to mention the cream on top. Whipped cream, to be precise.

We ate in reverent silence enjoying each perfect spoonful of that amazing homemade comfort food.

I was just fighting the temptation to lick my bowl when the doorbell rang.

"Another guest?" I set my bowl in the sink.

Tasha walked to the door and came back with Shawn Warren at her side.

"Just stopping in to check on y'all." His eyes gravitated to the banana pudding.

"Here you go, honey." Bessie Mae filled another bowl with the delicious dessert and set it on the island.

"You sure?" he asked.

"Well, of course. We're very neighborly around here." These words came from Tasha as she shared a genuine smile.

He took a seat and dove right in.

Nadine arrived next with Coco in her arms. Tasha apologized that we were all still there, but Nadine seemed thrilled to see us.

"You have no idea how lonely it gets over at my place. Please, stay awhile. We'll all watch the fireworks together. I heard they're going to start at nine."

Looked like we still had a couple of hours to kill. We nibbled on the leftover foods and eventually found ourselves back in the parlor, where Bessie Mae talked Bob into playing for us.

"My skills aren't what they used to be," he said. "These poor old hands need some WD-40."

"Then use one of the player piano rolls," she countered. "You can't go wrong that way."

He grudgingly took a seat at the piano and fidgeted with the player piano roll—that long strip of perforated paper, meticulously punched with tiny holes that dictated the melody to be played, then began to pump the pedals.

As he did so, the piano roll unwound and passed through the piano's mechanism, the perforations triggering the keys to move. "Let Me Call You Sweetheart" began to play, the vibrant strains of the old, familiar song filling the room.

Bob's frown eased into a gentle smile as the music poured forth. I found myself completely mesmerized by the unexpected magic of the scene transpiring in front of me. The piano keys danced up and down on their own, a delightful thing to watch, filling the room with the lovely melody.

In that moment, I saw the truth: Behind the facade of a gruff and solitary demeanor, Bob Reeves had a soft side. And it was clear he had a passion for music.

I felt the most amazing wave of nostalgia and warmth wash over me as my aunt's trembling voice chimed in with the lyrics. I'd heard her sing before, of course. She used to be in the choir at church, offering the occasional solo. But today, her voice sounded, somehow. . .younger. Or, perhaps it was the look of sheer joy on her face as the words rang out across the room. *Let me call you sweetheart, I'm in love with you!*

We all looked on in complete silence, the whole thing profoundly mesmerizing.

Well, until the end, when we broke into spontaneous applause.

"Wow! You two are the perfect duet!" Nadine said. "You've made my day."

"That was better than any Fourth of July fireworks," Tasha said.

"You should do a special at the church sometime," Dallas chimed in. "That was amazing."

"No thanks." Bob closed the piano lid. "That's enough for one night."

Only, it wasn't. I was reminded of something important. I asked Mason to come with me, and we headed out to my truck to fetch the song roller we'd discovered in the attic yesterday. When I came back in, I handed it to Bob, as if presenting him with a gift.

"What's this?" he asked.

"I'm not really sure." I took my seat on the plush leather sofa once again. "We found it yesterday in the attic at the little house, and I've been dying to know what song it is."

A couple of minutes later he had the roll firmly affixed in place against the tracker bar.

I watched as his feet went to work on the pedals once again. It didn't take long for a melody to come out. Unfortunately, it didn't sound familiar to me. But clearly it did to Bob and Bessie Mae.

My aunt let out a squeal and practically took to dancing. "Bob! It's our song!"

"Your song?" I asked.

"Yes. From *Annie Get Your Gun!*" She began to sing at the top of her lungs, "Anything you can do, I can do better."

"I can do anything better than you," he echoed.

On and on they went, in perfect harmony, their voices overlapping so naturally that it definitely wasn't feeling like a competition. In fact, this whole thing was starting to sound a lot more like the perfect duet.

CHAPTER
TWENTY-THREE

On Friday morning, I felt utterly exhausted. I concluded this must be what a marathon runner felt like on the day after the big race. My poor feet were weeping from hours of standing, and my voice—what little there was left of it after singing all those patriotic tunes—was hoarse and dry.

As much as I wanted to sleep in, I knew I could not. So I headed into town to work alongside other chamber members with the cleanup, a necessary task after such a big day.

When I arrived, it was easy to see that my fellow townspeople had stayed home today. Most of our stores and restaurants were pretty still, the parking lots mostly empty. I didn't blame folks for staying home.

Oh, but our poor chamber members! I'd never seen so many exhausted people. We had a lot of work to do, cleaning up after yesterday's events, but each committee took care of its own area, so it didn't all fall to a handful of people. At least there was that, even if we did move at a snail's pace.

In spite of our weariness, there was a lingering buzz of excitement in the air, mixed with the smell of leftover barbecue and fireworks smoke. We were all happy, it seemed, that the events of the day had come off without a flaw. The bake sale had raised a significant amount of money for the new gym at our church and the quilt show had funded one of the Methodist missionaries for a full year. That was something to be proud of.

The cupcake walk had provided funds for the Presbyterians to sponsor several children at their annual summer camp. And the car show had raised some necessary funds for the Assembly of God folks to offer a college scholarship to one of their recent graduates who was attending seminary in Waxahachie.

All in all, the day had been a rousing success. That was definitely something to celebrate.

I worked with a team of volunteers to pick up litter along the street that connected all of our churches. We also swept up a lot of confetti and streamers from the streets and sidewalks.

After that, we turned our attention to discarded fireworks at the Veterans Memorial Park. In spite of our exhaustion, everyone laughed and talked as we worked. The camaraderie made all of this work feel less like a chore and more like another event of its own, kind of like how we felt at Tasha's place on Sunday afternoon. There was something to be said for working as a team.

By late morning, the streets began to look clean again, the park pristine, and the town slowly returned to normal.

Well, mostly. I had seen Mason pass by a time or two, but we hadn't yet connected. I went looking for him around noon and finally located him in the fellowship hall of the Methodist church, taking down several of the larger PVC quilt racks.

He smiled as I drew near. "You doing okay today?"

I couldn't help the yawn that escaped but managed a quick, "Yeah. Just tired. And hot."

"Me too." He turned back to the PVC pieces, which almost tumbled down around him. "I don't think people realize how much work goes into a day like yesterday. I haven't worked this hard since I had to replace the motor in Tilly."

"Thanks for that, by the way." In spite of my sweaty self, I gave him a kiss on the cheek. "My girl is looking mighty fine because of you."

"Her owner is looking even finer."

I laughed. "Not today, she's not. I'm covered in sweat."

"Let's just call it a healthy glow." He continued to work but paused to look my way once again. "Hey, I wanted to tell you that I took a look at that projector we found in the attic."

"You did?" Wow. "When did you find time to do that?"

"I was too keyed up after all the activity yesterday. I couldn't fall asleep, so I ended up in my living room at two in the morning working on it."

"No way. I'm so sorry."

"It's okay, but I'm afraid the news isn't good."

"Oh, man." I plopped down into a folding chair and watched as he broke down the quilt rack into pieces.

He released a sigh. "Sorry, but it's a no-go. It's completely shot. I tried everything but couldn't fix it."

"So we're not able to watch the movies after all?"

"We can order a new one. They still sell them online."

"Pricey?" I asked.

"I have no idea." He pulled apart more PVC pieces and stacked them together then placed them into a long tube. "But I have a better idea. Do you trust me?"

"Sure. You know more about technological things than I do."

"I'm a mechanic, not really a technician. But I do have an idea that I think will solve the problem. I'll let you know when I'm ready. Okay?"

"Sure." I yawned. "Right now you could tell me that you were going to cancel our date and I would say it's okay. I'm so tired, nothing is making sense."

"Do you want to skip it?" he asked.

I thought about that before answering. "What if we just made it a late lunch after we're done working here? Would that be okay? I'd love to head home and take a nap."

"I hear you." He took a few steps toward the next quilt rack and made quick work of pulling it down. "I would do the same, but I'm working on a car for a friend when we wrap up here."

"Will lunch plans interfere with that?" I asked.

He shook his head. "Nope. I'll just tackle it when we're done. It's a small job." The PVC pipes in his hand separated and came clattering down to the floor. He groaned and reached down to pick them up.

"I'd better get over the Chamber office to help Dot clean up," I said. "Meet you later?"

"Mm-hmm."

We somehow made it through the cleanup by one o'clock. My date with Mason—if one could call it that—was definitely more abbreviated than usual.

Neither of us had the energy for anything fancy, especially in our current state of sweatiness, so we settled on burgers from Dairy Queen, followed by chocolate shakes.

Well, chocolate for me and strawberry for Mason. He'd always been a strawberry shake kind of guy.

I wasn't sure if it was the sugar, the heat, or the exhaustion, but I almost drifted off with the straw in my mouth. Mason's words jarred me back to attention.

"Hey, I wanted to let you know you inspired me to reach out to my aunt Lucy." He stirred his straw around in his shake cup.

"Oh?" I dabbed at my lips with a napkin and leaned back against the seat.

"Yeah. She was glad to hear from me. We had a good conversation."

"I think that's great, Mason."

"I'm sorry I let so much time go by. It felt really good to hear her voice. She sounds a lot like my mom, which was weirdly comforting."

"I'll bet."

"We committed to get together from time to time, to stay in touch."

"I think that's a good idea."

"Me too. She's one of the few family members I have left."

I paused to think that through. I had so many family members I couldn't count them on all of my fingers and toes. Well, including extended family, anyway. I couldn't imagine what it must've been like to be raised an only child.

"How are you doing with the loss of your dad?" I asked.

He shrugged and didn't say anything for a moment. "It's weird. I tuck it away most days, almost like it didn't really happen. You know?"

"Yeah. We all grieve differently. When Papaw died, I mourned very openly. But I can see how you might slip into denial as a safeguard."

"It's a way to protect the emotions, but only for a moment. And I'm still working through some of the financial stuff from his accident. That's been taking up some of my time and energy too."

"I'm sorry."

"Don't be." Mason finished his shake and then rose to put the cup into the trash.

I extended my hand to give him mine, then rose to join him. "I can't believe you still have to work today." I stifled another yawn as we made our way toward the door.

"Just a battery for a car. Nothing big. But I do have to stop by the auto parts store to pick it up."

"I'll be at home, in a deep sleep."

Only, of course, I didn't go right to sleep when I got home. Bessie Mae—God bless her—was still cleaning up after her big baking spree. I'd never seen so many dishes stacked up in our sink before. So I dove right in and helped her.

I decided to skip dinner altogether, since we'd had a late lunch. I showered and got in bed around seven o'clock and tried to watch a movie on my laptop, but I ended up dozing instead.

I found myself dreaming about cakes and cupcakes, all in shades of red, white, and blue.

The sound of my phone ringing woke me. I glanced at the time and was startled to see that it was five in the morning. Who would be calling me at this hour? A quick look at the screen revealed Tasha's name.

I fumbled with the phone to answer, nearly dropping it in the process. I managed a shaky "Hello?"

Tasha's voice sounded. "Sorry to wake you. I just didn't know who else to call."

"What's happened?" I asked. "Are you okay?"

"I just had a call from Nadine," she responded. "You're not going to believe it, RaeLyn. Someone broke in. . .again!"

CHAPTER
TWENTY-FOUR

"What?" I rubbed at my eyes and tried to make sense of what Tasha had just told me. "Are you sure?"

"Nadine woke up to a loud crashing sound behind the house. It was coming from the shed. From what she could gather, someone broke in and stole some stuff and then took off. She saw them running across the back lawn."

"Broke into the shed. . .or the house."

"Just the shed, I think. But still. . ."

I sat up in the bed and tried to force myself awake. "Could she tell who it was?"

"No, but she called Shawn right away. He went straight over and found a VW Bug a block away, parked on a cul-de-sac."

"A VW Bug?" I paused to think that through, then realized who it must belong to. "Conner Griffin?"

"Yes. He wasn't in the car, but it's definitely the one the church gave him. I just thought you would want to know."

"Of course." I kicked back the covers and scrambled out of bed. "And I guess this answers the question of who broke in the other night."

"Looks like it. He's like a phantom, moving in the night, that's for sure. But I feel so bad for Nadine. It really scared her. I can't afford for my guests to be frightened in the night. Can you even imagine the reviews on the website if this keeps up?"

I could imagine, all right. It would destroy her business before it ever got off the ground. "Maybe we could talk to Nadine, to calm her down?" I suggested.

"Yeah, maybe. But not until they find Conner and put him in jail. Otherwise she'll be a nervous wreck."

"True." Still, I knew that Mason would be devastated. He'd put so much hope in Conner.

I hated to wake him up but felt a phone call was in order. So when I ended the conversation with Tasha, I called him right away.

He answered with a groggy, "Hey, this is early, even for you."

"Yeah, sorry." I paused. Then I dove right in. "Just thought you'd want to know there was another break-in at Tasha's place. Deputy Warren found Conner's car parked a block away, empty."

"Man." He paused, and I could almost hear the wheels in his head clicking. "Not the news I hoped to wake up to."

"Right? He must be on the run. I don't know why else he would leave the car there."

"Unless it stopped running again," Mason countered. "I replaced the battery last night but told him that the alternator probably needed to be replaced, as well. He didn't have funds for that, at least not yet. I was hoping to buy him some time."

"It was his car you were working on?"

"Yeah." Mason yawned. "I found a refurbished battery really cheap and was hoping it would do the trick. He's going through a hard time, so he didn't have the money to tackle the alternator right away. Said he'd come back for that."

"And I'm guessing you didn't charge him to put the battery in."

"It's a battery, RaeLyn, not a new engine."

"Still. You're too good to him, Mason. Some people like to scam folks, and I think this guy is a scammer. And a thief. I don't know what he was stealing from the shed, but Tasha said he was making a lot of noise in there."

"Ugh."

"So much for thinking he was innocent the other day."

"Just because he showed back up again doesn't mean he's guilty of breaking in that night."

Why was Mason so defensive of this guy? It was really starting to bug me, especially now that he'd returned to the scene of the crime.

"It doesn't mean he's not, either," I countered. "But here he is, showing up in the middle of the night, breaking into the shed."

"Pretty sure that shed was unlocked. In fact, last time I checked, the handle didn't even latch properly."

"That's not the point," I argued. "He broke into it, just the same. No one shows up in the wee hours of the night—in their tiny little car, parked a block away—if their motives are good."

"Are we having our first fight?" Mason asked.

I grunted in response.

"Give me a chance to talk to him, will you? There might be some logical explanation."

"It would have to be a doozy. But you'll have to connect with Shawn Warren first. I think he's out looking for him."

"I'll head to Conner's house. Just give me a few minutes. I'll let you know what I find out."

"You're always extending acts of kindness to everyone, Mason," I said. "You're generous to all. And sympathetic. But I'm starting to wonder if you're being taken advantage of. Maybe we all are."

"I suppose that's possible. I just try to listen and make some sort of impression on folks, to gain their trust. But I'll keep my antennae up with Conner, I promise."

"Thank you." I released a slow breath.

I decided to call Tasha back, but she didn't answer. I could tell she was on another call, so I waited a few minutes—long enough to take a quick shower—then called again as I towel-dried my hair. By now, the sun was beginning to rise. I knew it wouldn't be long before my dad was up, feeding the cattle.

A short while later, I peered out the window and caught a glimpse of him heading out, bucket in hand.

About that time, my phone rang, and I saw Tasha's name on the screen.

"Sorry, I was on the phone with Shawn," she said as soon as I picked up. "He's such a great guy. I'm so glad he lives close by."

"What did he say about Conner? Did they find him?"

"No, they're still looking. They went by his place, but he wasn't there. No big surprise. I'm sure he's on the run, now that he knows people are looking for him."

"I talked to Mason. He's out looking too."

"Good."

"Do you know anything else?" I asked.

"Nothing. I'm giving Nadine a couple of hours to rest up, and then I'll head over there to take a look at the shed. I want to see if anything is missing."

"What was in there?"

"Just a few tools—the lawn mower, some rakes, stuff like that."

"Okay. I'll see you later in the day, I promise."

We ended the call, and I headed into the kitchen, where I found Bessie Mae whipping up some pancakes.

"You're up a lot earlier than usual," she said. "Was I making too much noise?"

"Not at all. I've been up a while, actually."

"Well, you did go to bed before the sun went down. That'll do it."

"Yeah."

She must've picked up on something in my expression because she immediately asked what was wrong.

I sighed as I reached to grab a coffee cup. "Where do you want me to start?"

"At the beginning, honey. Always at the beginning."

I filled my cup with hot coffee, almost spilling it in the process. "Whelp, remember there was a break-in at Tasha's place when I stayed with her last weekend?" I set the coffeepot down.

"Of course. Scared us to death, hearing about that. You were worried Bob did it, as I recall." She whisked the batter and then set the bowl down on the counter.

"I think we can assume he's innocent," I responded as I grabbed some creamer and poured it into my cup. "The police have their eye on someone else now."

"Who? Has something else happened?" Bessie Mae scooped some batter onto the hot skillet, and it began to sizzle.

"Yes, just a few hours ago, in fact." I gave the creamer a stir and took a seat at the table.

"Don't keep me in suspense, girl."

"At four in the morning, Nadine awoke to a noise coming from the shed on the back of the property. She looked out and saw a man running across the lawn."

"That would've scared me to death!"

"Me too." I stirred the coffee then took a sip. Ouch. Hot.

Dallas entered the kitchen and headed straight for the coffeepot. "I guess you got the call too?"

I nodded and sighed with dramatic effect.

"So who did it?" Bessie Mae almost lost her grip on the spatula she now held in her hand. "Who broke into the shed?"

"The same homeless guy who was camping out at her property before she took possession of the house," Dallas explained. "Police are out looking for him now."

"Oh dear." Bessie Mae paled. "That's not good."

"No, it's not." Dallas didn't look happy about any of this. I could tell he was worried.

"Good thing it was Nadine staying at Tasha's place and not that horrible ex-husband of hers," Bessie Mae said. "He would've written up a terrible review right there on the spot."

She was probably right about that.

Which almost made me wonder if he was behind it.

Just as quickly, that thought flitted out of my head. Conner was a loner. I couldn't see him communicating with Clayton Henderson.

A short while later the whole family gathered for a large breakfast of pancakes and sausage. I'd just settled in at the table when Mason rapped on the back door and then popped his head inside.

Bessie Mae pulled out another plate, slapped a couple of pancakes on it, then placed it on the table and gestured for him to sit.

He did, without question. And then she passed a cup of hot coffee his way.

Mason took a sip and then reached for the pancake syrup. "Okay, don't freak out."

I felt my anxiety rising. "Why would I freak out?"

He poured syrup over his pancakes then set the bottle back down. "I found Conner. He was actually at my shop, waiting for me to open up. He was there to ask for a tow."

"Okay. . ."

"He had no idea the police were looking for him, or that they had even been called. He said he drove out to the house to get some stuff he'd stored in the shed a few weeks back. Personal stuff, actually." Mason took a big bite of the pancake, and a look of pure contentment came over him.

"Stuff he stole?" I asked.

"Not at all. Personal family items. Things passed down from his mother."

"Like what?" Mom asked as she rose to refill her coffee cup.

"He showed me. There was an old photo album, her Bible, and a few other things that meant a lot to him. He hid them in the shed weeks ago and has been trying to figure out a way to get them back."

"Is that what he was doing there when Tasha and I were spending the night?" I asked. "Because there are better ways to ask for your stuff back than to break in and spray paint the front of a house with an ugly message."

"He insists he had nothing to do with that," Mason said. "But I did call Shawn Warren, and he's headed up to my shop now to have a talk with Conner. I've got a tow truck driver on the way to get his car."

"So now what?" My father asked. "Are they going to arrest him for trespassing?"

"I guess it depends on whether or not Tasha wants to press charges." Mason swiped at his lips with a napkin. "The ball's in her court."

"Well, she'd better," I argued. "He scared Nadine to death and he's just going to keep doing stuff like this unless they put him away."

"I guess." Mason leaned back in his chair. "I'm not saying what he did was right. I'll just be really disappointed for him if things end badly. He's been doing so well. You know?"

I didn't. . .but didn't want to argue with him. I would really have to pray that Tasha made the right decision here, for everyone.

"There's actually more to the Conner story than you know," Mason explained.

"Then spill the beans."

He reached for his coffee mug. "You remember I hired someone to fix the AC at Tasha's place a few days back?"

"Yes, of course. She was really grateful, especially since you wouldn't let her pay you."

"Well, what I didn't tell you was this: It was Conner. He's the one I hired." Mason took a drink of his coffee and set the cup down.

"What? He works on ACs?"

"He works on everything. He was a mechanic in the Air Force. The man can put together planes. And cars. And ACs. I haven't found anything yet that he can't do."

"No way." These words came from my dad. "Do you think he'd come and give our unit a look? It's not cooling like it should."

"Probably." Mason nodded then gazed tenderly into my eyes. "Sometimes people just need to be given a chance. You know?"

Yeah, I knew. But that still didn't explain why Conner Griffin had broken into the shed in the middle of the night. Until we had that question answered, I didn't care if he was the mayor of Mabank.

CHAPTER TWENTY-FIVE

We wrapped up our breakfast around eight thirty, and I fielded several texts from Tasha. When the meal was over, Mason decided to make a run up to the police station to check on Conner. Tasha asked me to meet her at her place at nine, and I agreed to do that, after asking Mom if she could watch over the shop.

"I guess that's okay." She headed to the sink to wash the breakfast dishes. "You and I have lunch at the tearoom with Dot at twelve thirty. Did you forget?"

I had forgotten, actually.

"I'll be back home by noon to ride with you," I promised.

"Your dad and Gage will take over at the shop when we leave," she said. "Don't be late."

I promised I would not. A few minutes later, I found myself once again headed back to that beautiful property on the lake, just outside of Payne Springs, the one now riddled with more problems than Tasha had probably ever imagined.

When I arrived, I found that Tasha was pulling into the driveway ahead of me. She got out of her car looking bleary-eyed. I didn't blame her. Neither did I blame her when she burst into tears a few seconds later. I gave her a minute to get the emotions out before handing her a tissue.

"Dry those eyes. We've got to be upbeat when we talk to Nadine."

"O-okay." She sniffled.

We walked to the front door and knocked, but no one answered. I could hear the hum of the vacuum cleaner inside, so I popped my head in the door and hollered out, "Hello!"

Nadine practically came out of her skin. She let out a shriek and dropped the handle of the vacuum. It hit the floor with a thud.

"Oh my stars, you scared me to death!"

"Sorry!" Tasha called out. "We knocked, but no one answered."

"I'm cleaning." Nadine turned off the vacuum. "It's how I calm myself. I clean."

Should I ask the woman to come back home with me to work on Dallas and Gage's room?

Tasha and I settled onto the sofa, and Nadine took a seat in one of the chairs. Coco leaped into her arms.

"That was some night," Nadine said. "Quite the adventure, if you don't mind my saying so. I didn't even have to pay extra for it!"

"Yes, well. . ." Tasha's words drifted off. "Speaking of money—I feel like I should pay you back some of the money you spent to stay here. It's the least I can do after what you've been through. You've been my most accommodating guest so far."

Should I mention Nadine was Tasha's *only* guest so far?

Nope. Things were bad enough already, and I knew how badly Tasha needed that money to make her mortgage payment.

Nadine looked stunned by this proposal. "Whyever would you do that?"

Tasha's gaze shifted to the floor. "Because, you didn't pay good money to come stay in a home where you wouldn't feel safe. It's not fair."

"I'll admit, it really scared me to wake up to a thief on the property," Nadine said. "But can I just be honest for a moment?"

"Sure." Tasha and I both spoke in unison.

"Staying here has been one of the best things I've done for myself in ages. I've been living in a bubble—a safe, pretty little bubble—in a fancy house with all of my needs met. It's kind of fun, in a weird sort of way, to step outside of that and see other parts of the world that I didn't know before."

"The parts where bad guys show up in the night?" I asked.

She waved her hand, as if to dismiss my concerns. "That man—whoever he was or is—didn't hurt me. He didn't even come near the house. I just heard a noise and Coco started barking. That's when I looked out the window and saw a shadow of someone skedaddling from the shed. It was all rather exciting. And can I just say, that Deputy Warren is a handsome fellow. He can come to my rescue any time he likes."

Well, then.

"You did the best thing by calling him," Tasha said.

"I'm just so glad you left me his card," Nadine said. "He's a great guy."

"Yes, he is." I did my best not to look Tasha's way.

Tasha rose and paced the living room. Then she finally stopped to speak. "Nadine, you're paid up for another four days, but I'll totally understand if you don't want to stay."

"Oh, but I must." She placed Coco on the floor. "I heard from the workers at my house, and the situation is more complicated than they thought. They've had to pull out some of the Sheetrock to get to the wiring. It's such a mess. So it will be several more days before I can go back. If you're okay with me staying, I'd sure love to. This place is starting to feel like my home away from home."

A look of relief passed over Tasha's face. "Absolutely, Nadine."

"Wonderful. Because I plan to rent it again in the fall. A couple of my college friends are coming in town for a getaway, and I think it would be fun to do it someplace other than my own house. What would you think of that?"

"I. . .I think that would be great," Tasha responded.

"We'll work out the details later, but I can't wait to have my friends over." Nadine's face lit in a comfortable smile. "They're going to love this place as much as I do. I just know it. Now follow me to the kitchen. I feel like cooking."

We moved to the kitchen and before I knew what hit me, Nadine was whipping up a quick brunch for us. Turned out, she was an amazing cook. I didn't tell her that Bessie Mae had just fed me a huge breakfast. Instead, I simply took—and ate—the hash browns, bacon, and eggs she offered us.

By the time we wrapped up, she decided to make some cupcakes. I could already feel my waistline expanding. If people didn't stop feeding me I'd need to shop for new clothes. And how could I possibly feign hunger at the tearoom if I'd eaten two breakfasts?

"This is what I do when I don't know what to do with myself," she explained. "I just love to bake."

"You and Bessie Mae would get along great in the kitchen," I said.

"Maybe." She rose and reached for a cupcake pan. "But, to be honest, I love to bake alone. It's how I process my thoughts. I whip up a cake or some cookies or even something fancy like a quiche. Then I take it up to the fire station and drop it off as a gift."

"I had no idea." I gave her an admiring look. "That's good of you."

"Now that I've met that handsome deputy I might switch to the sheriff's office." She laughed, then, just as quickly, shifted her gaze to the ground. "I'm sorry. That was just plain silly. Just because my husband filed for divorce and is seeing another woman doesn't mean I'm in the market for a new guy. Though, it did feel awfully nice to have one speak to me so kindly. I'm not used to that."

"It's sad that you're not used to that," Tasha said. "Because you deserve all the kindness in the world. And you deserve to be happy too."

I lost myself to my thoughts for a moment. Mason was such a great guy. I'd never heard him speak to anyone harshly—even during our almost-quarrel—especially not me. His faith was the driving force in his life, and it was genuine, not put-on, like Clayton's appeared to be.

Well, I assumed Clayton's was put-on, since he happened to be on the deacon board at church until his affair with Meredith was exposed. How could he treat Nadine this way and still sleep at night?

"In God's time." Nadine swiped at her eyes with the back of her hand. "Now, who wants to help me make these cupcakes?"

The woman might've said she liked to bake alone, but we sure had a great time mixing up the batter together and then spooning it into cupcake tins. Turned out, Nadine was just an ordinary gal, one who loved to go barefoot in the kitchen while baking cupcakes with her friends. Who knew?

And we were her friends now. That much was crystal clear. She might be older than us by quite a few years, but I could see that we would be great friends for the duration, if we set our minds to it. That idea was confirmed when she invited us to attend her girls' getaway in the fall. Tasha and I were both happy to accept.

At ten thirty-five, after popping the cupcakes into the oven, Nadine put a couple of sticks of butter on the island to soften up. We settled onto the barstools and sipped on glasses of sweet tea. I brought Nadine up to speed on the goings-on with Conner Griffin, after she asked for an update.

"So the man had personal items in the shed and was getting them out?" she asked.

"Yes," I said.

"He didn't take anything else?"

I shook my head. "From what I was told, the only things they found on him were personal possessions, things that had once belonged to his mother."

"So. . .heirlooms, then." Nadine seemed to lose herself to her thoughts.

I turned to face Tasha. "Have you checked the shed to make sure nothing else is missing?"

"No," she said. "Want to do that now?"

"We probably have just enough time while the cupcakes bake," Nadine said.

The three of us quickly made the trek down to the shed, where we found everything in perfect order. The tiny space was stuffed full of all sorts of items—a lawn mower, rakes, a shovel, and enough small tools to keep Tasha busy for years to come, if she so chose.

"I don't see a thing missing," Tasha said as she fussed with the door. "And Mason was right. The latch doesn't work."

"You talked to Mason?" He hadn't mentioned it.

"Yeah." She kept working on the latch. "He called right after he found Conner at his shop."

"Maybe there was nothing nefarious going on, then," Nadine suggested. "Maybe Conner was just embarrassed to ask for his things back. You know?"

"That's what Mason seems to think." I shrugged. "I told him there are better ways to go about it than showing up in the middle of the night and scaring folks to death."

"True." Nadine shook her head. "It's hard to know who to trust."

"Shawn told me that Conner does have a criminal record," Tasha explained. "A couple of previous incidents, including property damage and theft."

"Whoa." Nadine released a slow breath. "That's not good."

"All from years ago when he was battling addiction after he got back from Afghanistan," Tasha added. "I'm not saying these things directly implicate him in what happened last week, but I still think he had something to do with the break-in and the words painted on the front of the house." She turned to face Nadine. "I told you about that, right?"

"You did." Nadine fussed with her hair, tucking a loose strand behind her ear. "And it all sounds just awful. If I were a betting person I might put my money on Conner. But I just want to remind of you of something else, while you're piling up the evidence."

"What's that?" Tasha asked.

"Remember, I told you that Clayton wasn't keen on you opening your business."

"I remember."

"Well, back up several months, even before you found this piece of property. He was already mad, way back then. Whenever you would come around talking about vacation rentals, he was already seething."

"Whoa." Tasha looked stunned by this.

"Yep. He was pretty worked up. I never really understood why, exactly, but then it hit me—your parents own Fish Tales, the restaurant in town."

"Yes."

"They're successful," Nadine said. "And that restaurant has been around for years, so it's well established."

"Nine years, to be precise."

"Not a lot of businesses stay open that long. There's a history here of restaurants opening and then closing a couple of years later. But you guys—you've been successful."

"Yes." Tasha nodded.

"I'm telling you. . ." Nadine looked her directly in the eye. "Clayton strategically targeted you because of your success."

CHAPTER TWENTY-SIX

"Targeted us?" Tasha asked.

Nadine nodded. "Yep. He saw a successful family with a daughter with a competitive streak."

"Well, I wouldn't exactly say I'm competitive." Tasha did her best to shut the door of the shed, and then she turned to start the walk back to the house.

I cleared my throat.

"Okay, so I'm a *little* competitive. But this is putting a whole new spin on things, Nadine. Did you know he's actually offered to *buy* Fish Tales from my family?"

Nadine's eyes widened. "That's the last thing he needs, to be buying another business. He would sink it straight into the ground. The man can barely manage the ones he has right now. But I'm not surprised he's playing that hand. Like I said, he's got a particular problem with your family."

"That's crazy." Tasha turned to face Nadine. "Do you think he has it in him to sabotage me?"

"If you had asked me that a couple of years back, I would've said no. But the Clayton Henderson walking around Cedar Creek Lake right now isn't a man I know. . .at all."

"Gosh." Tasha's gaze shifted to the ground, and I wondered what she must be thinking. This was all pretty shocking.

Nadine remained a couple of steps behind us as we walked back toward the house. "I can't really say what Clayton is like right now. I mean, I was so gullible. I fell for so many of his lies over the years. I'm probably the last one to advise you."

"Or the best one," I countered.

"I do know this." She paused as we reached the back door. "He's such a coward. I can't imagine him turning up in the night with a can of spray paint to sabotage your place in person. But he *might* reach out to some of those so-called friends of his to do it for him."

"He has friends like that?" Tasha asked.

"Yeah. Way down deep, Clayton Henderson is a weak, petty man. He doesn't like to see anyone else succeeding if he's not. I can see how he might sabotage you just to leverage authority over you."

"Good grief." Tasha smacked herself on her forehead.

"I know. I wouldn't tell you all of this if I didn't think he was capable. Clayton likes to protect his interests and he considers this town—this whole area, really—his interest."

"The man can't possibly believe he wields that much power," I said.

"Oh, he does. And you don't want to get him riled up. He's got jealousy issues. And resentment issues." She turned to face me. "He wasn't even keen on your family's store opening, RaeLyn."

"Why?"

"Because it wasn't his idea. And there's nothing in it for him. Don't you see? He has to be the idea man and the one to pocket the profits."

Now I was the one saying, "Good grief."

"So seeing us thrive sets him off?" Tasha asked. "Is that what you're saying?"

"I don't have proof, unless you count my history with him. But that's my guess." Nadine paused. "I honestly think it goes back to his relationship with his father, or lack thereof. The man really needs counseling if we want to get to the core of his motivations. But it's obvious he wants to see other people fail while he succeeds."

Tasha looked my way and shrugged. "Oh well. He's going to have to get over that, because I plan to be very successful."

"So do I," I said as I reached for the handle of the back door.

"And I'm going to help you both by supporting you." Nadine clasped her hands together. "Now, let's get back in that kitchen before my cupcakes burn."

We walked inside and Nadine went straight to the oven. She peeked inside then closed the door.

"A couple more minutes is all."

She walked to the pantry and came out with some powdered sugar. Only then did I see all of the baking ingredients stuffed inside. The woman must've shopped for a bake-a-thon.

Still, I couldn't stop thinking about all she'd just told us about Clayton. I hadn't really imagined Clayton Henderson to be behind the break-in. It made more sense to think it was Conner all along, even if Mason disagreed with me.

Nadine put the sticks of butter into a bowl and began to beat them, the steady hum of the beaters serving as white noise to the thoughts spinning in my head.

"I still don't understand why, though," Tasha argued once Nadine paused from the mixer. "How could Clayton stand to benefit from seeing my place sabotaged?"

"That's easy," Nadine said as she added some powdered sugar to the bowl. "He can draw guests away and direct them to those new high-end cabins he's planning to build right here in Payne Springs. Less than a mile away." She began to beat the frosting once again.

"Wait." Tasha gave Nadine an incredulous look. "He's building cabins here? By my place?"

"Yes." Nadine stopped the mixer to add a little more powdered sugar and a dash of vanilla. "He bought the property six months ago, maybe longer. So he wasn't at all happy to hear that you got this place so close to his." The mixer started whirring again as she finished up the frosting.

"So that's what Meredith meant!" It all made sense to me now. "She was checking out the decor ideas for their new place—the lakefront cabins. No wonder Clayton wouldn't let her finish telling me about it."

Tasha groaned. "Why does that not surprise me?"

"The man is all about dominance. I'm telling you, he sees you as a threat." The timer on the stove dinged, and Nadine pushed the bowl of frosting aside as she reached for a hot pad. Seconds later she pulled the perfectly domed cupcakes out and set them on a wire rack to cool. Then she looked our way. "Sorry if I upset you."

"No." Tasha shook her head. "Don't be. I need to know what I'm up against, even if it's hard to hear." She paused, and then seemed to gather her wits about her. "I say we go for a drive. I have to see this property he bought."

"Sure. I'll come with," Nadine said. "Let's do it while the cupcakes are cooling. They can't be frosted yet, anyway."

That sounded good to me, though the smell of the cupcakes was teasing my taste buds. Why, I couldn't say. I'd already squeezed in a full day's food. I certainly didn't need more.

"I'll even drive," Nadine said. "I know right where it is. He took me out there a few months back to see what I thought of the area."

"What did you think?" Tasha asked.

Nadine's nose wrinkled. "It's pretty. But I think your place has a better view, honestly."

Five minutes later we were in her Lexus, cruising out of Tasha's neighborhood and toward a more rural neighborhood, just across the highway.

All around us, the lake properties were in full bloom. Wildflowers in every color. Luscious green grass. Dogwoods in vivid display. This side of the lake was every bit as pretty as Tasha's, if not more so. Of course, I wouldn't tell her that.

Only, my expression probably gave me away.

I gasped as we pulled onto the beautiful tree-lined road, and did my best not to carry on as she stopped in front of a spacious plot of land—probably five or six acres. Through the trees, I could make out the waters of the lake.

"He plans to clear all of this, of course," Nadine said. "It's really going to be beautiful."

"I can see that." Tasha's eyes narrowed to slits. "It's great. Of course it is. Only the best for Clayton Henderson."

She wasn't kidding. This was a serene, picturesque landscape, much like a postcard or a computer wallpaper. Tall pines and sturdy oaks framed the gentle slope stretching down to the water's edge.

Through the mesh of trees I could make out the lake. It was a shimmering expanse, its waters reflecting the sky. Wildflowers bloomed in abundance here. All in all, this was an idyllic setting, perfect for the cozy, budget-friendly cabins. Vacationers would be smitten, no doubt.

Nadine tapped the brakes and pulled the car off to the side of the road in front of the prettiest spot yet. She slipped the car into PARK and angled herself toward us.

"The cabins he's planning to build—unlike our big house on the Gun Barrel City side—will be more reasonably priced. For families. For retreats. That sort of thing."

Tasha groaned aloud. "So he's about to become my chief competition when it comes to drawing in middle-class families. I see how it is. Or, how it's going to be, anyway. The man might as well put a stake in my heart."

"He's also putting in a clubhouse and a pool," Nadine added as she gestured to the clearing on our right. "And a tennis court. It's going to be a larger project than our house on the lake because of all that, but he seems to think it will bring in a lot of money."

"Oh, I'm sure it will." Tasha looked as if she might be ill.

I felt a little nauseous thinking about it too. My mind slipped back to a story I'd heard a few months back about my grandfather. Once upon a time, he planned to build affordable cabins alongside the lake. But Clayton had stolen that dream from him. Now, was Clayton going to steal clientele from my best friend, as well? It was too much to bear.

"If he had this planned the whole time, how come I never heard of it?" Tasha asked.

Nadine bristled. "Oh, he didn't want anyone to know. It's supposed to be a surprise for the community. I don't even think Dot knows yet, and that's really saying something."

"No kidding," Tasha countered. "Dot knows everything."

"So if he's building here, why hasn't he started clearing the land yet?" I asked as I looked at the dense foliage. "I would think he would have done so by now."

Nadine fussed with the AC vent on the car's dash. "I think he ran into some kind of complication with the county. Something to do with mineral rights, maybe? I don't really remember."

"I've heard of that," I said. "It's weird. The surface landowner might not own the mineral rights."

"That *is* weird," Tasha said. "I guess I'd better give my contract another look to see what I bought."

"All I know is there was some question about surface rights versus mineral rights," Nadine said. "And it might affect buildings on the surface."

Here in this neck of the woods it was important to understand the nuances of mineral rights. My own family had rights on our land, and we'd been receiving checks from the gas company for years. Of course, they'd dwindled recently, but that money had been very helpful over the years.

Nadine pulled out her lipstick tube and ran the deep pink lipstick over her lips. "I feel sure he'll win that case. He usually gets whatever he wants. And he's working with this guy. . .kind of shady. He seems to think they can work around it." She paused and appeared to drift off to a quiet place. I had a feeling she was thinking about Meredith.

The whole thing made me feel sick to my stomach. So Clayton Henderson got to keep his big house in the city, the house on the lake for his ex, and now this beautiful piece of property to develop into a row of cabins that would surely rival all that Tasha was working for.

No wonder he wanted to see her shut down. He would create suspicion and draw potential guests away. He would offer competitive pricing. In short. . .he would dominate. Just like he always had.

CHAPTER TWENTY-SEVEN

I had a lot to process as I pulled away from Tasha's place a few minutes before noon. So much so, that I had a hard time staying focused on the road as I headed home.

I wasn't really upset with Mason, but I did find myself questioning his trust in Conner. I cared about my best friend. He cared about his new friend. And there wasn't much room to meet in the middle. So we really had to leave it up to Tasha to know whether or not to press charges.

I pulled into our driveway at noon straight up. Mom was already opening the door of her car as I climbed out of Tilly and walked her way.

"It's so hot out here," she said. "Figured I'd better get the AC going."

After a quick bathroom break and a change of blouse—mine being covered in sweat—we headed toward town. I tried to shift gears, to be fully engaged with my mother as she spoke.

Our preplanned lunch date had been set aside to talk about the upcoming fall festival at the church. Dot and Mom asked for my input to help draw in a younger crowd. I was happy to help, but this day was already packed so full of conversation—and food—that I wondered how I would manage it.

"I'm so glad your dad and Gage were willing to watch the shop," Mom said. "Wyatt Jackson brought in some antique tools this morning, and when I told them about it they were both practically giddy."

I could see that happening.

Mom pulled her car out onto the road and before long we were back where I'd just come from, the area near the lake by Tasha's place.

I brought my mother up to speed on all that had transpired, and she seemed a little unnerved. "I just think it's awful that someone is putting Tasha through this. But I've always worried about Clayton, especially since I heard that Nadine was staying there. I wouldn't put anything past that man when he gets worked up."

"You really think he would sabotage Tasha?"

"I don't know." My mother grew silent as she pulled the car into the parking lot at the tearoom. "I'm just saying I don't trust that man as far as I can throw him."

"Nadine said Clayton was even upset at our family for opening Trinkets and Treasures."

"What?" Mom looked genuinely stunned by this as she parked the car in a slot near the door. "Are you serious?"

"I am."

"Well, he'd better keep his distance from us. Your father and brothers won't have it if he messes with the Hadleys."

Oh boy. Didn't I know it.

"If he messes with us, I'm probably going to have a hissy fit," Mom said. "If there's one thing I can't abide, it's someone messing with my family."

"Nadine said she doesn't think he's the one who showed up in person that night at Tasha's place. She seems to think he's got people working for him who might be willing to do that sort of thing."

"Ugh."

"Whoever did this seemed to know Tasha and I were there that night."

"But, how?" Mom asked. "How would he have known that?"

"Good question." I paused to think that through. Who had we told about our overnight stay, besides family members? I would have to ask Tasha if she'd shared that info with anyone outside of our circle.

Dot pulled into the spot next to ours, and pretty soon all chatter about

Clayton was behind us. She and Mom were keen to talk about the fall festival, put on by our church's women's ministry.

So into the darling little tearoom we went, ready to shift gears from patriotic to autumn. The pretty little room was adorned with delicate floral wallpaper that put one in mind of yesteryear. The thin lace curtains also served to give the room its cozy, vintage charm.

As soon as we walked inside, we were greeted by the owners—petite twin sisters—Eva and Iva Gabriel. Folks in town jokingly called this middle-aged duo the Gabor sisters and it showed in both personality and attire.

Both were bleach blond, heavier on the bleach than the blond. And both loved their sparkly clothes, just like Tasha did. In fact, I'd often joked that they must be her long-lost aunts. Or cousins. Or something.

Only, these lovely Hispanic beauties definitely weren't related to my friend. And neither had ever married, which made them perfect to run the restaurant together. They had plenty of time to devote to the project.

Overhead the strains of elevator music played, soothing and inviting. I knew there would be glasses of peach tea on our table moments after we were seated, and homemade bread and butter to nibble on while we waited for our food.

Iva seated us at Dot's favorite table, near the back and away from the crowd, then passed off three laminated menus. "It's quieter here," she said.

I didn't care where we sat, honestly. I loved every square inch of this place. The odd mismatched sizes and shapes of the tables. The antique lace tablecloths. The overabundance of hand-painted tea cups. Mostly, I loved the color combinations—all of those sweet pastels and varying shades of white and cream.

Off in the distance, an unfamiliar blond woman waited on folks at a nearby table.

"I thought I knew everyone in town, but this gal I don't know." Dot gave her a curious look. "Is she new?"

A couple of moments later the young woman approached our table, all smiles. "My name's Summer. I'll be your server."

"Hey, are you the same Summer who works at Fish Tales?" I asked.

"Yes." Her smile broadened. "I've been there less than a week. I'm doing double-duty. Bouncing back and forth between the two restaurants."

"Nice to meet you." I extended my hand. "I'm RaeLyn Hadley. This is my mom and her best friend, Dot."

Summer's face lit in recognition. "Oh my goodness! I've heard all about the Hadleys from Tasha! She says you're the real deal."

"We're about as real as it gets." Mom glanced up from her menu. "Not sure if that's a good thing or a bad thing."

"I'm sure it's good." A smile warmed Summer's face. "Oh, wait a minute! You're the ones who own that adorable little antique store, the one in the barn? Trinkets and something-or-another?"

"Trinkets and Treasures," my mother interjected.

"That's us," I echoed.

Her face lit in recognition. "I was just there, picking up something for my mom. I think I met one of your brothers."

"Which one?" Mom laughed. "I have four sons."

"I think his name was. . ." She paused, and then said, "Gage?"

"Definitely one of my brothers," I said.

"Gage is my youngest," Mom said. "Jake—he's my oldest, married to Carrie. Logan—he's second oldest. Then the twins, Dallas and Gage."

I found it strange that Mom didn't mention Logan's girlfriend in the lineup. Maybe she was still holding out hope that he would drop her. The adorable girl standing in front of us right now must've looked like great potential to Mom, for one of her remaining boys. Sure enough, my mother quickly slipped into matchmaker mode as she sang Logan and Gage's praises.

I sometimes felt Mom was born in the wrong era. She would've made a great village yenta or Edwardian mother on the prowl for the viscountess for her son to wed.

The next couple of minutes were spent with Summer explaining how she ended up in the Mabank area. By the time she got to the point where her husband had passed away in a work-related accident, the smile had faded and her eyes were filled with tears.

"You poor thing." Dot reached out and grabbed her hand. "And here you are, having to work double-duty at two restaurants. That can't be easy."

"I don't mind." Summer released a sigh. "I need the income. I've got a little boy to take care of now, and I don't want to become too reliant on my parents. They're amazing, but I want to stand on my own two feet."

"I'm sure God will help you every step of the way," Dot said.

"Yes. He already has. It's been two years since David passed, and I'm trying to remind myself every day that God still has plans for my life."

"Plans for good, and not evil," Dot said. "Plans for a future, one filled with promise and possibility."

"Thank you." Summer rested her hand on Dot's shoulder. "I needed that reminder. Now, what can I get you ladies to drink?"

I went with the peach tea. Much to my surprise, Mom and Dot both ordered the raspberry at Summer's suggestion.

The doorbell jingled and another party of ladies entered. I recognized them as members of the Methodist Quilting Guild. Summer headed off to get them seated.

"That's just so sad," I said when she was out of hearing distance. "I can't imagine losing a husband at such a young age."

"I can," Dot said, and then leaned back in her chair.

I paused before saying anything. If Dot had ever been married, I knew nothing of it. I would have to ask Mom when we got back home. Did everyone in town have a backstory?

Thank goodness, Summer returned a few moments later with our flavored teas. I took a sip and felt myself slipping off into delirium. Peach tea often had that effect on me.

I didn't really need to see the menu—I pretty much had it memorized—but studied it anyway, until I decided on my order: a chicken salad sandwich on croissant with broccoli salad. Did I need to order lunch after the two breakfasts I'd already eaten? Nope. Would I do it anyway? You bet. Mom would never let me hear the end of it if I skipped a meal. Hopefully I could play at eating it and take the leftovers home for another day.

Mom opted for the tomato basil soup and a scoop of tuna salad. Dot wanted to try the club sandwich and fries.

After Summer took our orders, we grew silent for a moment. No doubt we were all thinking about what Summer had just shared with us about losing her husband. I found it all so sad but was glad she'd landed in Mabank. We'd treat her right. I would invite her to church, first thing.

All around us, the soft clinking of porcelain teacups and the gentle hum of conversation added a lovely backdrop to our thoughts as our conversation remained on halt. The mouthwatering aroma of sweet treats like Eva's freshly baked scones, hung heavy in the air around us. This was mixed with the pungent aroma of fragrant herbal teas. I was already feeling a little nauseous at the idea of food but did my best to hide it.

Before long Mom and Dot dove into a conversation about the fall festival, the purpose of today's little luncheon. On and on they went, sharing details, one after the other. I engaged with them as much as I could, even offering suggestions related to the various events I'd be in charge of. But my thoughts were really elsewhere today.

I couldn't wait to change the subject entirely, to tell Dot what I'd discovered about Clayton. But I needed to wait until there was a logical gap in the conversation before I could interject his name. Once I opened that Pandora's Box. . .whelp. . .it was going to be a mighty long conversation.

CHAPTER
TWENTY-EIGHT

Thank goodness, the conversation about the fall festival was abbreviated because Dot had forgotten to bring her schedule. I'd never known Dot to forget anything. She must still be exhausted after our big Fourth of July event.

This gave me an opportunity to wedge in my topic, and so I did, pausing only to take a sip of my peach tea first.

"Did you know that Clayton is talking about building a rental project along the Payne Springs side of the lake?"

"What?" Dot fanned herself with her napkin. "Another one?"

"Completely different from the house he built on the Gun Barrel City side," I explained. "This one is right by Tasha's place. All rentals. From what Nadine told us, they're going to be cute little log cabins, loaded with all of the necessities for an overnight camping experience for families. He's talking about putting in a pool, a tennis court, all kinds of things."

"That's going to go over like a ton of bricks," Dot said. "Every time I turn around he's up to something new, but his ventures always seem to peter out in the end."

"That's what Nadine said too."

Dot rolled her eyes. "He just got the permits to turn the old Italian restaurant on Market Street into a beauty salon. Did you realize Meredith is a beautician?"

Mom looked horrified by this. "She's the last person in town I'd want messing with my hair."

"I'm afraid most of the ladies in town will feel the same way. And besides, we've already got a beauty shop. Poor Lorelai will have a fit when she hears she's got competition."

I had no doubt she would. Everyone in town went to Curl Up & Dye.

Summer returned with our food at that very moment, and served it up with a smile. "Let me know if there's anything else you need," she said.

My mother took a bite of her tuna salad and then dabbed at her lips with her napkin. "Why does Clayton always feel the need to start these new businesses? I honestly don't get it."

Dot shook her head. "What I want to know is, how can he manage a beauty salon, and an entire community of rentals with all of the other businesses he's already running? What's he trying to prove, anyway?"

"That he's still the most well-to-do person in the county, in spite of his breakup from Nadine?" I picked up my sandwich but felt kind of sick looking at it.

"I guess." Mom shrugged. "I feel a little sorry for him."

"Why?" I lowered my voice and put my sandwich down. "He cheated on his wife."

"Oh, I don't mean that. I'm just saying, from the time we were younger, he always felt he had to prove himself. His father was something of a bully, and I'm afraid he didn't have much affection as a kid. His father pushed him to be the best—at everything."

"And he's still at it," Dot said. "But it all feels different, now that he's traded in Nadine for a younger model."

"I always forget you knew Clayton when you were younger," I said. "And Nadine too?"

Mom shook her head. "No, she was several years younger than us. And she came from Dallas. Her family visited the area when she was in her early twenties. Clayton was actually dating someone else at the time but ditched her for Nadine."

Oh my. Well, that certainly put a new spin on things.

"I've wondered if Clayton was behind the break-in at Tasha's inn." I managed a little bite of my sandwich then chased it down with a swig of tea.

"My goodness, I hope not." Dot looked downright astounded that I'd suggested such a thing. She swallowed down a couple of her fries and then seemed to lose herself to her thoughts.

"Here's what I don't understand. . ." Mom lowered her voice, her soup spoon dangling from her fingers. "How can the man show up in town with a new woman on his arm when he's not yet divorced from his wife? He's acting like this sort of behavior is totally normal. . .and it's not!"

"Agreed." Dot reached for her tea glass. "It's unthinkable."

Eva and Iva stopped by just then to ask us about the food. They must've sensed they'd walk up on a conversation.

"What did we miss?" Iva asked. "You ladies look like you're in the middle of a story."

"Yes, do tell," Eva chimed in. "Spill the tea."

"Spill the tea?" Mom looked confused. She glanced down at her tea glass then up at Eva.

"Tell us what's what," Eva said.

"We're just talking about Clayton Henderson." Dot lowered her voice. "I tend to think he believes the rules don't apply to him because he's bigger than they are."

"When you've got a god-complex," Eva said, "and he does—you honestly don't feel like you *have* to follow the same rules as everyone else."

"Take a look at Hollywood," Iva added. "Folks out there live as they please, breaking every rule in the book. Politicians do it too. They pass laws for other people but break them, themselves."

"Ugh." I wanted to hurl. The idea made me nauseous. Or maybe it was just all of the food. I couldn't possibly eat another bite.

"Your sandwich okay, honey?" Creases formed between Eva's finely plucked brows. "You've hardly touched it."

"Oh, yes ma'am." I picked it up and forced a smile. "Just ate a big breakfast, is all." I took a bite and set it back down.

"I'll never understand what makes some people such showboats," Iva chimed in. "Why demand so much attention?"

"I just feel like he has no conscience," I said. "How could you, and still be so blatant about your actions? And he's not giving a moment's thought to how all of this is making Nadine feel. She's humiliated, she's upset, she's. . ." I stopped suddenly, realizing I'd crossed a line in my very public proclamation about how Nadine was feeling. Suddenly I felt about as small as Clayton. When had I turned into a gossip? Ugh.

"We all feel for Nadine," Mom chimed in. "I've been thinking about inviting her to lunch one day soon."

"You should," Dot said. "I'll come too. We'll do a ladies day out."

"You'll do it right here," Iva said. "We'll give you our special room in back. It's more private."

"I'll watch the shop so you can go, Mom," I said. "I think Nadine would enjoy knowing that some of the townspeople are actually supportive of her."

The doorbell jangled, and I looked up to discover Tasha had entered the tearoom. She didn't look well. In fact, she looked downright ill, not at all how I'd left her.

"You look like you've seen a ghost," I said as she drew near.

"I called Dad's attorney."

"And?"

"He's still working on it."

Dot dabbed at her lips. "Well, since we've broached this subject, I might as well tell you that I've figured out why Belinda Keller is so desperate to gain possession of your house."

We all turned to face her.

"Why is that, Dot?" Tasha asked.

"Apparently her own home has gone into repossession."

"Oh, wow." I paused to think this through. "That's kind of sad, since she lost her husband and all."

Dot's brows arched. "Turns out she never had a husband."

At this news, Tasha pulled up a chair and sat at our table without so much as an invitation. I knew Mom and Dot wouldn't care.

"What?" This stopped me cold.

"I thought she was a starving widow?" Tasha asked.

Dot's voice lowered to a whisper. "She has a grown son from a prior relationship, but, based on my extensive research, she was never married."

"Dot!" I turned to face her. "How did you figure that out?"

"Easy, honey," she said. "A tiny little thing called the Internet. Public records are, well, public. And I hate to see a friend struggle." She patted Tasha's hand. "So I do what I can when I can."

"So Belinda's house is really being foreclosed upon." Tasha reached to grab my glass of tea, but I took it out of her hand before she could manage a swig.

"This is her third foreclosure or repossession, from what I've learned," Dot said. "She has a history of poor financial planning, one would say."

"What about other lawsuits?" I asked. "Does she have a history of filing them?"

"No idea, but I can certainly look."

"Please do. I wonder if this is something she does. . .filing lawsuits against people just to get the money."

"I suspect Belinda's resentment toward Tasha has more to do with the fact that she was excluded from her family circle," Dot said after a moment. "I'm sure she feels entitled to the property."

"Yes, but the courts say otherwise," I said.

"Of course. I'm just thinking about her emotional state, is all." Dot took a sip of her raspberry tea. "I think she sees Tasha's purchase of the home as a usurpation of what she perceives as her birthright."

"I've said that from the get-go," I said. "We just don't know what to do about it. The woman apparently had anger and resentment and she's using them against my friend. I'm not having it."

Mom flashed a concerned look my way. "Don't get yourself hurt, RaeLyn Hadley. There's no need to be overly brave. Let the police figure this out."

I would do my best not to get any deeper in it than I already was, but I didn't like the idea of anyone messing with my best friend.

The doorbell jangled again, interrupting my thoughts. This time Deputy Warren came in the front door with a couple of other officers. They were greeted by Summer. She led them to a table near ours. When he saw us, Warren headed our way, a confident smile on his face.

"Hey, I was planning to call you later today."

Okay, so his words were directed at Tasha, not the rest of us. But clearly, he had news.

"What's up?" she asked.

"Since you decided not to press charges against Conner, we released him. Mason has agreed to keep an eye on him. It really looks as if he just wanted to get his stuff. He's promised not to go back onto your property again."

"Fine." She fussed with her bag.

"Fine?" Creases formed between his brows. "Are you worried?"

"I don't know what I am right now," she said. "Clayton wants to shut me down, Bob Reeves has—had—a petition against me, Conner seems determined to scare me to death, and Belinda Keller is suing me. I'm starting to get a complex that everyone in town hates me."

CHAPTER
TWENTY-NINE

"Well, I sure don't hate you," Shawn Warren said with a glint in his eye. "So don't get too down in the dumps. Promise?"

"Yeah, I'll try not to." Tasha sighed. Loudly. This drew the attention of several patrons nearby, who looked concerned for her.

"Don't mind me," she said to the crowd as she waved her arms in mock despair. "Just having a dramatic moment. It's what I do."

When Warren walked away from the table, she turned her attention back to us. Mom, Dot, and I were all staring at her.

"What?" she asked.

"Um, I do believe that handsome officer is smitten with you, Tasha," Dot said. "And that was quite the performance you just put on, by the way. Who taught you to flirt like that?"

"Flirt?" Tasha looked more than a little confused. "I was just being myself."

Mom shot a glance my way. I knew she was thinking of Dallas. I was thinking of him too.

Tasha waved her hand at Summer to get her attention. "I wasn't flirting with anyone. Not on purpose, anyway. I just know that I need some peach tea or I'll never get through this crazy day."

A few minutes later, glass of peach tea in hand, Tasha had moved over to the counter to sit next to Warren. Summer stood across the counter from them, all laughter and smiles. She seemed to have a lovely effect on people, even my over-the-top friend.

I wrapped up my lunch with Dot and Mom, but could sense a lot of frustration in my mother as we pulled away from the restaurant a short time later.

"What are we going to do?" she asked as she eased the car out onto the road.

"About?"

"Tasha. And Dallas. I hate to see my boy brokenhearted. Do you really think she's interested in that handsome deputy?"

"Why does everyone keep calling him 'that handsome deputy'?" I asked.

Mom looked my way and said, "Duh."

"Okay, so he's movie star handsome. And yes, he has a crush on Tasha. He already told me as much. But she hasn't shared that she's interested in him. I think she's been completely oblivious to his interests."

"Until now. Dot had to go and open her mouth and share the news."

"I wouldn't worry about. Tasha's way too distracted with her new place to get attached at the moment, I'd say."

"You have to talk to her, RaeLyn." My mother tapped the brake as we approached a stop sign. "Make her see the light."

"Mom!" I stared at her, dumbfounded. "I can't make someone fall in love with someone, even if it's my brother we're talking about. I don't have those kinds of powers."

"I'm just saying, you could point out his good features," my mother said. "Before it's too late and she makes a poor decision."

Should I tell my mother that Tasha was probably more interested in the inspector than Deputy Warren? Nah. That would be a story for a later day. And besides, Tasha already told me she made poor decisions when she was hot. And tired. And hungry. I would have to catch her on a cold day. In the evening. After dinner.

Right now, I needed to get home, put these leftovers in the fridge, and let my stomach settle.

We arrived home to find Bessie Mae in the kitchen, with peaches simmering on the stove. She was deep in a conversation with Logan.

"You're not usually here at this time of day," Mom said as Logan turned to face us.

"I know." His brows quirked. "Bessie Mae and I were having a little heart-to-heart."

"About what?"

"Well, I have news." He pulled back one of the chairs at the table and gestured for Mom to sit.

She refused. "Nope. Not until you tell me what it is."

"Mom. Sit down and I'll tell you."

As if to encourage her, I took a seat and rested my elbows on the table. She eventually followed suit. Just about that time, Carrie walked in with the baby, carrying on about the heat. She must've figured out we were in the middle of something because she stopped speaking and dropped into a chair.

"What did I miss?" She pressed a pacifier into the baby's mouth and rocked her back and forth.

"Logan has news," I said.

Carrie looked his way, eyes wide. "Oh. I see."

"So what is this big mystery?" Mom asked. "Is it about your promotion?"

Logan shook his head. "No, I—"

"I hope they gave you a decent raise. You definitely deserve it."

"Thanks, but—"

"Does this promotion mean you're not going to have as much time around the ranch?" she asked. "Because we still need you to keep up with the finances, if you can. Your dad can't do it by himself. He was never very good with math."

"I'll still help. That's not really want I wanted to tell you. I want your permission to build a little house on the patch of land where the trailer sits."

"A house?" Mom looked perplexed by this. "Trailer's not big enough for you anymore?"

"Nope." A smile tipped up the edges of his lips. "Or, rather, it won't be. Soon."

Mom stopped in her tracks and then turned to face him. "What are you saying, Logan?"

"I'm going to propose to Meghan. And if she says yes, I want to give her a house on our family's property." He then dove into a lengthy description of what the house was going to look like, how the bank was going to help him fund it, and how many kids he hoped to one day have.

Mom sat in abject silence, but Bessie Mae and I were overjoyed. I rose, flung my arms around my brother's neck, and congratulated him.

"Don't congratulate me yet," he said. "I haven't even popped the question."

"Do you have a ring?" Carrie asked. "If so, you have to show us."

"I do." His gaze shifted to Bessie Mae, who—I now realized—must've been in on this. "Bessie Mae gave me the ring that Papaw slipped on grandma's finger when he proposed."

"I haven't seen that ring in ages," Carrie said. "How fun!"

Logan reached into his pocket and came out with a ring box. "I just came from having it cleaned at the jewelers in Athens. He tightened up a couple of the smaller diamonds. Said they were too loose."

This led to a lengthy conversation about how and where he planned to propose. Turned out, he hadn't thought that far ahead.

Mom disappeared into her bedroom, feigning a headache. Carrie and Logan moved their conversation to the living room, which left me alone in the kitchen with Bessie Mae. I gave her a warm look.

"I think it's so wonderful, don't you?"

"I do. Of course. Marvelous news. I just love seeing people in love."

"You okay?" I asked.

"Yes." She stirred the peaches and then put the lid back on the pan. "Making pie filling always helps me decompress."

"Why do we need to decompress?" I lifted the lid and peered into the pan to look at the sticky sweet peaches simmering below.

Bessie Mae released a breath. "I'm pretty wound up. Have a lot on my mind." She accidentally dropped the spoon into the pie filling and had to fish it out with the tongs.

Oh my. She was off her game.

"About Logan's proposal?"

"No. Nothing to do with that."

"What, then?" I asked.

"Oh, you know." She paused, and a mischievous smile tipped up the edges of her lips as she dropped the sticky spoon in the sink. "Stuff."

"Mm-hmm. I'm pretty sure I know what kind of stuff."

"Do you, now?" She gave me an inquisitive look.

I crossed my arms at my chest, ready to ask the tough questions. "Bessie Mae, can I ask you something?"

"Sure, honey."

"The more I see you and Bob together, the more I think, well. . ."

"You go right on thinking." She gave me a little wink. "I shall neither confirm nor deny. But do let your imagination run away with you, if you like. That's always fun."

"Can I just ask one question?"

"I may or may not answer it." She turned back to the peaches and gave them a stir.

"Why didn't you marry him?"

Bessie Mae froze in place. For a moment, I thought I'd hurt her. I wished I could take the question back, just like I wished I could help Dallas find true love with my best friend.

But, I couldn't.

An awkward silence grew up between us. Finally, my aunt turned down the burner on the stove and gestured for me to sit at the table. She took the chair next to mine.

"I will say this much—I always thought I would marry Bob Reeves. From the time I was fifteen, I was sure of it."

"But he went off to South Korea, and then. . ."

"I'm guessing you've heard the rumors about what happened after that." She picked up a napkin and fanned herself.

"About why he married Soo-Min?"

"Yes." She looked my way, as if waiting for a predicted response.

"I heard she was expecting before they were married. That's all I know."

"Oh, honey." Bessie Mae rested her hand on her heart, dropping the napkin in the process. "He didn't marry her for the reason people think. The baby she was carrying wasn't his."

Well, this was certainly news.

"His best friend—Billy—was killed in action. The poor man died trying to save his unit. Bob's life was spared because of Billy's heroic actions. Bob was hospitalized with serious injuries and almost didn't make it, himself."

"Oh wow." This put things in a new light.

"A few weeks later, Soo-Min broke the news that she was expecting Billy's child."

"Oh my goodness. Bessie Mae!" I clasped my hand over my mouth then pulled it away just as quickly. "Are you saying he married a complete stranger to give the child a father?"

"Out of love for his friend, and out of gratitude for the fact that Billy had saved his life. He figured that if Billy could sacrifice his own life for his unit, then raising the man's child was the least he could do in return."

My eyes flooded with tears. "This is the most amazing story I've ever heard."

"I agree." She sighed. "But when *I* heard the story all those years ago, it broke my heart into a thousand pieces." Her soft gray-blue eyes brimmed with tears. "We had dated in high school, and I felt sure he would return to marry me. I prayed for him every day after he left for Korea, knowing we would one day make a life together."

"Oh, Bessie Mae. You waited for him?"

A lone tear trickled down her cheek. "I did. And when I got the letter that he planned to marry Soo-Min, I thought my heart would never recover."

I reached over to give her a hug. "All these years, you've pined for him?"

She shook her head. "No, sweet girl. I tucked that pain so far away that I didn't even feel a thing after a while. I learned to be cordial to Soo-Min and even did my best to welcome her to the church. But she never really embraced me as a friend."

"Do you think she knew?" I asked.

Bessie Mae shrugged. "I never told her. And I don't think anyone else in town was close enough to her to share that information. I honestly just think she was missing her old life in South Korea."

"Sounds like it." My heart went out to the woman. How awful would it be, never to fit in?

"It wasn't until the other day at Tasha's place—when I saw him standing there looking so forlorn—that my heart opened up again." Bessie Mae swiped at her eyes with the back of her hand.

"This is the best—and worst—story ever!" I said. "And here, we were worried about Bob not liking us."

"He's a good man," Bessie Mae said. "Just a lonely man. He and Soo-Min had a companionship of sorts, but, from what I gathered, it never developed beyond that. So in his own way, he's been as single all of these years as I've been."

"And the little boy passed away in a tragic accident." I sighed. "Which makes me wonder why they stayed together after that?"

"Soo-Min moved here from a completely different country. She didn't really know anyone else. I think he felt a desire to protect her. There was nothing left to go back to in Korea. Her whole family had passed, from what he told me."

"So they were both stuck." I grew silent as I thought that through. This really was a tragic tale.

"I think they both did the best they could. Bob Reeves is a man of integrity. He would never go back on his word."

"Clearly. But what a story." I began to pace the room. "It makes me want to tell Tasha so she and I can reach out to him, to be a better neighbor."

"You're both doing just fine, sweetie," Bessie Mae explained. "I think the answer might be simpler than that. Bob and I have a little date coming up this weekend. I suspect, once we reconnect, you'll see a much softer side of him."

I reached to take my aunt's hand and gazed deep into her eyes. "Can I just say, my admiration for you is sky high. I'm so touched that you would handle this situation so beautifully all these years."

"Thank you, honey." Her nose wrinkled and she seemed to disappear on me for a moment. "But you know what the Duke always says, right?"

I didn't, but felt sure she was about to tell me.

"He says 'True grit is making a decision and standing by it, doing what must be done.'"

"And you did," I said. "For better or for worse."

"It was definitely worse," she said. "But I suspect better is on the way."

"If anyone deserves it, you do." I threw my arms around my aunt's neck and gave her a kiss on the cheek.

"Thank you. Now, you get on out there and give your dad a break. He's been in that shop all morning. Heaven only knows what he's placed on consignment. Last time he and Gage took over we ended up with the ugliest lamp I've ever laid eyes on."

I remembered it well. We were fortunate to have sold it a week later. We made a pretty penny, as I recalled, so maybe dad's instincts weren't as off-kilter as Bessie Mae feared.

CHAPTER THIRTY

After making a pit stop to touch up my hair, I headed out to the store to relieve my dad and brother.

I was surprised to find them engaged in a conversation with a man I'd never met before. He was kind of a shady-looking young guy with dark, greasy hair who didn't really seem interested in buying anything. Instead, he browsed the aisles of the store, gaze fixed on the people, not the stuff. He gave me a weird vibe, for sure, as he fingered all of our stuff but purchased none of it.

In the end, he did make a small purchase—a soda. And he used a debit card to pay for it. I couldn't say why, but I was happy to see him leave.

Once he was out of sight, I approached my dad. "What was that all about?"

He shrugged. "No idea. Said he was just passing through. Asked a bunch of questions about the area, like he was thinking about moving here."

"What kind of questions?"

"Asked about places to rent by the lake. Stuff like that. I think he owns a boat. He talked a lot about fishing."

"Oh, okay." We did see a lot of fishermen around here. Many stopped in the shop, hoping to purchase rods, reels, and so on. Unfortunately, we rarely kept those things in stock for long.

I took over for my dad and brother and was startled to see how big the crowd was as the afternoon wore on. At one point I wondered if they would buy us out. Thankfully, several people also came by with items to put on consignment. There was a never-ending flow of incoming and outgoing products at Trinkets and Treasures. But God always seemed to provide just enough and just in time, for the customers and for us.

When I closed up shop at five o'clock, I headed inside the house to help Mom and Bessie Mae with dinner. They had opted for a taco bar. This was one of my favorite Hadley meals. And on any other day I would have loved it. But I'd already had two and a half meals today—two breakfasts and a few nibbles of lunch. The idea of stuffing down a couple of tacos made me feel nauseous.

Still, it was unavoidable. The whole counter was lined with everything one could possibly want to build the tacos or nachos of their dreams— flour tortillas, corn tortillas, tortilla chips, crispy taco shells. Ground beef with taco seasoning. Salsa. Homemade queso. Shredded cheese. Shredded lettuce. Sliced jalapeños. Sour cream. Refried beans. Black beans. Spanish rice. And if that wasn't enough, there were always homemade sopapillas with honey and powdered sugar for dessert.

We did things right here at the Hadley place.

Which is why Mason was always invited to taco night. It sure beat going out to dinner. No restaurant could even come close.

By six thirty, the whole family was gathered around the table. Well, we didn't all fit around the table these days, but the overflow crowd sat on the barstools at the island next to the table. The conversation was pretty loud, but nobody seemed to mind.

I kept a watchful eye on my mother, who seemed to be watching Logan and Meghan. They were deep in conversation about something related to her shift at the hospital. I couldn't make heads or tails out of it, but my brother looked happier than I'd seen him in ages.

I played at eating, just like I'd done at lunch. Just enough that no one would question me. After dinner, Mason and I headed out past the gate and deep into the field to see the horses. I wanted to check in on Duchess, my favorite mare. She was moving pretty slow these days, and I wanted to make sure she was okay.

I called out for the horses and they came, one after the other—Jemima arrived first with her foal, Simon. Next came Delilah, the stalwart one. And finally, pulling up the rear, my gentle beauty, Duchess.

Her once-strong frame had softened. That happened with age. Oh, but those eyes still captivated me. She moved in our direction with deliberate grace, every step a reminder of all of the times we'd met in this very field.

Even now, her affectionate nuzzles brought me joy. And that beautiful brown coat with its soft white patches was as distinctive and charming as ever. I reached out to embrace her, while Mason turned his attention to Simon.

"I've always wanted to have horses," he said. "That's kind of hard to do, living in a room above the car shop."

"Maybe someday." I offered him a sweet smile.

Now that we were far enough away from itching ears, I decided to fill him in on everything I'd just learned from Bessie Mae about Bob Reeves and his marriage to Soo-Min. I poured out every last detail, and he listened quietly.

"Wow. I…" He turned his attention away from the horses as I wrapped up the tragic tale. "My respect for Bob Reeves just went *way* up."

"Mine too," I said. "He lived out that verse, 'Greater love has no one than this…'"

"To lay down one's life for one's friends." Mason paused. "It certainly puts Bessie Mae's story in perspective. All of these years, she never married. And now we know why."

I ran my hands down Duchess' neckline, and she rested against me. "She said she wasn't pining for him, but I believe that Pandora's Box has been reopened now. So I'm guessing we're about to see a love story play out better than any movie script."

"I guess so. Can you imagine falling in love in your eighties?"

I paused to think about that. If I said too much about the *L* word, he might think I was pushing it. I simply responded with, "I'm guessing it's the same, no matter your age."

"Maybe." He shrugged. "But when you're in your eighties, there's probably more pressure to move fast."

"Oh, I guess so."

I took his hand and we both began to walk toward the pond where the cattle were gathered.

My imagination got the best of me as I thought about Bob's story. Suddenly, I was hit with an idea. I stopped walking and looked into Mason's eyes.

"What?" he said.

"You said that Conner served in Afghanistan?"

"Yes." Mason brushed a loose hair from my forehead.

"And Bob served in post-war Korea."

"Right."

"What if the two of them were introduced to each other? Maybe they would have a lot in common?"

"I'm trying to imagine Bob Reeves befriending anyone. And I'm pretty sure he already knows Conner anyway. I think he's the one who called the police to report Conner squatting in the home."

"Oh, right." That did complicate things. But I still wasn't giving up on my idea. "So. . . what if we invited both of them out to lunch as our guests after church tomorrow?"

"After the week he's had, I'm not sure if Conner will come. You know?"

"You can make that happen, right? And I'm sure Bessie Mae can get Bob there. Want to give it a shot?"

"Sure." He paused, and I could almost see the wheels clicking in his head. "But I thought you were worried that one of these two men might be responsible for the break-in at Tasha's place?"

"All the more reason to keep a close eye on them, at least to my way of thinking." Personally, I thought my idea was brilliant. Mason didn't look quite so convinced. In fact, he looked downright distracted tonight. The guy clearly had something on his mind.

"I'm so confused right now about who broke in. I don't know what to think."

"I don't want to upset you, RaeLyn, but I'm convinced it's not Conner."

"Then who does that leave?" I asked.

"I don't know how—or if—Clayton could pull it off, but that guy really grates on my last nerve." Mason suddenly looked more tense than before. "I even wondered if he put someone else up to it."

"Who, though?" I asked. "Bob Reeves? Belinda Keller? Or maybe even. . ." The idea hit me a little too hard. "Nadine?"

"You think Clayton and Nadine are in cahoots?" Mason looked shocked by this proposition. "She can't stand him, though. And she's your friend."

"That's what she wants us to think, right?" Several crazy thoughts rolled around in my head all at once as my imagination took hold. The theory didn't make a ton of sense, but maybe Nadine was just an amazing actress. She had us fooled, if so.

After an awkward silence, I looked his way. "Are you okay?"

"Me?" He paused and then took hold of my hand and began to walk back toward the fence line. "Yeah. I just have something else on my mind altogether. Nothing to do with the break-in."

"Oh? You're acting kind of. . .weird."

He slipped his arm over my shoulder and pulled me close. "There's something I've been wanting to tell you for a while now."

"About the situation with Conner, you mean? I think I got your point. You think he's innocent. I'm not so sure."

"No, nothing about Conner."

Duchess drew near once more and tried to nudge her way between Mason and me. He looked at her and said, "You're not helping."

"About my suggestion that you run for mayor someday, because I still think you'd be a great politician?" I tried.

He laughed. "Definitely not. This has nothing to do with any of those things."

"Okay. . ." My heart skipped a beat. He had a serious look on his face that I rarely saw. Hopefully the news wouldn't be bad.

Mason rose and extended his hand. I took it and then stood next to him. He took a few steps toward the large white fence that separated the field from the yard. Once we reached the fence Mason pulled me into an embrace and gave me a kiss on the end of my nose.

"We've been together for over three months."

"Three months, three days, and four hours. . .but who's counting?"

He laughed. "Obviously we both are. But I didn't have it down to the hour."

"I don't either. I made up all of that. Just a wild guess." A giggle escaped me, and he gave me another kiss, this one on the lips.

"This is what I love about you," he said.

"Oh?" Had he really just slipped the *L* word into the conversation?

"I love your sense of humor."

"Oh, thank you. People say I'm very funny."

"I love the way you give of yourself to others."

"I don't know about that one," I countered. "I can be a little self-centered."

"You've poured yourself out on Tasha's behalf. And you're always there to help your family. I love that about you."

"Thank you." I slipped my arms around his waist. "What else?"

"I love that you're brave. Maybe a little too brave. You try to save the day for the people you love, even if it means putting yourself at risk."

"I'm working on that."

"I love that you've got a strong faith. I've been on the prowl for a gal with strong faith and a love of the Word."

"Have you now? Would this be a good time to tell you that I can list all sixty-six books of the Bible in order? And I've got the names of the disciples memorized in alphabetical order."

"Sure." He gave me another kiss. "But you've got nothing to prove when it comes to your faith."

"I feel the same about you." The man lived out his Christianity every moment of every day, after all.

"I love that you never mention that I smell like motor oil much of the time," he said.

I gave a little sniff and then said, "I love the smell of motor oil in the summertime. It's better than fresh-cut hay."

"Well, that's good, because I plan to go on smelling like this for a while. In my line of work, I have no choice." He followed this statement up with a kiss that nearly knocked me off my feet. Or maybe it was the scent of motor oil knocking me off my feet.

Then, just about the time I recovered, he leaned forward and whispered,

"But you know what I love most of all?"

I shook my head, unsure of where he was headed with this. "No. I don't. I really don't."

"You," he said with a smile as bright as sunshine. "I love *you*, RaeLyn Hadley. I always have and I always will."

And the kiss that followed convinced me that he meant it.

CHAPTER THIRTY-ONE

I wasn't sure if Conner would come back to church the following morning, but he did. He was in our Sunday school class with a donut in hand when I arrived. It felt a little strange—me considering him a suspect and all—but I greeted him and welcomed him to the group. Then I asked how his Fourth of July had gone.

Probably a dumb question, all things considered, but he shared with great enthusiasm how much he enjoyed working at the hot dog stand on the day of our big community event.

Mason arrived a short time later and joined our conversation, asking if Conner would join us for lunch at Fish Tales as his guest.

I saw the panic on the man's face. Either he was worried because he knew Fish Tales was Tasha's family restaurant, or maybe the idea of hanging out with the church crowd didn't appeal to him. But somehow—in that gentle, soothing way of his, Mason talked him into it.

Doubt filled my mind as I thought about how it would go. I suspected Conner would be a no-show. But at least the invitation had been extended. And if he did show up, we would finally have him in a position where we could ask some pointed questions...should the situation arise.

Bessie Mae worked her magic too, and by the time morning service began I got the news that Bob Reeves would be joining our family for lunch as well. I was less stunned by this news. This was going to be quite the get-together. No doubt about it.

As soon as service ended, Mason made a beeline to Conner to offer him a ride but was told he would meet us there.

"Sure you will," I whispered to no one but myself. The guy was probably going to take off in the opposite direction.

I learned from Logan that he and Meghan had plans elsewhere. I had my suspicions, as he whispered in my ear that he planned to take her to an amazing new place on the lake for a special date, but I didn't tell anyone else.

Bessie Mae offered to ride over to Fish Tales in Bob's little MG. It was so cute, watching her climb in it, that I took a picture to show her later. No doubt she would post it on social media with some sort of fitting John Wayne quip.

As I watched them pull away, I still couldn't stop thinking about all of the tiny cars in our world, of late. The VW Bug. The MG Midget. Belinda's tiny sedan. And Clayton Henderson's little silver Corvette. Had one of those cars been involved the night of the break-in? If so, how would I ever discover it?

Perhaps today wasn't the day to worry about that. Mason looked pretty excited about our lunch plans, and I didn't want to rain on his parade.

We arrived at Fish Tales to find a bigger-than-usual crowd. And Tasha's dad didn't seem happy to see Conner, who entered just behind us.

Tasha drew near and spoke in hushed tones. "He still thinks Conner had something to do with the break-in. But I asked him to give the guy a chance."

My gaze shifted to her father, who kept a watchful eye on Conner as he eased his way to the side of the group.

"Hey, I'm surprised he came at all," I said. "I was betting he wouldn't make it."

"It says something that he did. I think my dad is just scared for me."

I was scared for my friend too. If Mason had this wrong—if Conner was responsible for breaking in and painting those awful words on the front of the house—then we had a much bigger problem on our hands.

He could potentially turn on us at any moment and do something even more damaging.

"Check it out." She gestured to Dallas, who had engaged her father in conversation. "I wonder what he's up to."

I had no idea, but it was nice to see Dallas and Mr. Dempsey connecting.

Moments later, we settled in at the large table in the back of the room. We'd come in Fish Tales with a crew before but never this many. Between my family, Mason, Bob, and Conner, we were looking at more than a dozen people.

Mason made a point of seating Bob and Conner next to each other. Bob looked uncomfortable as he settled into his seat. I didn't really blame him. It hadn't been so very long ago that he'd called the cops on Conner, after all.

Summer showed up with menus, her long brown hair swaying with each step. She took our drink orders, her beautiful brown eyes sparkling with warmth and attentiveness. This gal really knew how to make the customers feel welcomed and valued, didn't she?

She recognized me at once and engaged me in conversation while taking my drink order. She did the same thing when she got to my mother and my youngest brother, who looked up from his menu.

"Hey, I know you." She flashed him a warm smile.

"Yeah." Gage glanced her way, recognition lighting his face. "You came in our store a while back, right?"

"Yes. I was picking up some canning jars for my mom."

"I remember. You also bought a toy for your son."

"I did."

They dove into a conversation, and she almost forgot to take the rest of the drink orders. Bessie Mae hollered out, "I'll have a water, easy ice."

Summer jumped back to attention with a quick, "Yes, ma'am!"

Then, somehow, Mason did what Mason always did. . .he managed to direct the conversation to the things Bob and Conner had in common.

And boy, did they have a lot in common.

Beyond their years in the military, both were wounded warriors, both had lost friends in battle, and both had struggled to acclimate after arriving home. Another thing they had in common were their stories. And boy, did they have a lot of them.

By the time our food arrived, the whole crowd was sitting in rapt awe, listening to them swap tales of their endeavors on their respective battlefields.

At one point, Tasha stopped by to refill our tea glasses. Her eyes bugged when she saw how we hung on Bob and Conner's every word. But she didn't ask any questions, which was probably for the best. I wasn't sure I had any answers. Yet.

But, just because these guys were getting along didn't mean one of them hadn't broken into the house a week ago. In fact, listening to them talk about their skills and abilities on the battlefield, I had to conclude that if anyone had the courage or the wherewithal to pull off such a shenanigan, one of these men would.

"Meet me at the counter?" Tasha whispered a moment later as she filled my tea glass.

I nodded and then excused myself and slid my chair back. A few moments later I was at the counter, wondering why she had pulled me aside. Tasha took me by the arm and practically dragged me into the kitchen.

"What in the world?" I asked. "What are we doing?"

"Remember I told you that Clayton wants to buy Fish Tales?"

"Yes."

"He's upped his offer. He sent a letter through his attorney yesterday offering my father a lot more money than before, and *way* more than the restaurant is worth."

"Is your dad going to do it?"

"I hope not." She chewed her lip. "I can't imagine my world without Fish Tales in it."

"Maybe you could still work here once he owns it? Maybe Clayton will make you manager or something. You know?"

"That's another thing." She refilled the tea pitcher and then turned my way. "He wants to change it up completely, turning it into some kind of upscale seafood restaurant. Something fancy."

"We don't need fancy in Mabank." I gestured to the very full restaurant. There was nothing snooty about any of us, and we liked it that way.

"Right? People love it because it's a down-home place to have lunch or dinner with your family. No one dresses up to come to Fish Tales." Tasha got so animated in her telling of this story that she sloshed the tea from the pitcher all over the floor.

"Except on Sundays," I said. "Bessie Mae always wears her finest on Sundays."

"You know what I mean, RaeLyn. It's casual dining, not some pretentious place where snobs hang out to eat forty-eight-dollar lobsters."

"Right."

"Just pray for my dad, that he makes the right choice," Tasha said. "I can't imagine anything worse than giving up our family business to someone like Clayton Henderson, especially after all Nadine told us about him. The idea makes my skin crawl."

It made mine crawl too. I loved this place exactly as it was—with its nautical decor, fishing nets and wooden oars on the walls, and colorful buoys, which gave the whole place kind of a cozy seaside vibe.

I'd shared more meals here than I could begin to count, every one of them with people I loved. The atmosphere was perfect for families and friends to enjoy. Knowing Clayton Henderson, he would mess all of that up, and we couldn't have that!

She reached for a mop to clean up the tea she'd spilled, and seemed to calm down a little. "Oh, and something else. I found out what Dallas was talking to my dad about earlier."

"Oh?"

"Yeah." She lowered her voice. "He told my father not to worry, because he's keeping an eye on me. And that if Conner Griffin even thinks about stepping out of line, he'll have Dallas Hadley to contend with."

"Wow. Go Dallas."

"I know, right? My dad was impressed. I'm a little impressed myself."

"Oh?"

"Yeah, I rarely see that side of him. I kind of like a gallant man." She peered around the corner of the kitchen in the general direction of my family's table. I seemed to lose her for a moment after that.

Until we left the kitchen and saw Shawn Warren entering the restaurant, a smile as bright as the Texas sunshine lighting up his face.

CHAPTER THIRTY-TWO

Deputy Warren saw us from a distance and waved. Then he walked toward us, his gaze fixed on Tasha as he took long steps in our direction.

"Hey, I was hoping I would see you guys here." The sparkle in those gorgeous blue eyes let me know his excitement was genuine. "How's it going at the house, Tasha?"

"Calmer. Are you here for lunch?"

"Yeah. I've got an hour before I have to be out on my shift. This is my favorite place to grab a bite to eat." His gaze lingered on her a bit longer than usual.

"Mine too." She laughed. "We have that in common."

"Yes." His coy smile seemed to captivate her. "We do."

Oh boy. Things were getting kind of sticky sweet in here. And, judging from the expression on Dallas's face as he watched from our table, a little heated too.

My brother took a big swig from his tea glass then held it up, as if to ask Tasha to return to the table.

"Silly boys." She giggled and headed over there to offer him a refill.

Deputy Warren took a seat at the counter, and Summer took his order. It didn't take long for her to have him laughing and talking, just as she'd done that day at the tearoom. This girl had some serious skills. Gage glanced their way, creases forming between his brows.

Oh boy. This was going to get exciting.

I walked back to the table and took my seat. By now, our war heroes had shifted gears and were talking about cars, a subject Mason loved, as well. I could tell they were excited and happy as they carried on about engines, carburetors, and so on, so I didn't mind when Tasha knelt down next to me and tapped me on the shoulder.

I looked her way. "What's up?"

"I'm picking up on some weird vibes from Shawn." She spoke in a hoarse whisper, her gaze shifting to the right and left.

"Oh?" I did my best to look surprised by her comment. Hopefully my face wouldn't give me away.

"Yeah, it's so weird. If I didn't know any better, I'd almost think he was. . ." She paused and then giggled.

"Interested in you?"

"Yeah." Her cheeks flushed pink. "Silly, I know."

"Why would you consider that silly?"

She brushed a loose strand of hair back and set the tea pitcher on the table. A little shrug followed. "I've never been that girl. You know?"

"What girl?"

"You, RaeLyn. Duh." She rolled her eyes. "The one the guys are interested in."

"Really?" Was she kidding? Tasha was the picture of perfection.

"I'm average," she said, her voice still low. "You know? That's why I dress it up with such fun and sparkly clothes. But underneath all the sparkle I'm just. . .me."

"You weren't wearing sparkle when Shawn was at your house the other day," I reminded her. "And you definitely weren't all jazzed up when the inspector stopped by."

"I guess that's true." Her nose wrinkled. "But this is feeling kind of weird. Awkward, even."

She rose and headed to a nearby table to refill drinks, but I couldn't stop thinking about what she'd said.

A short while later we wrapped up our meal. Mason was kind enough to pick up the tab for the whole group, which I found incredibly sweet. . . and a little odd. He was a working guy, not someone with a ton of money.

Still, I hate to rob him of his blessing. That's what Bessie Mae always said when someone tried to talk her out of paying for something.

After the bill was paid, Bob and Conner decided to head out to the parking lot to check out each other's cars.

"I haven't seen under the back hood of a VW Bug since the '70s," Bob said. "I've always been fascinated by German vehicles."

"Just replaced the alternator," Conner said. "And the battery."

"I had to do the same with mine a few weeks back," Bob said.

Conner gave the little Midget a closer look. "I drove an MG once when I was a teenager. Never forgot it. I had to fold up my body to fit in, but once I got in there it was a lot of fun."

We followed behind them, and before long both of them had their hoods up. It didn't take long for Tasha to join us. Then Warren came out to see where everyone was going.

While the guys were preoccupied looking at the cars' inner workings, I found myself distracted by the silver Corvette that crawled by. Clayton and Meredith. He gazed our way, eyes narrowed, then kept going.

"See? He's scoping out the joint." Tasha's words sounded from behind me. "The guy makes me so nervous."

"Me too." I bit my lip as the car came to a halt at the light. "Oh my gosh, look at his license plate!" I pointed to the DA-MAN1 plate and groaned. "He really thinks a lot of himself, doesn't he?"

"Too much, to my way of thinking."

The light turned, and Clayton's vehicle eventually disappeared from view.

Deputy Warren must've overheard our conversation because he approached with a concerned look on his face. "Everything okay over here?"

"Yeah. Just a little worried about Clayton," Tasha said. "I get a really weird vibe when he's around."

"Let me know if he bothers you." Warren gave her a penetrating look. "You've got my number."

"Yes, I do."

Was it my imagination, or did my friend bat her eyelashes?

He then explained that he needed to head out to work. Moments later Deputy Warren pulled away in his patrol car.

"I'm telling you, there's something weird about Shawn." She sighed. "Or am I just imagining it?"

"You're not imagining it. He asked me just the other day if you were seeing anyone."

She gasped and her cheeks turned pink. "He did?"

"He did. And I don't know why any of this surprises you. You're one of the most beautiful people I've ever known, inside and out."

"Puh-leeze."

"I mean it. You're a natural beauty, and that's emphasized by how you always give of yourself to others. So don't let me ever hear you say that you're not pretty. There's a beauty in you that shines through, like the star you are. And in case you think people don't notice, well—think again."

"People like Shawn Warren."

"And probably Cody too." I took her arm and eased her away from the cars where the guys were deep in conversation. "But I want to let you know, in case you haven't already figured it out, that there's someone else who's been with you for weeks now, seeing you in every conceivable type of situation. He's seen you dolled up, he's seen you dressed down. He's seen you with paint in your hair and with sweat running down your face. And he's so crazy about you that he can't walk or talk straight. That's why he's always there, whenever you call."

"Oooh." She released a sigh and shifted her gaze to my brother, who happened to glance our way at that very moment. "Dallas is pretty amazing."

"He is. And I'm not just saying that because he's my brother. He genuinely adores you and would do anything to prove it."

"He already has." She paused, and appeared to be thinking.

"Why do you think he's poured himself out at your new place over the last few weeks? It's not his love of carpentry work, I can assure you. It was all for you."

"I've noticed his attentions, of course," she said. "The thing about Dallas is, he feels so comfortable. So natural."

"Isn't that the best foundation for a relationship?" I asked.

"I guess."

"He might not always know how to say the right thing, but he's definitely the one with his whole heart invested. His whole yellow-rose-of-Texas heart, my friend."

"Yellow rose of—" She paused and clasped a hand over her mouth before pulling it away, eyes bugged. "Oh, RaeLyn! Why didn't you tell me Dallas sent those flowers?"

"We were both hoping you'd figure it out on your own."

"I'm too dense to see what's in front of me, apparently." She smacked herself on the forehead. "I'm such a goober."

"You're not. You're distracted by bright and shiny objects. And I have to admit, Deputy Warren is *definitely* a bright and shiny object. He's one handsome fella."

"He is." She sighed. "Movie star handsome. But Dallas is cute too."

"Inside and out," I said.

Something caught my eye on the far side of the parking lot. I found myself distracted by another couple that had pulled themselves away from the crowd for a one-on-one conversation. My aunt. . .and the man she clearly loved.

"One thing is for sure." I jabbed Tasha with my elbow.

"What's that?"

I gestured to Bob Reeves, who had slipped his arm around my aunt's waist. "That fellow right there?"

"Yeah? What about him?"

"I think we can say with absolute certainty that he's not the one who broke into your house that night."

"Agreed." Tasha nodded. "We can officially lay that suspicion to rest."

"And. . ." I watched Bessie Mae reach over and give Bob a tender kiss on the cheek. "I think we can also safely say that it won't be long before that fellow is my uncle."

CHAPTER
THIRTY-THREE

Just as we all got ready to leave the restaurant, a call came through from Logan with the news that he had proposed to Meghan. A rousing cheer went up from everyone in the parking lot at the news that she'd said yes.

Well, almost everyone. Mom still seemed a bit stunned by it all, but I knew she would eventually come around.

Perhaps it was the excitement of the moment, but Dallas finally worked up the courage to ask Tasha out on a date. Okay, so it was a double date with Mason and me, but she agreed.

On Tuesday evening, we drove all the way to Tyler to see an action movie at a new theater, one with comfy reclining seats and sky-high screens. Afterward, we went for a very late dinner at an amazing restaurant I'd never been to, one that Mason chose.

I ordered the most delicious fettuccine Alfredo with chicken, as well as a Caesar salad. And when Mason insisted on ordering dessert, I caved and got the Tiramisu and a cup of espresso.

"I hope I don't regret this," I said as I took my first bite. "All of this caffeine this late in the day? I'll be up all night."

"If I know you, you'll write this week's article in double-time." Mason laughed and then took a bite of his limoncello dessert. "Oh, wow. This is great."

"I'm already plotting out my article," I countered. "I plan to steal some of Landon's lesson to put in it."

"Oh?" This came from Dallas. "Which part?"

"About how God uses the community around us to show us that we're loved. And lovable. It's a good message for the church and a good message for our town. This past week at the Fourth of July event really showed me all that can be accomplished when we work together."

Instead of responding to me, Dallas reached down to pick up Tasha's purse after it slipped off the back of her chair.

"Don't want to lose this." He passed it back her way.

She took hold of it, her hand lingering on his.

Mason arched his eyebrows and then took a drink of his coffee.

Across the table from us, Dallas and Tasha dove into a lively conversation about plumbing. I shot my brother a funny look, but he ignored it and kept going. Surely Tasha wasn't genuinely interested in plumbing.

Or, maybe she was. She took bite after bite of her dessert—a double dark chocolate something-or-another—but kept up with Dallas as he shared about how to choose the perfect toilet to work with a septic system.

If this wasn't true love, I didn't know what was.

Just as the check arrived, Tasha's phone dinged. After a lengthy pause, Dallas looked her way. "You gonna take that?"

"Oh, sure." She jabbed her fork prongs into the chocolate cake. "I was just trying to be polite by resisting."

He laughed. "Well, don't be polite on my account. Might be important."

She reached into her purse and came out with the phone. After glancing at the screen, she looked up, bug-eyed.

"Oh my goodness, look at this!" She held up the phone and tipped it in our direction. "Someone wants to rent the house next week!"

"Who is it?" Dallas asked. "Anyone we know?"

She squinted to read the print on her phone then shook her head. "I don't know this name. Rick Kohlman. He wants the place for three nights, starting. . .Wednesday."

"Oh, wow," I countered. "Day after tomorrow?"

"Looks like it." She looked back down at her phone, as if double-checking.

"Will Nadine be gone by then?" Mason asked.

She nodded. "Yes. I heard her place will be ready tomorrow morning, so she'll be checking out then. That's a pretty quick turnaround, but I think I can handle it. And I sure need the money. I have to pay my—"

"Mortgage," we all said in tandem and then laughed.

"Yes, that," she countered.

"This is good news, then." Dallas rested his hand on hers. "You're getting what you need—guests."

"I am." Her cheeks flushed. "It's all very exciting. And a little over-whelming. There's so much to do."

"Like?"

"Cleaning the place after the guests sign out. Putting fresh sheets on the bed. Washing towels. Stuff like that."

"Ah. Gotcha."

"Maybe one day I can afford to hire a cleaning service, but we're not there yet."

"Trust me, there won't be anything to clean after Nadine leaves." I pushed my espresso cup aside. "The woman is her own built-in cleaning service."

"Still, I'll have to change the linens and mop the floors and. . ."Tasha went into a lengthy discussion of all that had to be done.

"We can help," Dallas said. "Just let me know what you need."

She gave him an appreciative look. "You're too good to me, Dallas."

His gaze shifted to his hands, and I waited for him to say some-thing brilliant in response.

"Has this new guy filled out an application?" Dallas asked. "Or is this just an inquiry?"

Tasha did a bit of scrolling on her phone and then shook her head. "No app yet. But I'll ask him to do that. Right now." She started scroll-ing on the phone and then paused to look at Dallas. "If you're okay with it, I mean."

He looked baffled by this. "Why wouldn't I be okay with it?"

"I'm interrupting our. . .date. . .to take care of a business matter. I don't want to be rude."

"This is real life," he said. "And if you're excited, I'm excited."

I could tell that he meant it.

A few seconds later her phone dinged.

"Is that him?" Dallas asked.

She glanced down at her phone and her face flushed pink. "Um, no. Something else."

She shot a look my way and then asked if I would accompany her to the ladies' room.

"That last text was from Shawn Warren," she said as we found ourselves alone in the restroom.

"Oh?"

"He asked if I was free on Saturday night."

"Oh boy."

"Crazy timing. What should I tell him?"

"Well, are you busy on Saturday night?" I asked.

She chewed on her lip. "I have no idea."

"You are cordially invited to dinner at our place on Saturday night," I said. "It's Bessie Mae's eighty-third birthday. Mom and I are cooking fried chicken."

"Oh, man. I love fried chicken."

"There you go."

She whipped out a lipstick container and swiped it across her lips. "This is all so awkward. You know?"

"I'm not used to seeing this side of you, Tasha."

"I know. It's so silly. You have to forgive me for being a little giddy." She tucked her lipstick container back in her purse. "I've never had multiple guys interested in me at the same time before."

"Yes, you have," I countered. "You had plenty of guys crazy about you in high school. And college too."

"Not really." She zipped her purse closed. "I mean, I had a couple of summer romances, but they weren't the guys for me. We ended up having nothing in common. And I'm afraid that will happen again if I'm not careful. So how do I choose between these great guys God is dropping in my path?"

I responded to her reflection in the mirror. "First of all, pray about it. You don't want a flash-in-the-pan relationship. You want a guy that you could see yourself marrying someday, someone who loves this area as much as you do."

"True." She chewed on her lip. "That might leave Cody out. He lives in Kaufman, and I don't think he plans to move."

"Cody? Who was talking about Cody?"

"No one. I'm just saying." She started fussing with her hair.

"Tasha, this isn't really as hard as you're making it. You just have to imagine what your life is going to look like five years from now. Or ten. Or twenty. When you see yourself then, who do you still see in the picture?"

Her lips curled up in a smile.

"Well, when you put it like that, it's easy. The steady one. The loving one. The faithful one who'll still be by my side is the one sitting next to me at dinner tonight."

"I'm not saying you have to decide today. But I think you're on the right track."

"Dallas does have a very calming presence. I like that about him."

"Calming?" I almost snorted. "You should hear him fighting with Gage at the house. They bicker like pole cats. And my room is right across from theirs, so I get the brunt of it."

"He's not like that with me. He's empathetic. Understanding."

"I've seen that side of him too, especially when he's with you. I think you bring out a whole different side of my brother we didn't know existed. It's been fun to watch."

She nodded as she stared at her reflection in the bathroom mirror. "I guess it's time to start looking at him less as my best friend's brother and more as a really great man."

"Who happens to have a major crush on my best friend," I countered. "There is that."

"You think?" She shifted her purse to her other shoulder.

"I know. And you do too. Dallas adores you."

"It feels good to be adored." She offered a shy smile. "A little weird, but good. Remember how long I had a crush on Logan? He never once looked my way."

"I remember, but here's the thing…God knows. Like, He knows who we're going to end up with. He knows how He'll get us there. And He knows our hearts well enough to guide us every step of the way. Logan ended up with Meghan. They're a great match. And you? Well, you'll end up with the perfect guy for you."

"You're very wise, RaeLyn Hadley." Tasha sighed. "I wish I had half your wisdom."

"I'm not so sure about that. But God did bless me with four brothers, so I feel like I know a little something about how guys operate." Okay, so I hadn't exactly figured out all of the nuances of my relationship with Mason, but we were working on it.

"God gave me no siblings at all." Tasha sighed. Then—just as quickly—she slipped her arm through mine. "That's not true, actually. He gave me you. You're the closest thing to a sister I'll ever have."

"Aw." I gave her a hug. "If you end up with my brother we'll be real sisters. Imagine that."

"Something to pray about," she said. "But, that's actually one of the things I'm worried about. What happens if it doesn't work out with Dallas and me? You're my best friend, RaeLyn. I don't want to risk losing our friendship over a broken romance. You know?"

"First of all, that would never happen. Even if you and Dallas don't end up a couple, you'll always be my best friend."

"You say that now."

"I'll always say that." In fact, I couldn't imagine a scenario without my best friend in it.

We walked back out to the table to discover it had already been cleared. Had we really taken that long?

The guys were standing near the exit—looking like they wanted to make a clean getaway. Turned out, they were deep in conversation about cars. Mason looked up as we approached.

"Want to take a little walk around the lake behind the restaurant?" he asked. "They've done it up nice with lights and stuff."

How could a girl turn away "done it up nice with lights and stuff?"

"Sure," I said, and then slipped my arm through his.

We took the lead with Dallas and Tasha lagging behind us. Mason hadn't been kidding. There was a pretty little man-made lake back here, completely with a fountain in the middle, all lit up and on vivid display against the starry night skies overhead.

I sighed and leaned in close. "Thanks for everything."

"I didn't do anything special."

"You did." I paused to give him a kiss on the cheek. "You're always thinking about other people, and tonight is no exception. Thanks for always being so kind to my best friend. And my brother."

He gave me an inquisitive look. "RaeLyn, I love hanging out with your family and your friends. They're my friends too. You never have to thank me for that."

"Well, I just want you to know that I see how much you genuinely care about others, and that means a lot to me."

"Thanks." He paused and looked over his shoulder at my brother and Tasha. "Can we stop for a minute?" He pointed to a wrought iron bench near the water.

"Sure."

Tasha and Dallas kept on walking, which put some distance between us as Mason and I settled onto the bench. I watched as my brother reached for her hand.

Progress.

"There's something I need to talk with you about." Mason's words startled me back to attention.

"Oh?"

"Yeah." He leaned forward with his elbows on his knees.

"You're making me nervous."

"Sorry." A definitive pause followed. "But I've got to tell you something, and it's pretty important. And the timing feels just right."

CHAPTER
THIRTY-FOUR

"I don't talk much about what happened to my dad," Mason said. "About his death, I mean."

Ah. So that's what this was about. I reached to take his hand and gave it a gentle squeeze, preparing myself for whatever he was about to say.

"I don't know how much I shared with you about the big rig that hit him, but the guy driving it works for a big transport company."

"Yeah, I think I knew that. The driver was injured, right?"

"Yeah, but he was only in the hospital a few days."

"That's good."

"I certainly didn't go looking for this, but my dad's insurance company filed suit against the transport company."

"Oh, wow."

"...and won."

"Oh." I stared at him, not quite understanding what this meant.

"A lot of money." He rose and began to pace back and forth in front of me, finally stopping to look me in the eye. "And I'm his sole beneficiary."

"Whoa."

"I'm so torn up about it. All the money in the world won't bring my dad back. But I know he would want me to use it to make something of myself. So I've been thinking and praying about what to do."

"I'm sure you have."

"Most of it will sit in the bank—or investments—for the time being. But I do want to look at buying some land at some point soon. Living above the shop isn't the best scenario long-term. You know? There's only so long a guy can go on eating tamales that smell like—"

"Motor oil."

"I was going to say solvents and gasoline, but I guess you've just proven my point. It's time to start looking elsewhere."

"Oh, Mason. . .I'm relieved for you, and not because of the motor oil." I rose and threw my arms around his neck. "Thank you for telling me."

"I've only known a few days," he said. "I wasn't sure what to do. . . or say. It just feels weird to benefit from something this tragic."

"I think it's God's way of reminding you that He sees you," I said. "He cares about you. And He's going to go on taking care of you, even after all the pain you've been through."

"Yes. He is. He has."

I offered all the encouragement I could—both with words and the tender embrace that followed. And, by the time we caught up with Tasha and Dallas, Mason was all laughter and smiles once again.

We still had a long drive back to Mabank from Tyler. Not that I minded. Nights like these were so special that they could linger as much as they liked.

Mason drove, and I sat next to him in the passenger seat. I could hear Tasha and Dallas quietly talking in the back seat. At one point I turned just enough to see that they were holding hands. Things were moving along nicely.

A moment later, Tasha spoke, her words quite animated. "I have decided I'm going to win over Bob Reeves."

"Oh?" I turned around to face her. "How are you going to do that?"

"Easy. I'm going to bake him cookies."

"But you don't bake."

"I know someone who does. Two someones. And then—" She paused. "I'm going to get involved in the neighborhood. I'm signing up for some sort of committee."

"Like what?" Dallas asked.

"Oh, you know: Neighborhood clean-up days. Barn raisings. That sort of thing."

"Barn raisings?" Mason laughed.

"Well, the modern-day equivalent, whatever that looks like. The point is, I'm going to kill Bob and my other neighbors with kindness, so they have no qualms about me. We don't have to be adversaries. We can come together, overcoming our differences, and the neighborhood will be better off for it. Just call me Tasha the bridge builder."

"My goodness." I gave her an admiring look. "Maybe you will outshine Clayton as a leader in the community."

She rested her hand on her heart. "I, Tasha Dempsey, local entrepreneur, am committed to building connections in the community and forging lasting friendships."

"Amen," Mason said.

Her voice grew louder and more animated, as if she'd stepped in front of a microphone to deliver a political speech. "My actions shall serve as a testimony to the transformative power of communication and goodwill amongst all peoples in the Cedar Creek area and beyond. In short, I shall help the community overcome their differences and will, instead, foster positive change for future generations."

"Good grief," I said.

"Watch and see," she responded.

"Maybe Tasha is the one who should run for mayor." Mason's words stirred us back to attention. "She's certainly got the speech-giving part down pat."

"Wait, what? Run for mayor?" This really seemed to get her excited. "Do tell."

I laughed. "Yeah, I told Mason he should consider running for mayor someday, but you would be good at it too."

"Nope. I'm going to be too busy running all of my businesses," she said. "You can be mayor, Mason. I'll be visiting your office a lot to tell you about my entrepreneurial ventures. You can talk the people into going along with them. You're good at that."

They lit into a conversation that had us all laughing before long. I could almost picture Mason and Tasha running the town.

Somehow Tasha shifted gears back to Bob Reeves. "Point is, I have to win him over long-term. I can't abide the idea of being disliked by my neighbors. The Bible says I should love my neighbor as myself, and well. . ." She laughed. "I do love myself."

I was pretty sure my brother didn't mean to snort out loud, but he did.

"Winning him over might be easier than we think," I said. "If he and Bessie Mae become a couple, you won't even have to worry about baking him cookies. And you know Bessie Mae. She can win over even the toughest critic."

"That's certainly true," Tasha said.

Dallas admitted that it sounded great, as well.

"I love a good challenge," Tasha interjected. "And it will be fun to get involved with my neighbors. I've never owned a home before. It's important to all get along if we're going to live together."

Should I remind her that she wasn't actually going to be living in this house, at least not much? Probably not.

She went on and on about how she planned to prove that she was a responsible and conscientious member of the Payne Springs community. And I had a feeling she would carry through and actually do all—or at least some—of the things she had listed earlier.

Dallas chimed in to say that he planned to get to know Bob a little better too.

"I kind of feel like he's a lonely old man who needs a friend," he said. "But at lunch yesterday I figured out we have a ton of things in common."

"Like what?" Tasha asked.

"He loves to fish. I love to fish."

"I love to fish too," she said.

"He's into woodworking. I'm into woodworking."

"I didn't know you were into woodworking, Dallas," Tasha said. "You're a man of many talents."

He laughed. "I'm just saying, if I stop by from time to time we'll have plenty to talk about. And it would be good to keep an eye on him. He's no spring chicken."

"He's young enough to have rediscovered the love of his life," Tasha said. "There's something to be said for that."

There was, indeed. And once Bessie Mae became a more permanent fixture in Bob's life, he might not have as much time to fish as Dallas thought.

In the moment, I found myself distracted as a car zipped by us. A familiar silver Corvette.

Only, something definitely seemed amiss.

I turned to face Mason, "Okay that was weird."

"What's that?"

I rested my hand on his arm. "Can you speed up a little?"

"Why?" Mason gave me a funny look, as if to ask if I was serious. "What's happening?"

"Clayton Henderson's sports car just passed us. The silver Corvette."

"And?"

"Belinda Keller was sitting in the passenger seat."

CHAPTER THIRTY-FIVE

"Are you sure it was Belinda Keller?" Tasha asked.

I nodded. "Yep. I'd know that profile anywhere."

"Was she driving the car?" Mason asked as he stepped on the gas.

"Nope. She was sitting in the passenger seat. There was a man driving, but I couldn't tell much about him. All I had were the road lights to go by."

"And you're convinced it was Clayton's Corvette?" Dallas asked. "That's a pretty popular model. And color. Maybe they just have a similar car."

"A woman who's going through a financial downturn has a Corvette?" That made no sense at all.

"But if she was in the passenger seat it might be the driver's vehicle," he countered. "I'm sure there's a perfectly logical explanation."

I doubted it. "I couldn't make out the license plate, but let's catch up to them and then we'll know for sure."

Mason hit the gas and off we went down highway. The dark, moonlit road stretched in front of us as we rounded the bend, headlights slicing through the night as we shifted in and out of traffic.

Suddenly, I spotted the Corvette, its sleek frame unmistakable as it approached an intersection ahead of us.

"Look!" I pointed as we drew near the vehicle. "There it is."

"How are we going to do this?" Tasha asked. "I don't want her to see us. They might be armed."

"She doesn't know me," Mason said. "So I'm safe."

"Same," Dallas added.

So Tasha and I did what any two normal country girls would do in a situation like this—we ducked. I felt my heartbeat thumping in my chest as I stayed hunkered down, out of sight. The guys were eerily silent for a moment, which only made the pounding of my heartbeat in my ears even louder.

Mason tapped the brakes, and I felt the truck slow as we pulled up next to the Corvette at the stoplight. Out of the corner of my eye I watched as he slanted his gaze toward the vehicle. Creases formed between his eyes right away.

"Well?" Tasha asked.

"Is it Clayton?" My words came out as a hoarse whisper, as if I expected the people in the other vehicle to overhear me.

"No, but sure looks like his car." Mason squinted, as if trying to get a better view.

"I can see the license plate from back here," Dallas said from his spot in the backseat. "It's definitely his plates."

"I don't recognize the guy driving," Mason said. "Younger. Dark hair. Looks kind of rough."

I peered up to make absolutely sure it was Belinda in the passenger seat. She glanced my way and I ducked back down.

Yep. Definitely Belinda. I caught a glimpse of the man behind the wheel and my stomach did a flip. He looked vaguely familiar, but I couldn't remember where I'd seen him before.

The car shot off, and we tagged along behind. Tasha and I rose from our spots.

"Okay, this is weird," Dallas said. "Why would another couple be driving Clayton's car?"

"I have no idea. Unless he sold it." It was the only explanation I could come up with on the fly.

"Is there a way to know that?" Tasha asked.

"Maybe Nadine could find out for us?" I suggested. "Can you call her to find out?"

"Great idea!" Tasha's phone lit up as she punched in Nadine's number.

"Heavens," Nadine said after Tasha filled her in. "Maybe he has sold it. I just heard from my attorney that Clayton's lakefront property deal fell through. I suspect this divorce is hitting his pocketbook pretty hard."

"He lost the lakefront deal?" Tasha almost squealed with delight. "Sorry. That was probably rude. But I'm glad it's not going through."

"Me too," Nadine said. "But now you've got me curious as to why he'd let that Corvette go. It was his baby. Give me a few minutes to call my attorney, and I'll be right back with you. If he just pocketed that much money, I'm entitled to half of it."

"Does your attorney know Clayton?" Tasha asked.

"They used to be good friends, and he always keeps his ear to the pavement. If there's something going on, he might have heard about it through some of their mutual friends."

"Okay."

We drove back to my house, our overlapping conversation more animated than before. It made no sense for Belinda to be seated in Clayton's Corvette unless he really had sold it to her. But if that was the case, she was definitely lying about her financial problems. On the other hand, Dot said the foreclosure was real. Right? What was this woman up to?

"I can't imagine Clayton letting go of that car," Tasha said.

"I can," Mason countered. "He sold his Lexus a couple of months ago. And the last time he brought in one of his older model cars he talked about possibly selling off a few of them because they're so expensive to maintain. I got the feeling he was ready to put his car days behind him. I think he's bored with it."

"Why, though?" Tasha asked. "Is he really going through financial woes?"

"No idea," Mason said.

None of this made much sense. The woman who had lost her home to foreclosure was riding around in a Corvette. The man who owned the town and claimed to be the most successful among us was, in reality, selling off his assets. What was the connection here?

"Why would he try to put off the appearance that everything is great?" I asked.

"I think the prospect of losing his wealth or facing public scrutiny would be too much on top of what he's already going through with the divorce," Dallas said. "So all of the big talk about his new businesses might just be that. . .big talk."

"Still, I can't get past why he would have sold it to Belinda, of all people. That's too much of a coincidence."

"Maybe he sold it to the man behind the wheel," Mason suggested. "Not to Belinda at all."

"And it's just a coincidence that the woman who showed up at my door demanding I give her my house was in the passenger seat?" Tasha groaned. "Nope. Not buying it."

I had no idea, but everything about this felt wrong. And confusing.

Tasha paused. "Then again, how can Belinda afford to sue me? She hired one of the most expensive firms in town."

"Which one?" Dallas asked.

"Harding, Benson, and Collingsworth." Tasha spit out the names as easily as her own. "I know they're pricey because my dad mentioned it when he got the paperwork from Clayton the other day."

"Wait, what paperwork?" Dallas asked.

"Clayton is trying to talk my parents into selling him our restaurant," she said. "And the offer came with a cover letter from Clayton's attorney at Harding, Benson, and Collingsworth. My dad thought it was presumptuous to involve an attorney in a real estate offer and went off on a tangent about how pricey they are. That's the only reason I know."

"Very weird," Dallas said.

Tasha sighed. "But my point is, Belinda's using the same law firm."

"I'm sure lots of people use the same attorney," Mason said. "Nothing really weird about that."

"If they live in Mabank," Tasha said. "But Belinda doesn't live in Mabank. She lives in Tyler. It would make more sense that she was working with an attorney closer to home."

"Right. It is kind of weird that she would use someone in this area," Dallas said.

"Someone who's known as being top dollar," Tasha added.

"Yes. Very weird. Unless. . ." The idea hit me hard and fast. "Unless someone has been guiding her every step of the way—introducing her to an attorney, helping her behind the scenes, hoping to get control of the house in a way that wouldn't make him look suspicious."

"What are you talking about, RaeLyn?" Tasha asked.

"I'm talking about Clayton Henderson. What if he and Belinda Keller are working in cahoots? That would explain why Belinda is riding down the road in Clayton's car. Maybe it was part of the deal. You know?"

"You really think so?" Tasha asked.

In that moment, it certainly felt like a very real possibility.

"I wouldn't be so sure," Mason said. "If you're basing all of this on a stranger driving Clayton's car, I'm still going to go with the idea that he sold it to them. Like I said, he told me he's getting tired of the upkeep on all of those old cars. Selling them has been on his to-do list for a while now."

That made sense, but my radar was still up. Way up.

I didn't have any idea what these folks were up to, but I suspected it wasn't good.

Tasha phone rang and she said, "Nadine!" then answered. Nadine agreed to be put on speaker phone.

"My attorney hasn't heard anything about Clayton selling that Corvette," she said. "And I'm certainly not going to call Clayton to ask. I know the affair with Meredith has put a financial strain on him. So has the divorce, of course. So I guess anything's possible."

"This story just gets stranger and stranger," I said.

"Maybe I could call that handsome deputy and ask him to check to see if the Corvette was reported stolen or something." Nadine's voice brightened. "Maybe he would know."

Now there was an interesting angle.

We ended the call and began to talk about the possibility that the vehicle could, very well, be stolen.

Up ahead the Corvette reappeared, slowing down at a four-way stop in Athens. The gorgeous vehicle gleamed under the moonlight, moving with ease past other vehicles. As we drew near once again, the headlights of Mason's truck reflected off the polished chrome accents on the car.

"Looks like we're all headed the same direction," Mason said. "Makes me wonder."

"Me too."

This time I decided not to duck. Instead, I gave the man behind the wheel a closer look. He turned to glance my way and recognition flashed on his face as our eyes met.

My heart leaped to my throat, and I quickly turned Mason's way. "I just remembered why that guy looks so familiar."

"Why is that?" he asked.

"He came in our shop the other day. He was all by himself, kind of hanging around. I got a weird vibe from him."

"Did he buy anything?" Dallas asked.

"No." I paused, as a memory hit. "Wait a minute. Yes, he did. He bought a soda. And he used a debit card to pay for it. Oh, my goodness! We might've just hit the jackpot, y'all."

"Are you thinking what I think you're thinking?" Mason asked.

"I am." I rested my hand on his arm as the light in front of us turned green. "How fast can you get me back to Trinkets and Treasures?"

Turned out, he managed that task in record time. We were in the parking lot of the store ten minutes later, the tires of Mason's truck grinding to a halt against the gravel below. We came pouring out like supersleuths on a mission and rushed to the shop's front door.

It didn't take long for Riley to come running toward us. She barked repeatedly, as if to ask, "What am I missing? What's going on here?" I petted her on the head to let her know we were okay. But my adrenaline was definitely through the roof.

I used the key to open the lock, and then we all walked inside. I flipped on the light and tried to collect my thoughts.

"I have the receipts in here." I walked behind the counter and reached for the lock box on the shelf under the register. Seconds later, I had it open.

"What day was it again?" Tasha asked.

"I think it was Friday. No, Saturday. The day I ate all day."

I fumbled through the bag of receipts but couldn't find the one in question. I ended up dumping them out on the counter, and we all dove in.

"Bingo!" Dallas came up with a receipt, which he turned our way.

"One item. Soda. Saturday."

"Is there a name on it?" I snatched the receipt from his hand and squinted to see the faded print. It took a minute, but I finally made it out. Rick Kohlman.

Rick Kohlman.

The same name on the new application for Tasha's house.

I showed it to her and she went into an immediate panic.

Our sleuthing skills went right out the window as the reality set in. Before long, we were all talking over one another.

"Who is this guy?" Dallas asked. "And why is he driving Clayton Henderson's Corvette?"

"More important, why does he want to stay in my house?" Tasha added.

"Only one way to know for sure who he is." I reached for my phone and looked him up on social media. It didn't take long to discover a Rick Kohlman in Tyler, Texas.

And it only took a minute to scroll through his friends list and discover a picture of his mother. . .Belinda Keller.

CHAPTER THIRTY-SIX

We called Warren right away. Turned out, he had just ended his call with Nadine, so he started by telling us about their discussion.

"I checked the system and don't see the car listed as missing," he said. "But I can drive by Clayton's place and talk to him in person. That's probably the best way to get to the bottom of this, honestly."

"It might be better not to, just yet," I said. "We have some other questions we're trying to get answers to first."

"Like what?" Warren asked.

"Like, whether or not he's working with these people," Mason countered. "And if you confront him right away, he might actually get away with it. I say we wait and catch him in the act with some of these folks."

Warren sighed. "Yeah, I think Nadine suspects that as well. If that's the case, this whole thing's about to blow sky-high. I can't imagine how the town will react if he's behind the break-in at Tasha's place."

After telling him there was more to consider, I then filled him in on what we'd just learned about Belinda and her son.

"Do you have a name for the guy?" Warren asked.

"Yes. Rick Kohlman. He inquired about renting Tasha's place this week. Same guy that was just driving Clayton's car up Highway 31 with

Belinda in the passenger seat."

"Definitely sounds fishy. Either they stole Clayton's car or he really is in on it, like you said. Hang on a second and let me check something." Warren disappeared on us and came back a short while later, the concern in his voice amped up. "Listen, stay away from that guy. Let us take it from here."

"Why?" Tasha asked. "What's wrong with him?"

"Rick Kohlman is actually Jonathan Richard Kohlman, and he's been involved in a handful of real estate scandals in Kaufman."

"Real estate scandals?" The pitch of Tasha's voice rose. "What do you mean?"

"He set himself up as a broker and rented out empty houses that he didn't own. Pocketed the money and moved on to the next house."

"That's awful!" Tasha said. "Was that the plan with my place?"

"I suspect it was more personal with your house, since it was his mother's family home," Deputy Warren said. "But regardless, this isn't a good guy. So don't go getting brave or anything. Promise me?"

"I don't have a brave bone in my body," Tasha responded. "So you have no worries there."

I wasn't so quick to answer.

"Definitely don't let him anywhere near your home," Warren said. "And if I were you—lawsuit or no lawsuit—I would file a restraining order against the mother."

"So how do I prove that they're faking the will? I mean, the woman is suing me," Tasha said.

"That's a question for your attorney," Warren countered. "I can't advise you on that one."

"Right."

After they ended the call, it took a while for us to calm down. My parents must've seen the lights on because they showed up with Bessie Mae sometime around ten fifteen, just as we started trying to figure out a plan of action.

Mom convinced me I should come inside and go to bed.

"Nothing good happens after midnight," she said.

"It's ten fifteen," I countered.

"You get my point. Sleep on it and decide what, if anything, to do tomorrow. And for pity's sake, RaeLyn, leave it in the hands of the police."

"Says the woman who went with me in person to rescue Tilly from her thief a few short months ago."

"Well, that was different," she argued. "It didn't seem as dangerous because we knew the person who had stolen it."

Like *that* made any sense.

I said good night to Tasha and gave Mason a kiss.

"Listen to your mom," Mason said as he held me tight for a moment. "Don't do anything dangerous."

"Who, *moi*?" I rolled my eyes. "I seriously doubt I'll be the one to rush in and save the day. But let's pray the police are able to solve this. I want my friend to be able to enjoy her new place without all of this drama. You know?"

After we parted ways I went with my family into the house. I took a quick shower and then decided to try to write my article for the week. I was more than a little distracted, which didn't help.

I borrowed a verse from Landon's lesson a couple of Sundays back, the one about God placing the lonely in families. Then I dove in, sharing my thoughts on what it felt like to live in such a close-knit community like we had here in the Mabank/Gun Barrel City area. Having experienced this crazy evening with my friends, I felt the camaraderie more than usual.

After pressing send on the article, I fell into a fitful sleep. I dreamed we were chasing Belinda and her son down the highway, all the way to Tasha's house. Once we arrived, Conner Griffin emerged from the shed, pushing a lawn mower. Bob Reeves came running from his house next door, shouting that he was going to call the police if we didn't all keep it down. Nadine decided to bake cupcakes for all of them. From there, everyone ended up in the lake on an airboat.

When I awoke early on Wednesday morning, I had a splitting headache. I took a hot shower and some headache meds and then dressed for the day. When I got out to the kitchen, Mom gave me a look that said, "Are you okay?"

I just grunted in response and reached for the coffeepot. Before I could take a sip, my phone rang. I answered the call from Tasha right away, hoping there wouldn't be any more trouble.

"Tasha? Everything okay?"

"Yeah. I'm at the house with Nadine. She's checking out today, so I came over to clean."

"Why the rush, if you're turning down that guy's app?"

"Something amazing happened. I have a big family coming in tomorrow afternoon at four, all the way from Houston. Ten people. They're coming up for the big fishing competition."

"Oh, that's great."

"Yes, well. . .can you meet us over here? Nadine seems a little down in the dumps now that she has to go home. I was hoping you could bring some donuts so we could hang out and visit while I clean."

"Sure. Any kind in particular?"

She gave me some ideas, and I grabbed my laptop and headed out a few minutes later, swinging by the donut shop before heading to her house.

When I got there, I found Tasha and Nadine in the kitchen, deep in conversation about Clayton. I set the donuts and my laptop down on the island and headed over to the coffeepot, pausing only to grab a mug along the way.

"I still can't figure out if he's in on this," Nadine said. "I mean, I thought I knew the guy. I was married to him for years. But then he turned out to be someone I didn't know at all."

"Someone capable of committing a crime?" I filled my mug with coffee and added a healthy dose of creamer.

Nadine shrugged and her eyes filled with tears. "This is going to sound crazy, but I still can't picture him going that far."

"I say we do a little more digging." I opened my laptop and asked Tasha for the Wi-Fi information.

"It's right here, on the refrigerator." She handed me the card with the passwords, and a couple of moments later I was online.

I went straight to my Facebook account to see if I could find Rick Kohlman on my Facebook account using this device. It took a little digging, but there he was—Rick Kohlman from Tyler, Texas.

"I say we look through his recent posts and pictures. I have a feeling everything we've been seeing on Belinda's page is staged. But she has no way of knowing that we have her son's info, so his posts are probably real."

"That makes sense." Tasha reached for a donut then leaned in to look at the pictures as they came up. "This makes me wonder if she even lost her house to foreclosure at all. You know?"

"She did. Dot checked into it and she's lost multiple properties. But that makes me think she's been scamming people for a while now. And I think we're about to find out who her accomplice is."

I looked through the pictures on Rick's account, and one stood out. "Wow. Check this out." I angled the computer so Tasha and Nadine could see. "Looks like he just posted less than an hour ago from a pretty high-class place."

"Where is that?" Tasha asked. She took a bite of the donut, and chocolate squirted out on her face. She dabbed at it with her fingers.

I squinted and tried to figure it out. "I don't know, but it looks super fancy."

"I feel like I know that place." Nadine reached over and enlarged the screen. "Oh, I do! That's the Gaylord in Grapevine, on the other side of Dallas. Clayton and I were there at a big banquet last winter. The lobby is out of this world." She pointed at the picture. "See? You can make out all of the Texas-themed replicas, like Spindletop and the Alamo. Parts of it even look like the San Antonio Riverwalk."

"Oh, you're right." I gave it another look. "I should have recognized that lobby. We stayed there once at a church convention."

Still, I couldn't figure out what Rick was doing there.

"Wait a minute now. . ." Tasha leaned in close and stared at the picture. "Is this who I think it is?" She pointed at a shadowy image seated off in the distance. "Is that Mommy Dearest?"

"No way. Belinda always looks really frumpy. And poor. This woman looks. . ." I squinted to give the photo a closer look. "Anything but poor."

In fact, she had on designer clothes and a lot of makeup and appeared to be sipping an expensive cocktail.

Tasha rose and paced the room. "So let me get this straight. Belinda shows up at my door with a big sob story about needing a place to stay. She's driving a beater car, wearing old clothes. Then, a few days later, she's cruising down the road in Clayton's Corvette. Then, the day after that, we see pictures of her all dolled up at a fancy hotel."

"Sipping drinks with a man we now know to be her son," Nadine added.

I couldn't make sense of any of this. "I think there's more to the story."

"This makes no sense," Tasha said. "I was actually starting to feel sorry for her."

"Me too."

Only, seeing the photos of them now, laughing, talking, and sipping expensive drinks? Whelp, my compassion just sailed right out the window.

I went through several more photos, all at the same location, and all dated today, July 9th. I landed on one that startled me. I enlarged it, not quite believing my eyes as something shocking popped out at me.

"Oh. My. Stars."

"What, RaeLyn?" Tasha raised her arms, clearly worked up.

"Check out the woman sitting across from them, the one with the low-cut dress."

I turned the laptop in their direction, and Tasha pressed in for a better view, blocking the rest of us.

"Who is it?" Nadine asked. "Who's the woman in the picture?"

We both turned to look at her at the same time and said the same thing: "Meredith Reed."

Nadine's gaze narrowed to slits and she rose and grabbed her keys.

"What are you doing?" I asked, my heart skipping to my throat.

"Buckle up, kids," she responded, a glint of excitement in her eyes. "We're going to Grapevine."

CHAPTER THIRTY-SEVEN

"Are you suggesting we drive to Grapevine, Texas?" I asked. "Because I'm not sure that's the best—"

Nadine nodded and grabbed her purse. "You betcha. Let's go."

"It's an hour and a half drive," I argued. "Maybe two. They'll be gone by the time we get there."

"Nope. In that photo he just posted, they're sitting outside the restaurant having drinks. That tells me they haven't even started their meal yet. I say we hit the road, and we'll get there about the same time they finish."

"But Warren asked us to stay out of it," I argued. "And Mason will kill me if I throw myself in the middle of a real-life crime scene. If we survive it, I mean."

"We don't have to do anything but make sure it's them," she said. "At that point we can call the police in Grapevine."

"And tell them what?" Tasha asked. "They won't even know what we're talking about."

"We'll ask them to call Deputy Warren. He can fill them in. But I think it's important to nab them while they're all together. That way we have proof that they're working as a team. If the trail leads nowhere, fine.

But if it leads somewhere. . ."

I wasn't sure what to think, honestly. Even if Meredith and Belinda were friends, so what? What did that prove?

Moments later, we climbed into Nadine's car, and she punched the address for the Gaylord Hotel into her GPS. We took off, heading west on 175.

We were just west of the high school when Tasha decided to call my brother's friend Anthony.

"Why?" I asked.

"If he knows Belinda, he surely knows Rick. Right? Maybe he's got some information that might be helpful."

"Right," I agreed. "And maybe he can shed some light on why they're at the Gaylord."

Tasha punched in Anthony's number and moments later had him on speaker phone. He listened quietly while she brought him up to speed on all that had transpired.

"I don't know why my stepsister and nephew would be working with Meredith Reed," he said. "But I can definitely see them living the high life. That's what they do. One minute they're telling everyone they're flat broke, the next they're jetting off to someplace expensive on someone else's dime."

"Whose dime, though?" Tasha asked.

"Clayton Henderson," he said. "That's my guess. But as to whether he realizes it or not, I can't say."

"What's the motive here?" Nadine asked.

"Money, of course," he said. "Always money. My sister never had a real relationship with anyone in our family. She bolted years ago. I think she had a lot of unforgiveness issues with my mom and stepdad, her real dad."

"I see." Tasha released an exaggerated sigh.

"She was jealous of me. I had a better relationship with her dad than she did. But then again, I never came begging like she did. I always paid my own way."

"I hate to get personal," Tasha said. "But when you sold me the house, the proceeds all went to you. Right?"

"That's the crazy thing," he said. "I felt bad for her, so I sent her a portion of the money. Ten thousand dollars."

"Which would've been enough to save her house, surely," Tasha said.

"And have a few drinks at the Gaylord," I chimed in. "So maybe she's just there in a borrowed car having drinks with her friend Meredith. This could be that simple."

"Who knows." Anthony paused. "She definitely cashed the check, so she didn't walk away from this thing empty-handed, which is why it made no sense that she was still fighting so hard to claim she had a different will." He paused. "You know her claims about the other will were bogus, right?"

"I was served papers," Tasha said. "A guy showed up and. . ." She gasped. "Oh!"

"What?" we all asked in unison.

"I just realized where I saw that guy driving the Corvette before. He was the one who showed up at my house with those papers."

"I can assure you, they were fake," Anthony said. "There's no lawsuit."

"But the papers were on stationery from a prominent law firm," Tasha explained. "They're local and everything."

"Anyone could copy that stationery," he countered.

"Why is she so intent on taking my house away from me?" Tasha asked. "If she made money off of it, she should be happy."

"Pretty sure I know," Nadine chimed in. "And I'm going to call Clayton right now to ask him myself. I think he pulled her into his scheme just to hurt you, Tasha. This all goes back to him. I know it."

Tasha ended the call with Anthony just as we saw a sign for Kaufman up in the distance.

Nadine punched in Clayton's number, and soon he was on Bluetooth for all of us to hear.

"Nadine?" His voice sounded strange. "That you?"

"What are you up to, Clayton?" Nadine asked. "Why would you put poor Tasha through all of this?"

"All of what?"

"Pitting that Belinda Keller woman against her. Sabotaging her new house. Why did you do it, Clayton? Wasn't it bad enough to hurt me?

You have to hurt my friends too?"

"I have no idea what you're talking about. And I'm dealing with problems of my own that have nothing to do with Tasha Dempsey, trust me. I'm having a day over here." He began to rant, but I couldn't make out much of it because Tasha's phone started ringing.

Tasha answered the call, which turned out to be from Warren. She put him on speaker too.

Nadine was still on her very heated call with Clayton. Before long, there were multiple voices overlapping in the vehicle, all of them loud. I did my best to separate the stories, one from the other. Someone had to play referee in this game. Looked like I was it.

Deputy Warren's voice sounded from Tasha's speaker phone. "Hey, I just thought you'd want to know, Clayton Henderson just reported his vehicle stolen."

"The Corvette?" Tasha called out to be heard.

"Yes. What's with all the noise on your end?" Warren asked. "You okay?"

"Yep," she hollered as Nadine and Clayton continued to argue. "We're fine."

"He loaned it to Meredith yesterday morning, and she took off with it and never came back. He said he was giving her the benefit of the doubt, but he's pretty sure she is gone for good. We tried to track it, but she removed the tracking device."

Clayton must've heard Deputy Warren's spiel because he said, "That's right. She removed the tracking device."

"We know where the car is," Tasha said, looking back and forth between both phones. "We're headed there now."

"Oh no you're not," Warren countered. "Please pull off the road and leave this to us."

My phone rang at that very moment, and I looked down to see Mason's name on the screen.

I answered and pressed the phone to one ear, pushing my index finger in the other. "Hello?"

The voices in the car had reached a decibel unkind to human ears by now, but I did my best to speak above them as I said, "Hello?"

"What's going on over there?" Mason asked. "Sounds like you're in a barroom brawl."

"I kind of am."

"RaeLyn. . .where are you?"

"Oh. You know."

"RaeLyn."

"In Nadine's car," I hollered to be heard above the din of voices. "We found out that—"

"Clayton's car was stolen. I just heard it from Dot."

"How did she know?" I asked.

"How does she know anything? She's Dot."

"We just got that news too. Crazy, right? The victor has become the victim."

"Huh? Victor? Victim?"

"Meredith was playing Clayton," I said. "Isn't that crazy?"

To which Clayton responded, "Yes, she was! And I'm going to find her and make her pay!"

Another loud conversation ensued from Clayton's end.

"You're with Clayton Henderson?" Mason asked.

"Not exactly. But. . .sort of," I hollered back.

Off in the distance I heard Tasha telling Warren that he would find the car at the Gaylord in Grapevine. Clayton must've heard that part because he dove into the conversation, thinking it was meant for him. Before long, we had total chaos on our hands, with Clayton saying he was headed to Grapevine too.

"Where. Are. You. RaeLyn?" Mason asked.

"In Kaufman."

"*Why* are you in Kaufman?"

"Can't a girl go to Kaufman without folks wondering what she's up to?" I asked.

"Not if that girl is you."

I groaned. "Mason, don't worry. You're such a worrier."

"With good reason. Please come back. Now."

I somehow got Nadine's attention at that very moment. She ended her call with Clayton just about the time Tasha hung up from talking to Deputy Warren.

That left just one person on the line, and he wasn't happy at the moment.

"Could I call you back in a bit?" I asked. "We're kind of busy right now. I think Shawn Warren is calling the police in Grapevine to arrest Meredith and the others, but I need to make sure."

"Why are we arresting Meredith?" Mason asked.

"Oh, you missed that part. She's the one who stole Clayton's car. And she's currently having drinks at the Gaylord in Grapevine. We saw it all on social media, which is why we were—"

"Is this the part where you tell me you were headed to Grapevine, RaeLyn?" he asked.

"It wasn't my idea," I countered, doing my best to keep my voice cheerful.

"RaeLyn, for the love of all that's holy, turn that car around and come home!"

"I would, but I'm not the one driving."

Thank goodness Nadine got the message and gave me a thumbs-up. Then she made an illegal U-turn and pointed her car back toward Mabank.

CHAPTER
THIRTY-EIGHT

It wouldn't be completely accurate to say that Mason was mad at me, exactly, but he didn't really take the news of our Grapevine trip very well. On the other hand, the fact that we only made it as far as Kaufman helped a lot. And the arrest of Meredith, Belinda, and Rick a few hours later did alleviate his pain to some extent, though I certainly got an earful about the role I had played in trying to catch them in the act.

It took a few days for the whole story to come out, but when it did, I covered it all in a special *Mabanks Happenings* edition on Thursday afternoon of that same week.

Turned out, Meredith really was working with Belinda and her son, Rick, an old friend of hers. We were a little surprised—and weirdly disappointed—to learn that Clayton wasn't in on it. . .at all. He'd been suckered by Meredith, who had managed to get her hands on his car, as well as one of his ATM cards. Poor guy never knew what hit him until the bank clued him in that thousands of dollars were missing from his account.

At least he got his Corvette back. There was that.

I was grateful when the trio landed in jail, primarily because it meant

Tasha could finally relax. It also meant the Hadley family could focus solely on the one person who mattered most this week. . .Bessie Mae.

We settled in to celebrate her birthday on Saturday evening. I didn't know a lot of people who had made it to eighty-three in such great health, but she had, and she deserved to be celebrated.

Mason had asked if he could bring a special guest to dinner. He and Conner arrived around six. Conner looked healthier and happier than before. I had it on good authority things were going well for him at the restaurant. He had also picked up some hours at Mason's car shop to help pay off that alternator.

I greeted him like the guest he was, and he presented Aunt Bessie Mae with a bouquet of flowers—yellow roses. We'd been seeing a lot of those lately.

Meghan and Logan arrived around six fifteen, and she made her way from person to person, showing off her ring and talking about their upcoming wedding plans, which would take place next spring. I loved seeing her like this. And the joy on my brother's face made my heart soar. He deserved it.

Bessie Mae had a special guest too. By now, I had to admit, it was fun to see my aunt and Bob Reeves enjoying one another's company. Turned out, he loved John Wayne movies almost as much as she did. And I felt sure the man had never eaten better in his life. We were seeing him at our place around mealtime more and more.

I watched as he reached to take her hand, wrapping his fingers around hers. The loveliest smile lit her face.

And I had that amazing sense of joy that flooded over me, the same sense of joy I'd experienced when riding with Papaw in Tilly as a child. A sense of belonging. A sense of knowing when something was right. A good fit.

That's what Bessie Mae and Bob Reeves were. A good fit.

We shared Bessie Mae's favorite meal, one Mom and I had cooked without any help from her. Chicken-fried chicken was a staple around here, and we loved ours with mashed potatoes, gravy, and home-grown green beans.

Then came the birthday cake.

"I sure hope you didn't put eighty-three candles on it," Bessie Mae said. "I don't have enough air in me to blow out that many candles."

I disappeared into the utility room and fetched the Italian cream cake from the fridge. Only two candles on top, an 8 and a 3. But I went ahead and lit them before heading back into the kitchen.

At this point, we all erupted in song. Bessie Mae blew out the candles and we dove into that cake lickety-split. Mom pulled out a couple of tubs of Blue Bell and before long we were in our usual sugared-up state of delirium.

Mason rose and tapped his tea glass with a spoon to get our attention. I gave him a curious look.

"What are you up to?"

"You'll see." He cleared his throat to get the attention of everyone in the room. Before long, he finally had us all facing him.

"I've got something I think you'll all enjoy," he said. "And I think the timing is right, all things considered."

"For what?" I asked.

"Home movies."

I felt overjoyed as I realized what he'd done. "Oh, Mason. You figured out a way?"

"A way to do what?" Bessie Mae asked.

"We found the old home movies in the attic, Bessie Mae," I said. "The ones you told me about."

"I found a place in Dallas to have them digitized," Mason explained.

"Are you serious? You can do that?" My aunt clasped a hand over her mouth, clearly overjoyed.

"I can, and I did," Mason explained. "And we're about to watch them together for the first time, if you folks are ready."

Oh, we were ready, all right.

He started the first one, which was all in black and white. I had mentally prepared myself to see Bessie Mae as a young girl but wasn't psychologically prepared to see my Papaw, her older brother. The moment he came on our TV's screen, I felt my breath catch in my throat.

"Oh, Charles!" Bessie Mae rose and moved toward the TV. She placed her hand on the screen, as if trying to touch him. "I remember the day this happened. It was Christmas morning."

We watched, transfixed, as little Bessie Mae—who couldn't have been more than four or five—opened her Christmas presents with her older brother taking turns opening his as well.

"I remember that doll!" She let out a squeal. "Oh my stars. I think that's one of the ones y'all found in the attic at the little house awhile back." It didn't take long for tears to flow down Bessie Mae's cheeks.

One by one we watched all of the movies. It took two and a half hours, but—as a family—we were able to watch Bessie Mae and Papaw grow up. For the first time, I saw my great-grandparents in action. And I also saw something else—our family acreage. Before any of us were born.

The place looked a lot different back then. Our house was missing, of course. And the big barn. The antique store didn't exist. But even in black and white, I could still make out the fields that still stole my heart.

Finally it came time to start the last movie. Bessie Mae wasn't psychologically prepared for this one. Neither was Bob Reeves, apparently.

They gasped aloud as the film started, showing both of them in action at Mabank High School.

"Bessie Mae!" Mom pointed to the screen. "That's you? On stage? Singing?"

"Yes ma'am." Her cheeks flushed pink. "And Mr. Reeves is my accompanist."

Bob's gaze shifted to the floor and then back to the television, as if not really believing what he was watching.

We all focused on the scene in front of us as Bessie Mae sang—in crystal clear voice—"You Can't Get a Man with a Gun."

I couldn't get over what a powerhouse she was on stage. Not just her singing voice but her acting abilities as well.

And talk about a knockout!

"Bessie Mae, you were—are—gorgeous," I stammered. "Like, super-model gorgeous."

"She always was," Bob agreed. "Hasn't changed a bit."

My aunt laughed. "That might be stretching it a bit, Bob. But thank you."

As I watched my aunt in her portrayal of Annie Oakley in the 1959

242

high school production, two things stood out. One: I had so much to learn about my family's history. And, two: Bessie Mae's fascination with westerns went back a lot farther than I had realized.

As the movie ended, Mason decided a personal serenade was in order. He walked over to our family piano, opened the lid, then gestured for Bob to take a seat.

"What are we doing?" he asked.

Mason pulled out a piece of sheet music and set it down.

Bob stared at it, and then smiled. "Are you serious?"

"Never more so." Mason gestured for Bessie Mae to join them. My aunt looked a bit panicked as she saw Mason had selected the very song we'd just heard her sing all those years ago.

I made a quick dash to my room and came back with my cowgirl hat—the fancy white one with the pink trim. I plopped it onto Bessie Mae's head.

"Oh, honey, I just can't." With the wave of a hand she appeared to dismiss my idea. "I don't sing anymore. I would sound like an old toad, croaking in pain."

"I heard you just the other day, and you sounded amazing." I gestured for Bob to play, and he began. I was mesmerized to hear just how good he was. Those first few notes came pouring out, and then came the opening words. So much for needing WD-40. Before long, Bessie Mae was belting out the song, just as she had done in 1959. The old gal hadn't lost her touch.

It didn't take long for Dallas to grab his guitar and join in. Between my brother and Bob Reeves, it was sounding like we had a couple of pros in the building. Perhaps we did.

Bessie Mae carried on with dramatic flair. We seemed to lose her to the joy of the moment. And she wasn't the only one enjoying it. The more she sang, the brighter the smile on Bob's face. And, as I watched the two of them in action, I slowly backed out of the scene. They didn't need me anyway. I was just there as a prop.

As we all looked on, it was easy to see these two as a proper duo. She was the brave western girl, looking for love but unwilling to give up her personal passions. Nothing had changed there.

From the looks of things, Bob had some passions too. I watched, mesmerized, as his fingers ran up and down the keyboard. It was like watching a completely different man as he played. Perhaps this was all a part of the bigger work God was doing in Bob's life, reawakening the passion for music. That spark had certainly fanned into flame, right here, in front of us all.

Watching them also reminded me that their days of sharing those gifts weren't over just yet. These two still had plenty to offer.

When the song ended, Bob spontaneously started playing "Anything You Can Do I Can Do Better," which he sang in perfect duo with Bessie Mae. Before long, we were all singing the various parts, guys on one team and ladies on the other. I couldn't remember when I'd ever had so much fun.

When the song ended, we all began to talk over one another. Dallas and Bob dove into a lengthy discussion about their love of musical styles. Tasha went off on a tangent about the costume Bessie Mae had worn in the high school production. Mason and Conner talked about cars.

And me? Well, I just watched it all, a blissful observer.

I kept thinking about that Sunday school lesson a couple of weeks back—the one about how God puts the lonely in families. He'd certainly done that here, hadn't He? Some were family by blood. Others fit in like puzzle pieces meant to be part of the overall picture. And some—like Bob Reeves—surprised us, gently sliding into place, as if the puzzle had been waiting for him all along. Maybe it had. Maybe Bessie Mae had been holding that spot open for him all these years.

My gaze shifted to Mason, as he laughed and talked with Conner. My sweet, precious Mason. The one I loved. The one who loved me. He was more than a good man. He was a great man.

Just about the time we were ready to wrap up for the night, Bob got our attention. "I've got one more song, if you don't mind. A very special number for a very special lady." He turned to face my aunt. "Bessie Mae Hadley, this one's for you."

He took a seat at the piano once again, and, seconds later, "Let Me Call You Sweetheart" poured out. We all sat in silence, listening to the beautiful melody pouring from his very talented fingertips. There was no need for vocals. He'd practiced this one so that the melody rang out loud and clear from the instrument itself. I'd never heard anything so fine.

When the song ended, Bob Reeves swung back around to face her once more, his gaze firmly fixed on her. "You were my sweetheart then. You're my sweetheart now. And, Bessie Mae Hadley, I'd like you to be my sweetheart from now until eternity."

And then, with the whole Hadley clan looking on, Bob Reeves managed to get down on one knee in front of my precious aunt, who had tears running in rivulets down her face.

"Will you marry me, Annie Oakley?" he asked. "Be my bride?"

She could barely answer, the tears were flowing so rapidly now. But as Bessie Mae nodded, as her shaky "Yes!" gave her response, the applause from all in attendance was deafening.

I looked Mason's way and smiled. He walked my way and slipped his arm around my waist and then led me out of the house, across the porch, and over to the swing, where we both sat down.

"Looks like you're about to be in wedding-planning mode," he said.

"Yeah, I'm thinking it's going to be a rush to the altar. Looks like you were right about that."

"I'm right about a lot of things," he said, and then planted a little kiss in my hair.

"Oh?"

"Yeah. Once upon a time, I saw a girl coming down the hall at Mabank Jr. High. She had dark hair, a splattering of freckles, and braces. She also had more than enough attitude to knock me backward off my feet."

"True. I've always had attitude."

"I know. And I said to myself, 'Mason, one day that girl is going to be yours. If you can just keep her in line.'"

"Keep her in line." I snorted. "That's funny."

"Right?"

"What ever happened to that girl?" I asked.

"She ran off to Grapevine where she got arrested and ended up serving time in the county jail."

I punched him on the arm. "No, really. What ever happened to her?"

"I'd like to say they let her out on good behavior, but that never happened."

"Mason. Seriously."

"I'll tell you what happened." He drew me close and whispered in my ear, "She made me the happiest guy on earth, and we both lived happily ever after on a big parcel of land in East Texas where we raised half a dozen rotten kids who turned out to be just like their Mama."

"Very funny." I punched him again. Though, he probably had the rotten kids part right.

And that's when it occurred to me that he might not be joking around.

"Wait. Are you saying. . ."

"That I want to spend the rest of my life trying to corral the *real* Annie Oakley?" Mason laughed, and then pulled me close. "Yes, RaeLyn Hadley. That's *exactly* what I'm saying."

And the diamond ring in his hand convinced me that he meant every single word.

Bessie Mae's Oatmeal-Craisin Pecan Cookies

(double batch/party size)

Cream:

1 cup butter

Add and Cream Well:

1 cup packed brown sugar
1 cup sugar

Combine and Beat In Until Smooth:

2 eggs
2 teaspoons vanilla

Sift Together and Add to the Above Ingredients:

2 cups sifted flour
1 teaspoon baking soda
1 teaspoon salt

When Beaten Smooth, Add:

3 cups uncooked quick rolled oats

Add:

1 cup Craisins
1 cup chopped pecans

Beat well. Drop cookies 2 inches apart on cookie sheet and bake for 10 to 12 minutes at 375 degrees.

Bessie Mae's Italian Cream Cake

This recipe makes three 9-inch rounds.

INGREDIENTS

Cake:

1 white cake mix

1 yellow cake mix

6 eggs

½ cup vegetable oil

1 stick butter

1 cup water

1 cup milk

2 teaspoons vanilla

1 small box instant vanilla pudding (powder)

1 cup chopped pecans

1 cup sweetened coconut (flakes)

Frosting:

1 cup (two sticks) room temperature butter (salted)

1 block room temperature cream cheese

1 cup shortening

1 teaspoon clear vanilla extract

1 bag (7 to 8 cups) powdered sugar

Cream (to thin)

Filling / Topping:

Toasted chopped pecans

Toasted sweetened coconut flakes

INSTRUCTIONS

For the Cake:

Combine all ingredients except nuts and coconut. Mix well.
Work in nuts and coconut. Grease and flour three 9-inch pans.
Divide batter between three pans and bake at 350 degrees for about 30 minutes.

Frosting:

Bring butter and cream cheese to room temperature. Mix until soft and creamy. Add shortening and continue to beat until incorporated. (You can leave out shortening if you prefer traditional cream cheese frosting.) Add extract and then lower speed of your mixer to add powdered sugar (more or less to desired consistency) and add a drizzle of cream if needed to thin.

Filling and Icing the Cake:

Level all three cakes.

Put one cake on your cake board and add layer of cream cheese frosting.

Pipe ring around edge of cake and add some toasted pecans and coconut inside of ring.

Continue to stack and fill.

Turn top cake upside down, so that it's bottom up.

Ice cake with crumb coat and chill.

Once chilled, ice liberally with frosting.

Add chopped (toasted) pecans and coconut to sides and top then pipe trim or rosettes to add further decor.

JANICE THOMPSON, who lives in the Houston area, writes novels, nonfiction, magazine articles, and musical comedies for the stage. The mother of four married daughters, she is quickly adding grandchildren to the family mix. Visit janiceathompson.com.

THE LITTLE RED TRUCK MYSTERIES

The Hadley family opens Trinkets & Treasures antique store
in their old barn. Soon the ranchers turned antique dealers
must become sleuths to solve a string of mysteries.

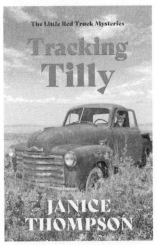

Tracking Tilly
BOOK 1
by Janice Thompson

The Hadley family ranch is struggling, so RaeLyn, her parents, and
brothers decide to turn the old barn into an antique store. The only
thing missing to go with the store is Grandpa's old red truck, Tilly, that
was sold several years ago. Now coming back up on the auction block,
Tilly would need a lot of work, but RaeLyn is sure it will be worth it—
if only she can beat out other bidders and find out who stole Tilly after
the auction ends. RaeLyn finds herself in the role of amateur sleuth,
and the outcome could make or break the new family venture.

Paperback / 978-1-63609-908-8

COMING SOON!

Mistletoe and Mayhem
Book 3
by Janice Thompson

It's less than a week until Christmas and just a few days away from RaeLyn and Mason's wedding on the Hadley ranch. Unfortunately, an arsonist set a wildfire that is rapidly traveling across several counties and headed right for the Hadley acreage. Can firefighters put it out in time or will the family homestead go up in flames, taking the business with it and ruining the wedding of their dreams? Who would want to cause such chaos and destruction?

Paperback / 979-8-89151-172-9